G. A. Lazenby

W9-AXJ-745

ROLLING STONES

The last photograph of O. Henry, taken by W. M. Vander-
weyde (New York) in 1909

ROLLING STONES

BY
O. HENRY

Author of "The Four Million," "The Voice of the City," "The Trimmed Lamp" "Strictly Business," "Sixes and Sevens," Etc.

PUBLISHED BY
DOUBLEDAY, PAGE & COMPANY
FOR
REVIEW OF REVIEWS CO.
1915

O. HENRY

O. Henry, Afrite-Chef of all delight—
Of all delectables conglomerate
That stay the starved brain and rejuvenate
The Mental Man! The æsthetic appetite—
So long enhungered that the "inards" fight
And growl gutwise—its pangs thou dost abate
And all so amiably alleviate,
Joy pats his belly as a hobo might
Who haply hath obtained a cherry pie
With no burnt crust at all, ner any seeds;
Nothin' but crisp crust, and the thickness fit.
And squashin'-juicy, an' jes' mighty nigh
Too dratted, drippin'-sweet for human needs,
But fer the sosh of milk that goes with it.

*Written in the character of "Sherrard
Plummer" by James Whitcomb Riley*

*By permission of James Whitcomb Riley and
his publishers, The Bobbs-Merrill Company*

CONTENTS

CONTENTS

INTRODUCTION

This the twelfth and final volume of O. Henry's work gets its title from an early newspaper venture of which he was the head and front. On April 28, 1894, there appeared in Austin, Texas, volume 1, number 3, of *The Rolling Stone*, with a circulation greatly in excess of that of the only two numbers that had gone before. Apparently the business office was encouraged. The first two issues of one thousand copies each had been bought up. Of the third an edition of six thousand was published and distributed *free*, so that the business men of Austin, Texas, might know what a good medium was at hand for their advertising. The editor and proprietor and illustrator of *The Rolling Stone* was Will Porter, incidentally Paying and Receiving Teller in Major Brackenridge's bank.

Perhaps the most characteristic feature of the paper was "The Plunkville Patriot," a page each week — or at least with the regularity of the somewhat uncertain paper itself — purporting to be reprinted from a contemporary journal. The editor of the Plunkville *Patriot* was Colonel Aristotle Jordan, unrelenting enemy of his enemies. When the Colonel's application for the postmastership in Plunkville is ignored, his columns carry a bitter attack on the administration at Washington.

THE ROLLING STONE

is a weekly paper published in Austin, Texas, every Saturday and will endeavor to fill a long-felt want that does not appear, by the way, to be altogether insatiable at present.

THE IDEA IS

to fill its pages with matter that will make a heart-rending appeal to every lover of good literature, and every person who has a taste for reading print; and a dollar and a half for a year's subscription.

OUR SPECIAL PREMIUM

For the next thirty days and from that time on indefinitely, whoever will bring two dollars in cash to *The Rolling Stone* office will be entered on the list of subscribers for one year and will have returned to him on the spot

FIFTY CENTS IN CASH

The editor's own statement of his aims

Introduction

With the public weal at heart, the *Patriot* announces that "there is a dangerous hole in the front steps of the Élite saloon." Here, too, appears the delightful literary item that Mark Twain and Charles Egbert Craddock are spending the summer together in their Adirondacks camp. "Free," runs its advertising column, "a clergyman who cured himself of fits will send one book containing 100 popular songs, one repeating rifle, two decks easywinner cards and 1 liver pad free of charge for $8. Address Sucker & Chump, Augusta, Me." The office moves nearly every week, probably in accordance with the time-honored principle involving the comparative ease of moving and paying rent. When the Colonel publishes his own candidacy for mayor, he further declares that the *Patriot* will accept no announcements for municipal offices until after "our" (the editor's) canvass. Adams & Co., grocers, order their $2.25 ad. discontinued and find later in the *Patriot* this estimate of their product: "No less than three children have been poisoned by eating their canned vegetables, and J. O. Adams, the senior member of the firm, was run out of Kansas City for adulterating codfish balls. It pays to advertise." Here is the editorial in which the editor first announces his campaign: "Our worthy mayor, Colonel Henry Stutty, died this morning after an illness of about five minutes, brought on by carrying a bouquet to Mrs. Eli Watts just as Eli got in from a fishing trip. Ten minutes later we had dodgers out announcing our candidacy for the office. We have lived in Plunkville going on five years and have never been elected anything yet. We understand the mayor business thoroughly and if elected some people will wish wolves had stolen them from their cradles. . . ."

The page from the *Patriot* is presented with an array of perfectly confused type, of artistic errors in setting up, and when an occasional line gets shifted (intentionally, of course) the effect is alarming. Anybody who knows the advertising of a small country weekly can, as he reads, pick out, in the following, the advertisement from the "personal."

> Miss Hattie Green of Paris, Ill., is
> Steel-riveted steam or water power
> automatic oiling thoroughly tested
> visiting her sister Mrs. G. W. Grubes
> Little Giant Engines at Adams & Co.
> Also Sachet powders Mc. Cormick Reapers and
> oysters.

All of this was a part of *The Rolling Stone*, which flourished, or at least wavered, in Austin during the years 1894 and 1895. Years before, Porter's strong instinct to write had been gratified in letters. He wrote, in his twenties, long imaginative letters, occasionally stuffed with execrable puns, but more than often buoyant, truly humorous, keenly incisive into the unreal, especially in fiction. I have included a number of these letters to Doctor Beall of Greensboro, N. C., and to his early friend in Texas, Mr. David Harrell.

In 1895-1896 Porter went to Houston, Texas, to work

Introduction

on the Houston *Post*. There he "conducted" a column
which he called "Postscripts." Some of the contents
of the pages that follow have been taken from these old
files in the fair hope that admirers of the matured O. Henry
will find in them pleasurable marks of the later genius.

Before the days of *The Rolling Stone* there are eleven
years in Texas over which, with the exception of the
letters mentioned, there are few "traces" of literary
performance; but there are some very interesting drawings, some of which are reproduced in this volume.
A story is back of them. They were the illustrations
to a book. "Joe" Dixon, prospector and inveterate
fortune-seeker, came to Austin from the Rockies in 1883,
at the constant urging of his old pal, Mr. John Maddox,
"Joe," kept writing Mr. Maddox, "your fortune's in
your pen, not your pick. Come to Austin and write an
account of your adventures." It was hard to woo
Dixon from the gold that wasn't there, but finally Maddox
wrote him he must come and try the scheme. "There's
a boy here from North Carolina," wrote Maddox. "His
name is Will Porter and he can make the pictures. He's
all right." Dixon came. The plan was that, after
Author and Artist had done their work, Patron would
step in, carry the manuscript to New York, bestow it on
a deserving publisher and then return to await, with the
other two, the avalanche of royalties. This version of
the story comes from Mr. Maddox. There were forty
pictures in all and they were very true to the life of the
Rockies in the seventies. Of course, the young artist had

no "technique" — no anything except what was native. But wait! As the months went by, Dixon worked hard, but he began to have doubts. Perhaps the book was no good. Perhaps John would only lose his money. He was a miner, not a writer, and he ought not to let John go to any expense. The result of this line of thought was the Colorado River for the manuscript and the high road for the author. The pictures, fortunately, were saved. Most of them Porter gave later to Mrs. Hagelstein of San Angelo, Texas. Mr. Maddox, by the way, finding a note from Joe that "explained all," hastened to the river and recovered a few scraps of the great book that had lodged against a sandbar. But there was no putting them together again.

So much for the title. It is a real O. Henry title. Contents of this last volume are drawn not only from letters, old newspaper files, and *The Rolling Stone*, but from magazines and unpublished manuscripts. Of the short stories, several were written at the very height of his powers and popularity and were lost, inexplicably, but lost. Of the poems, there are a few whose authorship might have been in doubt if the compiler of this collection had not secured external evidence that made them certainly the work of O. Henry. Without this very strong evidence, they might have been rejected because they were not entirely the kind of poems the readers of O. Henry would expect from him. Most of them, however, were found in his own indubitable manuscript or over his own signature.

Introduction

There is extant a mass of O. Henry correspondence that has not been included in this collection. During the better part of a decade in New York City he wrote constantly to editors, and in many instances intimately. This is very important material, and permission has been secured to use nearly all of it in a biographical volume that will be issued within the next two or three years. The letters in this volume have been chosen as an "exhibit," as early specimens of his writing and for their particularly characteristic turns of thought and phrase. The collection is not "complete" in any historical sense.

1912.   H. P. S.

This record of births and deaths is copied from the Porter Family Bible, just lately discovered.

BIRTHS

ALGERNON SIDNEY PORTER
Son of
SIDNEY AND RUTH C. PORTER
Was born
August 22, 1825

MONDAY EVENING, May 29, 1858
Still-born Son of
A. S. AND M. V. PORTER

MONDAY, August 6, 1860, 9 o'clock P. M.
SHIRLEY WORTH
Son of
A. S. AND M. V. PORTER

THURSDAY, September 11, 1862, 9 o'clock P. M.
*WILLIAM SIDNEY
Son of
A. S. AND M. V. PORTER

SUNDAY, March 26, 1865, at 8 o'clock A M
DAVID WEIR
Son of
A. S. AND M. V. PORTER

* O. HENRY

*MARY JANE VIRGINIA SWAIM
Daughter of
WILLIAM AND ABIAH SWAIM
Was born
February 12, 1833

DEATHS

MARY VIRGINIA PORTER
TUESDAY EVENING, September 26, 1865
At 7:30 o'clock

ATHOL ESTES PORTER
SUNDAY EVENING, July 25, 1897
At 6 o'clock

ALGERNON SIDNEY PORTER
SUNDAY MORNING, September 30, 1888
At 20 minutes of 2 o'clock

* MOTHER OF O. HENRY

ROLLING STONES

THE DREAM

[This was the last work of O. Henry. The *Cosmopolitan Magazine* had ordered it from him and, after his death, the unfinished manuscript was found in his room, on his dusty desk. The story as it here appears was published in the *Cosmopolitan* for September, 1910.]

MURRAY dreamed a dream.

Both psychology and science grope when they would explain to us the strange adventures of our immaterial selves when wandering in the realm of "Death's twin brother, Sleep." This story will not attempt to be illuminative; it is no more than a record of Murray's dream. One of the most puzzling phases of that strange waking sleep is that dreams which seem to cover months or even years may take place within a few seconds or minutes.

Murray was waiting in his cell in the ward of the condemned. An electric arc light in the ceiling of the corridor shone brightly upon his table. On a sheet of white paper an ant crawled wildly here and there as Murray blocked its way with an envelope. The electrocution was set for eight o'clock in the evening. Murray smiled at the antics of the wisest of insects.

There were seven other condemned men in the chamber. Since he had been there Murray had seen three taken out to their fate; one gone mad and fighting like a wolf caught

3

in a trap; one, no less mad, offering up a sanctimonious lip-service to Heaven; the third, a weakling, collapsed and strapped to a board. He wondered with what credit to himself his own heart, foot, and face would meet his punishment; for this was his evening. He thought it must be nearly eight o'clock.

Opposite his own in the two rows of cells was the cage of Bonifacio, the Sicilian slayer of his betrothed and of two officers who came to arrest him. With him Murray had played checkers many a long hour, each calling his move to his unseen opponent across the corridor.

Bonifacio's great booming voice with its indestructible singing quality called out:

"Eh, Meestro Murray; how you feel — all-a right — yes?"

"All right, Bonifacio," said Murray steadily, as he allowed the ant to crawl upon the envelope and then dumped it gently on the stone floor.

"Dat's good-a, Meestro Murray. Men like us, we must-a die like-a men. My time come nex'-a week. All-a right. Remember, Meestro Murray, I beat-a you dat las' game of de check. Maybe we play again some-a time. I don'-a know. Maybe we have to call-a de move damn-a loud to play de check where dey goin' send us."

Bonifacio's hardened philosophy, followed closely by his deafening, musical peal of laughter, warmed rather than chilled Murray's numbed heart. Yet, Bonifacio had until next week to live.

The cell-dwellers heard the familiar, loud click of the

steel bolts as the door at the end of the corridor was opened. Three men came to Murray's cell and unlocked it. Two were prison guards; the other was "Len" — no; that was in the old days; now the Reverend Leonard Winston, a friend and neighbor from their barefoot days.

"I got them to let me take the prison chaplain's place," he said, as he gave Murray's hand one short, strong grip. In his left hand he held a small Bible, with his forefinger marking a page.

Murray smiled slightly and arranged two or three books and some penholders orderly on his small table. He would have spoken, but no appropriate words seemed to present themselves to his mind.

The prisoners had christened this cellhouse, eighty feet long, twenty-eight feet wide, Limbo Lane. The regular guard of Limbo Lane, an immense, rough, kindly man, drew a pint bottle of whiskey from his pocket and offered it to Murray, saying:

"It's the regular thing, you know. All has it who feel like they need a bracer. No danger of it becoming a habit with 'em, you see."

Murray drank deep into the bottle.

"That's the boy!" said the guard. "Just a little nerve tonic, and everything goes smooth as silk."

They stepped into the corridor, and each one of the doomed seven knew. Limbo Lane is a world on the outside of the world; but it had learned, when deprived of one or more of the five senses, to make another sense supply the deficiency. Each one knew that it was nearly eight, and that Murray was to go to the chair at eight. There is also in the many Limbo Lanes an aristocracy of crime. The man who kills in the open, who beats his enemy or pursuer down, flushed by the primitive emotions and the ardor of combat, holds in contempt the human rat, the spider, and the snake.

So, of the seven condemned only three called their farewells to Murray as he marched down the corridor between the two guards — Bonifacio, Marvin, who had killed a guard while trying to escape from the prison, and Bassett, the train-robber, who was driven to it because the express-messenger wouldn't raise his hands when ordered to do so. The remaining four smoldered, silent, in their cells, no doubt feeling their social ostracism in Limbo Lane society more keenly than they did the memory of their less picturesque offences against the law.

Murray wondered at his own calmness and nearly indif.. ference. In the execution room were about twenty men, a congregation made up of prison officers, newspaper reporters, and lookers-on who had succeeded

Here, in the very middle of a sentence, the hand of Death interrupted the telling of O. Henry's last story. He had planned to make this story different from his others, the beginning of a new series in a style he had not previously attempted. "I want to show the public," he said, "that I can write something new — new for me, I mean — a story without slang, a straightforward dramatic plot treated in a way that will come nearer my idea of real story-writing." Before starting to write the present story, he outlined briefly how he intended to develop it: Murray, the criminal accused and convicted of the brutal murder of his sweetheart — a murder prompted by jealous rage — at first faces the death penalty, calm, and, to all outward appearances, indifferent to his fate. As he nears the electric chair he is overcome by a revulsion of feeling. He is left dazed, stupefied, stunned. The entire scene in the death-chamber — the witnesses, the spectators, the preparations for execution — become unreal to him. The thought flashes through his brain that a terrible mistake is being made. Why is he being strapped to the chair? What has he done? What crime has he committed? In the few moments while the straps are being adjusted a vision comes to him. He dreams a dream. He sees a little country cottage, bright, sun-lit, nestling in a bower of flowers. A woman is there, and a little child. He speaks with them and finds that they are his wife, his child — and the cottage their home. So, after all, it is a mistake. Some one has frightfully, irretrievably blundered. The accusation, the trial, the conviction, the sentence to death in the electric chair — all a dream. He takes his wife in his arms and kisses the child. Yes, here is happiness. It was a dream. Then — at a sign from the prison warden the fatal current is turned on.

Murray had dreamed the wrong dream.

A RULER OF MEN

[Written at the prime of his popularity and power, this characteristic and amusing story was published in *Everybody's Magazine* in August, 1906.]

I WALKED the streets of the City of Insolence, thirsting for the sight of a stranger face. For the City is a desert of familiar types as thick and alike as the grains in a sand-storm; and you grow to hate them as you do a friend who is always by you, or one of your own kin.

And my desire was granted, for I saw, near a corner of Broadway and Twenty-ninth Street, a little flaxen-haired man with a face like a scaly-bark hickory-nut, selling to a fast-gathering crowd a tool that omnigeneously pro-claimed itself a can-opener, a screw-driver, a button-hook, a nail-file, a shoe-horn, a watch-guard, a potato-peeler, and an ornament to any gentleman's key-ring.

And then a stall-fed cop shoved himself through the congregation of customers. The vender, plainly used to having his seasons of trade thus abruptly curtailed, closed his satchel and slipped like a weasel through the opposite segment of the circle. The crowd scurried aim-lessly away like ants from a disturbed crumb. The cop, suddenly becoming oblivious of the earth and its inhabi-tants, stood still, swelling his bulk and putting his club

8

through an intricate drill of twirls. I hurried after Kansas Bill Bowers, and caught him by an arm.

Without his looking at me or slowing his pace, I found a five-dollar bill crumpled neatly into my hand.

"I wouldn't have thought, Kansas Bill," I said, "that you'd hold an old friend that cheap."

Then he turned his head, and the hickory-nut cracked into a wide smile.

"Give back the money," said he, "or I'll have the cop after you for false pretenses. I thought you was the cop."

"I want to talk to you, Bill," I said. "When did you leave Oklahoma? Where is Reddy McGill now? Why are you selling those impossible contraptions on the street? How did your Big Horn gold-mine pan out? How did you get so badly sunburned? What will you drink?"

"A year ago," answered Kansas Bill systematically. "Putting up windmills in Arizona. For pin money to buy etceteras with. Salted. Been down in the tropics. Beer."

We foregathered in a propitious place and became Elijahs, while a waiter of dark plumage played the raven to perfection. Reminiscence needs must be had before I could steer Bill into his epic mood.

"Yes," said he, "I mind the time Timoteo's rope broke on that cow's horns while the calf was chasing you. You and that cow! I'd never forget it."

"The tropics," said I, "are a broad territory. What

part of Cancer of Capricorn have you been honoring with a visit?"

"Down along China or Peru — or maybe the Argentine Confederacy," said Kansas Bill. "Anyway 'twas among a great race of people, off-colored but progressive. I was there three months."

"No doubt you are glad to be back among the truly great race," I surmised. "Especially among New Yorkers, the most progressive and independent citizens of any country in the world," I continued, with the fatuity of the provincial who has eaten the Broadway lotus.

"Do you want to start an argument?" asked Bill.

"Can there be one?" I answered.

"Has an Irishman humor, do you think?" asked he.

"I have an hour or two to spare," said I, looking at the café clock.

"Not that the Americans aren't a great commercial nation," conceded Bill. "But the fault laid with the people who wrote lies for fiction."

"What was this Irishman's name?" I asked.

"Was that last beer cold enough?" said he.

"I see there is talk of further outbreaks among the Russian peasants, " I remarked.

"His name was Barney O'Connor," said Bill.

Thus, because of our ancient prescience of each other's trail of thought, we travelled ambiguously to the point where Kansas Bill's story began:

"I met O'Connor in a boarding-house on the West Side. He invited me to his hall-room to have a drink, and we became like a dog and a cat that had been raised together. There he sat, a tall, fine, handsome man, with his feet against one wall and his back against the other, looking over a map. On the bed and sticking three feet out of it was a beautiful gold sword with tassels on it and rhinestones in the handle.

"'What's this?' says I (for by that time we were well acquainted). 'The annual parade in vilification of the ex-snakes of Ireland? And what's the line of march? Up Broadway to Forty-second; thence east to McCarty's café; thence ——'

"'Sit down on the wash-stand,' says O'Connor, 'and listen. And cast no perversions on the sword. 'Twas me father's in old Munster. And this map, Bowers, is no diagram of a holiday procession. If ye look again ye'll see that it's the continent known as South America, comprising fourteen green, blue, red, and yellow countries, all crying out from time to time to be liberated from the yoke of the oppressor.'

"'I know,' says I to O'Connor. 'The idea is a literary one. The ten-cent magazine stole it from "Ridpath's History of the World from the Sand-stone Period to the Equator." You'll find it in every one of 'em. It's a continued story of a soldier of fortune, generally named O'Keefe, who gets to be dictator while the Spanish-American populace cries "Cospetto!" and other Italian maledictions. I misdoubt if it's ever been done. You're not thinking of trying that, are you, Barney?' I asks.

"'Bowers,' says he, 'you're a man of education and courage.'

"'How can I deny it?' says I. 'Education runs in my family; and I have acquired courage by a hard struggle with life.'

"'The O'Connors,' says he, 'are a warlike race. There is me father's sword; and here is the map. A life of inaction is not for me. The O'Connors were born to rule. 'Tis a ruler of men I must be.'

"'Barney,' I says to him, 'why don't you get on the force and settle down to a quiet life of carnage and corruption instead of roaming off to foreign parts? In what better way can you indulge your desire to subdue and maltreat the oppressed?'

"'Look again at the map,' says he, 'at the country I have the point of me knife on. 'Tis that one I have selected to aid and overthrow with me father's sword.'

"'I see,' says I. 'It's the green one; and that does credit to your patriotism, and it's the smallest one; and that does credit to your judgment.'

"'Do ye accuse me of cowardice?' says Barney, turning pink.

"'No man,' says I, 'who attacks and confiscates a country single-handed could be called a coward. The worst you can be charged with is plagiarism or imitation. If Anthony Hope and Roosevelt let you get away with it, nobody else will have any right to kick.'

"'I'm not joking,' says O'Connor. 'And I've got

$1,500 cash to work the scheme with. I've taken a liking to you. Do you want it, or not?'

"'I'm not working,' I told him; 'but how is it to be? Do I eat during the fomentation of the insurrection, or am I only to be Secretary of War after the country is conquered? Is it to be a pay envelope or only a portfolio?'

"'I'll pay all expenses,' says O'Connor. 'I want a man I can trust. If we succeed you may pick out any appointment you want in the gift of the government.'

"'All right, then,' says I. 'You can get me a bunch of draying contracts and then a quick-action consignment to a seat on the Supreme Court bench so I won't be in line for the presidency. The kind of cannon they chasten their presidents with in that country hurt too much. You can consider me on the pay-roll.'

"Two weeks afterward O'Connor and me took a steamer for the small, green, doomed country. We were three weeks on the trip. O'Connor said he had his plans all figured out in advance; but being the commanding general, it consorted with his dignity to keep the details concealed from his army and cabinet, commonly known as William T. Bowers. Three dollars a day was the price for which I joined the cause of liberating an undiscovered country from the ills that threatened or sustained it. Every Saturday night on the steamer I stood in line at parade rest, and O'Connor handed over the twenty-one dollars.

"The town we landed at was named Guayaquerita, so they told me. 'Not for me,' says I. 'It'll be little old Hilldale or Tompkinsville or Cherry Tree Corners when

I speak of it.   It's a clear case where Spelling Reform ought to butt in and disenvowel it.'

"But the town looked fine from the bay when we sailed in.   It was white, with green ruching, and lace ruffles on the skirt when the surf slashed up on the sand.   It looked as tropical and dolce far ultra as the pictures of Lake Ronkonkoma in the brochure of the passenger department of the Long Island Railroad.

"We went through the quarantine and custom-house indignities; and then O'Connor leads me to a 'dobe house on a street called 'The Avenue of the Dolorous Butterflies of the Individual and Collective Saints.'   Ten feet wide it was, and knee-deep in alfalfa and cigar stumps.

"'Hooligan Alley,' says I, rechristening it.

"''Twill be our headquarters,' says O'Connor.   'My agent here, Don Fernando Pacheco, secured it for us.'

"So in that house O'Connor and me established the revolutionary centre.   In the front room we had ostensible things such as fruit, a guitar, and a table with a conch shell on it.   In the back room O'Connor had his desk and a large looking-glass and his sword hid in a roll of straw matting.   We slept on hammocks that we hung to hooks in the wall; and took our meals at the Hotel Ingles, a beanery run on the American plan by a German proprietor with Chinese cooking served à la Kansas City lunch counter.

"It seems that O'Connor really did have some sort of system planned out beforehand.   He wrote plenty of letters; and every day or two some native gent would stroll

round to headquarters and be shut up in the back room
for half an hour with O'Connor and the interpreter. I
noticed that when they went in they were always smoking
eight-inch cigars and at peace with the world; but when
they came out they would be folding up a ten- or twenty-
dollar bill and cursing the government horribly.

"One evening after we had been in Guaya — in this
town of Smellville-by-the-Sea — about a month, and me
and O'Connor were sitting outside the door helping along
old tempus fugit with rum and ice and limes, I says to him:

"'If you'll excuse a patriot that don't exactly know
what he's patronizing, for the question — what is your
scheme for subjugating this country? Do you intend to
plunge it into bloodshed, or do you mean to buy its votes
peacefully and honorably at the polls?'

"'Bowers,' says he, 'ye're a fine little man and I intend
to make great use of ye after the conflict. But ye do not
understand statecraft. Already by now we have a network of strategy clutching with invisible fingers at the
throat of the tyrant Calderas. We have agents at work
in every town in the republic. The Liberal party is
bound to win. On our secret lists we have the names of
enough sympathizers to crush the administration forces
at a single blow.'

"'A straw vote,' says I, 'only shows which way the hot
air blows.'

"'Who has accomplished this?' goes on O'Connor. 'I
have. I have directed everything. The time was ripe
when we came, so my agents inform me. The people are

groaning under burdens of taxes and levies. Who will be their natural leader when they rise? Could it be any one but meself? 'Twas only yesterday that Zaldas, our representative in the province of Durasnas, tells me that the people, in secret, already call me "El Library Door," which is the Spanish manner of saying "The Liberator.'"

"'Was Zaldas that maroon-colored old Aztec with a paper collar on and unbleached domestic shoes?' I asked.

"'He was,' says O'Connor.

"'I saw him tucking a yellow-back into his vest pocket as he came out,' says I. 'It may be,' says I, 'that they call you a library door, but they treat you more like the side door of a bank. But let us hope for the worst.'

"'It has cost money, of course,' says O'Connor; 'but we'll have the country in our hands inside of a month.'

"In the evenings we walked about in the plaza and listened to the band playing and mingled with the populace at its distressing and obnoxious pleasures. There were thirteen vehicles belonging to the upper classes, mostly rockaways and old-style barouches, such as the mayor rides in at the unveiling of the new poorhouse at Milledgeville, Alabama. Round and round the desiccated fountain in the middle of the plaza they drove, and lifted their high silk hats to their friends. The common people walked around in barefooted bunches, puffing stogies that a Pittsburg millionaire wouldn't have chewed for a dry smoke on Ladies' Day at his club. And the grandest figure in the whole turnout was Barney O'Connor. Six foot two he stood in his Fifth Avenue clothes, with his eagle eye and his black moustache that tickled his ears. He was a born dictator and czar and hero and harrier of the human race.   It looked to me that all eyes were turned upon O'Connor, and that every woman there loved him, and every man feared him.   Once or twice I looked at him and thought of funnier things that had happened than his winning out in his game; and I began to feel like a Hidalgo de Officio de Grafto de South America myself. And then I would come down again to solid bottom and let my imagination gloat, as usual, upon the twenty-one American dollars due me on Saturday night.

"'Take note,' says O'Connor to me as thus we walked, 'of the mass of the people.   Observe their oppressed and melancholy air.   Can ye not see that they are ripe for revolt?   Do ye not perceive that they are disaffected?'

"'I do not,' says I. 'Nor disinfected either. I'm beginning to understand these people.   When they look unhappy they're enjoying themselves.   When they feel unhappy they go to sleep.   They're not the kind of people to take an interest in revolutions.'

"'They'll flock to our standard,' says O'Connor. 'Three thousand men in this town alone will spring to arms when the signal is given.   I am assured of that. But everything is in secret.   There is no chance for us to fail.'

"On Hooligan Alley, as I prefer to call the street our headquarters was on, there was a row of flat 'dobe houses with red tile roofs, some straw shacks full of Indians and dogs, and one two-story wooden house with balconies a little farther down. That was where General Tumbalo, the comandante and commander of the military forces, lived. Right across the street was a private residence built like a combination bake-oven and folding-bed. One day, O'Connor and me were passing it, single file, on the flange they called a sidewalk, when out of the window flies a big red rose. O'Connor, who is ahead, picks it up, presses it to his fifth rib, and bows to the ground. By Carrambos! that man certainly had the Irish drama chaunceyized. I looked around expecting to see the little boy and girl in white sateen ready to jump on his shoulder while he jolted their spinal columns and ribs together through a breakdown, and sang: 'Sleep, Little One, Sleep.'

"As I passed the window I glanced inside and caught a glimpse of a white dress and a pair of big, flashing black eyes and gleaming teeth under a dark lace mantilla.

"When we got back to our house O'Connor began to walk up and down the floor and twist his moustaches.

"'Did ye see her eyes, Bowers?' he askes me.

"'I did,' says I, 'and I can see more than that. It's all coming out according to the story-books. I knew there was something missing. 'Twas the love interest. What is it that comes in Chapter VII to cheer the gallant Irish adventurer? Why, Love, of course — Love that makes the hat go around. At last we have the eyes of midnight hue and the rose flung from the barred window. Now, what comes next? The underground passage — the intercepted letter — the traitor in camp — the hero thrown into a dungeon — the mysterious message from the señorita — then the outburst — the fighting on the plaza — the ——'

"'Don't be a fool,' says O'Connor, interrupting. 'But that's the only woman in the world for me, Bowers. The O'Connors are as quick to love as they are to fight. I shall wear that rose over me heart when I lead me men into action. For a good battle to be fought there must be some woman to give it power.'

"'Every time,' I agreed, 'if you want to have a good lively scrap. There's only one thing bothering me. In the novels the light-haired friend of the hero always gets killed. Think 'em all over that you've read, and you'll see that I'm right. I think I'll step down to the Botica Española and lay in a bottle of walnut stain before war is declared.'

"'How will I find out her name?" says O'Connor, laying his chin in his hand.

"'Why don't you go across the street and ask her?' says I.

"'Will ye never regard anything in life seriously?' says O'Connor, looking down at me like a schoolmaster.

"'Maybe she meant the rose for me,' I said, whistling the Spanish Fandango.

"For the first time since I'd known O'Connor, he laughed. He got up and roared and clapped his knees, and leaned against the wall till the tiles on the roof clattered to the noise of his lungs. He went into the back room and looked at himself in the glass and began and

laughed all over from the beginning again. Then he
looked at me and repeated himself. That's why I asked
you if you thought an Irishman had any humor. He'd
been doing farce comedy from the day I saw him without
knowing it; and the first time he had an idea advanced to
him with any intelligence in it he acted like two twelfths of
the sextet in a 'Floradora' road company.

"The next afternoon he comes in with a triumphant
smile and begins to pull something like ticker tape out of
his pocket.

"'Great!' says I. 'This is something like home. How
is Amalgamated Copper to-day?'

"'I've got her name,' says O'Connor, and he reads off
something like this: 'Dona Isabel Antonia Inez Lolita
Carreras y Buencaminos y Monteleon. She lives with her
mother,' explains O'Connor. 'Her father was killed in
the last revolution. She is sure to be in sympathy with
our cause.'

"And sure enough the next day she flung a little bunch
of roses clear across the street into our door. O'Connor
dived for it and found a piece of paper curled around a
stem with a line in Spanish on it. He dragged the interpreter out of his corner and got him busy. The interpreter
scratched his head, and gave us as a translation three
best bets: 'Fortune had got a face like the man fighting';
'Fortune looks like a brave man'; and 'Fortune favors
the brave.' We put our money on the last one.

"'Do ye see?' says O'Connor. 'She intends to encourage me sword to save her country.'

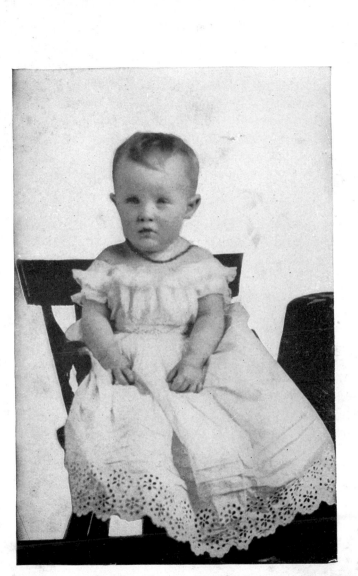

O. Henry at the age of two

Hill City Quartette

R. K. Edmondson Jr.   H. H. Long

W. S. Porter   C. E. Hillyer

1886

"'It looks to me like an invitation to supper,' says I.'

"So every day this señorita sits behind the barred windows and exhausts a conservatory or two, one posy at a time. And O'Connor walks like a Dominecker rooster and swells his chest and swears to me he will win her by feats of arms and big deeds on the gory field of battle.

"By and by the revolution began to get ripe. One day O'Connor takes me into the back room and tells me all.

"'Bowers,' says he, 'at twelve o'clock one week from to-day the struggle will take place. It has pleased ye to find amusement and diversion in this project because ye have not sense enough to perceive that it is easily accomplished by a man of courage, intelligence, and historical superiority, such as meself. The whole world over,' says he, 'the O'Connors have ruled men, women, and nations. To subdue a small and indifferent country like this is a trifle. Ye see what little, barefooted manikins the men of it are. I could lick four of 'em single-handed.'

"'No doubt,' says I. 'But could you lick six? And suppose they hurled an army of seventeen against you?'

"'Listen,' says O'Connor, 'to what will occur. At noon next Tuesday 25,000 patriots will rise up in the towns of the republic. The government will be absolutely unprepared. The public buildings will be taken, the regular army made prisoners, and the new administration set up. In the capital it will not be so easy on account of most of the army being stationed there. They will occupy the president's palace and the strongly fortified government buildings and stand a siege. But on the very day of the outbreak a body of our troops will begin a march to the capital from every town as soon as the local victory has been won. The thing is so well planned that it is an impossibility for us to fail. I meself will lead the troops from here. The new president will be Señor Espadas, now Minister of Finance in the present cabinet.'

"'What do you get?' I asked.

"'Twill be strange,' said O'Connor smiling, 'if I don't have all the jobs handed to me on a silver salver to pick what I choose. I've been the brains of the scheme, and when the fighting opens I guess I won't be in the rear rank. Who managed it so our troops could get arms smuggled into this country? Didn't I arrange it with a New York firm before I left there? Our financial agents inform me that 20,000 stands of Winchester rifles have been delivered a month ago at a secret place up coast and distributed among the towns. I tell you, Bowers, the game is already won.'

"Well, that kind of talk kind of shook my disbelief in the infallibility of the serious Irish gentleman soldier of fortune. It certainly seemed that the patriotic grafters had gone about the thing in a business way. I looked upon O'Connor with more respect, and began to figure on what kind of uniform I might wear as Secretary of War.

"Tuesday, the day set for the revolution, came around according to schedule. O'Connor said that a signal had been agreed upon for the uprising. There was an old cannon on the beach near the national warehouse. That had been secretly loaded and promptly at twelve o'clock was to be fired off. Immediately the revolutionists would seize their concealed arms, attack the comandante's troops in the cuartel, and capture the custom-house and all government property and supplies.

"I was nervous all the morning. And about eleven o'clock O'Connor became infused with the excitement and martial spirit of murder. He geared his father's sword around him, and walked up and down in the back room like a lion in the Zoo suffering from corns. I smoked a couple of dozen cigars, and decided on yellow stripes down the trouser legs of my uniform.

"At half-past eleven O'Connor asks me to take a short stroll through the streets to see if I could notice any signs of the uprising. I was back in fifteen minutes.

"'Did you hear anything?' he asks.

"'I did,' says I. 'At first I thought it was drums. But it wasn't; it was snoring. Everybody in town's asleep.'

"O'Connor tears out his watch.

"'Fools?' says he. 'They've set the time right at the siesta hour when everybody takes a nap. But the cannon will wake 'em up. Everything will be all right, depend upon it.'

"Just at twelve o'clock we heard the sound of a cannon —BOOM!—shaking the whole town.

"O'Connor loosens his sword in its scabbard and jumps for the door. I went as far as the door and stood in it.

"People were sticking their heads out of doors and windows. But there was one grand sight that made the landscape look tame.

"General Tumbalo, the comandante, was rolling down the steps of his residential dugout, waving a five-foot sabre in his hand. He wore his cocked and plumed hat and his dress-parade coat covered with gold braid and buttons. Sky-blue pajamas, one rubber boot, and one red-plush slipper completed his make-up.

"The general had heard the cannon, and he puffed down the sidewalk toward the soldiers' barracks as fast as his rudely awakened two hundred pounds could travel.

"O'Connor sees him and lets out a battle-cry and draws his father's sword and rushes across the street and tackles the enemy.

"Right there in the street he and the general gave an exhibition of blacksmithing and butchery. Sparks flew from their blades, the general roared, and O'Connor gave the slogan of his race and proclivities.

"Then the general's sabre broke in two; and he took to his ginger-colored heels crying out, 'Policios,' at every jump. O'Connor chased him a block, imbued with the sentiment of manslaughter, and slicing buttons off the general's coat tails with the paternal weapon. At the corner five barefooted policemen in cotton undershirts and straw hats climbed over O'Connor and subjugated him according to the municipal statutes.

"They brought him past the late revolutionary head-quarters on the way to jail. I stood in the door. A policeman had him by each hand and foot, and they dragged him on his back through the grass like a turtle. Twice they stopped, and the odd policeman took another's place while he rolled a cigarette. The great soldier of fortune turned his head and looked at me as they passed. I blushed, and lit another cigar. The procession passed on, and at ten minutes past twelve everybody had gone back to sleep again.

"In the afternoon the interpreter came around and smiled as he laid his hand on the big red jar we usually kept ice-water in.

"'The ice-man didn't call to-day,' says I. 'What's the matter with everything, Sancho?'

"'Ah, yes,' says the liver-colored linguist. 'They just tell me in the town. Verree bad act that Señor O'Connor make fight with General Tumbalo. Yes. General Tumbalo great soldier and big mans.'

"'What 'll they do to Mr. O'Connor?' I asks.

"'I talk little while presently with the Juez de la Paz — what you call Justice-with-the-peace,' says Sancho. 'He tell me it verree bad crime that one Señor Americano try kill General Tumbalo. He say they keep Señor O'Connor in jail six months; then have trial and shoot him with guns. Verree sorree.'

"'How about this revolution that was to be pulled off?' I asks.

"'Oh,' says this Sancho, 'I think too hot weather for revolution. Revolution better in winter-time. Maybe so next winter. Quien sabe?'

"'But the cannon went off,' says I. 'The signal was given.'

"'That big sound?' says Sancho, grinning. 'The boiler

in ice factory he blow up — BOOM! Wake everybody
up from siesta. Verree sorree. No ice. Mucho hot day.'

"About sunset I went over to the jail, and they let me
talk to O'Connor through the bars.

"'What's the news, Bowers?' says he. 'Have we taken
the town? I've been expecting a rescue party all the
afternoon. I haven't heard any firing. Has any word
been received from the capital?'

"'Take it easy, Barney,' says I. 'I think there's been
a change of plans. There's something more important
to talk about. Have you any money?'

"'I have not,' says O'Connor. 'The last dollar went
to pay our hotel bill yesterday. Did our troops capture
the custom-house? There ought be plenty of government money there.'

"'Segregate your mind from battles,' says I. 'I've
been making inquiries. You're to be shot six months
from date for assault and battery. I'm expecting to
receive fifty years at hard labor for vagrancy. All they
furnish you while you're a prisoner is water. You depend
on your friends for food. I'll see what I can do.'

"I went away and found a silver Chile dollar in an old
vest of O'Connor's. I took him some fried fish and rice
for his supper. In the morning I went down to a lagoon
and had a drink of water, and then went back to the jail.
O'Connor had a porterhouse steak look in his eye.

"'Barney,' says I, 'I've found a pond full of the finest
kind of water. It's the grandest, sweetest, purest water
in the world. Say the word and I'll go fetch you a bucket

of it and you can throw this vile government stuff out the window. I'll do anything I can for a friend.'

"'Has it come to this?' says O'Connor, raging up and down his cell. 'Am I to be starved to death and then shot? I'll make those traitors feel the weight of an O'Connor's hand when I get out of this.' And then he comes to the bars and speaks softer. 'Has nothing been heard from Dona Isabel?' he asks. 'Though every one else in the world fail,' says he, 'I trust those eyes of hers. She will find a way to effect my release. Do ye think ye could communicate with her? One word from her — even a rose would make me sorrow light. But don't let her know except with the utmost delicacy, Bowers. These high-bred Castilians are sensitive and proud.'

"'Well said, Barney,' says I. 'You've given me an idea. I'll report later. Something's got to be pulled off quick, or we'll both starve.'

"I walked out and down to Hooligan Alley, and then on the other side of the street. As I went past the window of Dona Isabel Antonia Concha Regalia, out flies the rose as usual and hits me on the ear.

"The door was open, and I took off my hat and walked in. It wasn't very light inside, but there she sat in a rocking-chair by the window smoking a black cheroot. And when I got closer I saw that she was about thirty-nine, and had never seen a straight front in her life. I sat down on the arm of her chair, and took the cheroot out of her mouth and stole a kiss.

"'Hullo, Izzy,' I says. 'Excuse my unconventionality,

but I feel like I have known you for a month. Whose Izzy is oo?'

"The lady ducked her head under her mantilla, and drew in a long breath. I thought she was going to scream, but with all that intake of air she only came out with: 'Me likee Americanos.'

"As soon as she said that, I knew that O'Connor and me would be doing things with a knife and fork before the day was over. I drew a chair beside her, and inside of half an hour we were engaged. Then I took my hat and said I must go out for a while.

"'You come back?' says Izzy, in alarm.

"'Me go bring preacher,' says I. 'Come back twenty minutes. We marry now. How you likee?'

"'Marry to-day?' says Izzy. 'Good!'

"I went down on the beach to the United States consul's shack. He was a grizzly man, eighty-two pounds, smoked glasses, five foot eleven, pickled. He was playing chess with an india-rubber man in white clothes.

"'Excuse me for interrupting,' says I, 'but can you tell me how a man could get married quick?'

"The consul gets up and fingers in a pigeonhole.

"'I believe I had a license to perform the ceremony myself, a year or two ago,' he said. 'I'll look, and ——'

"I caught hold of his arm.

"'Don't look it up,' says I. 'Marriage is a lottery anyway. I'm willing to take the risk about the license if you are.'

"The consul went back to Hooligan Alley with me.

O. Henry in Austin, Texas. 1896

Emigrants' Camp

(*An early Drawing by O. Henry*)

Izzy called her ma to come in, but the old lady was picking a chicken in the patio and begged to be excused. So we stood up and the consul performed the ceremony.

"That evening Mrs. Bowers cooked a great supper of stewed goat, tamales, baked bananas, fricasseed red peppers and coffee. Afterward I sat in the rocking-chair by the front window, and she sat on the floor plunking at a guitar and happy, as she should be, as Mrs. William T. B.

"All at once I sprang up in a hurry. I'd forgotten all about O'Connor. I asked Izzy to fix up a lot of truck for him to eat.

"'That big, oogly man,' said Izzy. 'But all right — he your friend.'

"I pulled a rose out of a bunch in a jar, and took the grub-basket around to the jail. O'Connor ate like a wolf. Then he wiped his face with a banana peel and said: 'Have you heard nothing from Dona Isabel yet?'

"'Hist!' says I, slipping the rose between the bars. 'She sends you this. She bids you take courage. At nightfall two masked men brought it to the ruined château in the orange grove. How did you like that goat hash, Barney?'

"O'Connor pressed the rose to his lips.

"'This is more to me than all the food in the world,' says he. 'But the supper was fine. Where did you raise it?'

"'I've negotiated a stand-off at a delicatessen hut downtown,' I tells him. 'Rest easy. If there's anything to be done I'll do it.'

"So things went along that way for some weeks. Izzy was a great cook; and if she had had a little more poise of character and smoked a little better brand of tobacco we might have drifted into some sense of responsibility for the honor I had conferred on her. But as time went on I began to hunger for the sight of a real lady standing before me in a street-car. All I was staying in that land of bilk and money for was because I couldn't get away, and I thought it no more than decent to stay and see O'Connor shot.

"One day our old interpreter drops around and after smoking an hour says that the judge of the peace sent him to request me to call on him. I went to his office in a lemon grove on a hill at the edge of the town; and there I had a surprise. I expected to see one of the usual cinnamon-colored natives in congress gaiters and one of Pizzaro's cast-off hats. What I saw was an elegant gentleman of a slightly claybank complexion sitting in an upholstered leather chair, sipping a highball and reading Mrs. Humphry Ward. I had smuggled into my brain a few words of Spanish by the help of Izzy, and I began to remark in a rich Andalusian brogue:

"'Buenas dias, señor. Yo tengo — yo tengo ——'

"'Oh, sit down, Mr. Bowers,' says he. 'I spent eight years in your country in colleges and law schools. Let me mix you a highball. Lemon peel, or not?'

"Thus we got along. In about half an hour I was beginning to tell him about the scandal in our family when Aunt Elvira ran away with a Cumberland Presbyterian preacher. Then he says to me:

"'I sent for you, Mr. Bowers, to let you know that you can have your friend Mr. O'Connor now. Of course we had to make a show of punishing him on account of his attack on General Tumbalo. It is arranged that he shall be released to-morrow night. You and he will be conveyed on board the fruit steamer *Voyager*, bound for New York, which lies in the harbor. Your passage will be arranged for.'

"'One moment, judge,' says I; 'that revolution ——'

"The judge lays back in his chair and howls.

"'Why,' says he presently, 'that was all a little joke fixed up by the boys around the court-room, and one or two of our cut-ups, and a few clerks in the stores. The town is bursting its sides with laughing. The boys made themselves up to be conspirators, and they — what you call it? — stick Señor O'Connor for his money. It is very funny.'

"'It was,' says I. 'I saw the joke all along. I'll take another highball, if your Honor don't mind.'

"The next evening just at dark a couple of soldiers brought O'Connor down to the beach, where I was waiting under a cocoanut-tree.

"'Hist!' says I in his ear: 'Dona Isabel has arranged our escape. Not a word!'

"They rowed us in a boat out to a little steamer that smelled of table d'hôte salad oil and bone phosphate.

"The great, mellow, tropical moon was rising as we steamed away. O'Connor leaned on the taffrail or rear balcony of the ship and gazed silently at **Guaya——** at Buncoville-on-the-Beach.

He had the red rose in his hand.

"'She will wait,' I heard him say. 'Eyes like hers never deceive. But I shall see her again. Traitors cannot keep an O'Connor down forever.'

"'You talk like a sequel,' says I. 'But in Volume II please omit the light-haired friend who totes the grub to the hero in his dungeon cell.'

"And thus reminiscing, we came back to New York."

There was a little silence broken only by the familiar roar of the streets after Kansas Bill Bowers ceased talking.

"Did O'Connor ever go back?" I asked.

"He attained his heart's desire," said Bill. "Can you walk two blocks? I'll show you."

He led me eastward and down a flight of stairs that was covered by a curious-shaped glowing, pagoda-like structure. Signs and figures on the tiled walls and supporting columns attested that we were in the Grand Central station of the subway. Hundreds of people were on the midway platform.

An uptown express dashed up and halted. It was crowded. There was a rush for it by a still larger crowd.

Towering above every one there a magnificent, broad-shouldered, athletic man leaped into the centre of the struggle. Men and women he seized in either hand and hurled them like manikins toward the open gates of the train.

Now and then some passenger with a shred of soul and self-respect left to him turned to offer remonstrance; but the blue uniform on the towering figure, the fierce and conquering glare of his eye and the ready impact of his ham-like hands glued together the lips that would have spoken complaint.

When the train was full, then he exhibited to all who might observe and admire his irresistible genius as a ruler of men. With his knees, with his elbows, with his shoulders, with his resistless feet he shoved, crushed, slammed, heaved, kicked, flung, pounded the overplus of passengers aboard. Then with the sounds of its wheels drowned by the moans, shrieks, prayers, and curses of its unfortunate crew, the express dashed away.

"That's him. Ain't he a wonder?" said Kansas Bill admiringly. "That tropical country wasn't the place for him. I wish the distinguished traveller, writer, war correspondent, and playwright, Richmond Hobson Davis, could see him now. O'Connor ought to be dramatized."

THE ATAVISM OF JOHN TOM LITTLE BEAR

[O. Henry thought this the best of the Jeff Peters stories, all the rest of which are included in "The Gentle Grafter," except "Cupid à la Carte" in the "Heart of the West." "The Atavism of John Tom Little Bear" appeared in *Everybody's Magazine* for July, 1903.]

I SAW a light in Jeff Peters's room over the Red Front Drug Store. I hastened toward it, for I had not known that Jeff was in town. He is a man of the Hadji breed, of a hundred occupations, with a story to tell (when he will) of each one.

I found Jeff repacking his grip for a run down to Florida to look at an orange grove for which he had traded, a month before, his mining claim on the Yukon. He kicked me a chair, with the same old humorous, profound smile on his seasoned countenance. It had been eight months since we had met, but his greeting was such as men pass from day to day. Time is Jeff's servant, and the continent is a big lot across which he cuts to his many roads.

For a while we skirmished along the edges of unprofitable talk which culminated in that unquiet problem of the Philippines.

"All them tropical races," said Jeff, "could be run out better with their own jockeys up. The tropical man knows what he wants. All he wants is a season ticket to the cock-fights and a pair of Western Union climbers to go up the bread-fruit tree. The Anglo-Saxon man wants him to learn to conjugate and wear suspenders. He'll be happiest in his own way."

I was shocked.

"Education, man," I said, "is the watchword. In time they will rise to our standard of civilization. Look at what education has done for the Indian."

"O-ho!" sang Jeff, lighting his pipe (which was a good sign). "Yes, the Indian! I'm looking. I hasten to contemplate the redman as a standard bearer of progress. He's the same as the other brown boys. You can't make an Anglo-Saxon of him. Did I ever tell you about the time my friend John Tom Little Bear bit off the right ear of the arts of culture and education and spun the teetotum back round to where it was when Columbus was a little boy? I did not?

"John Tom Little Bear was an educated Cherokee Indian and an old friend of mine when I was in the Territories. He was a graduate of one of them Eastern football colleges that have been so successful in teaching the Indian to use the gridiron instead of burning his victims at the stake. As an Anglo-Saxon, John Tom was copper-colored in spots. As an Indian, he was one of the whitest men I ever knew. As a Cherokee, he was a gentleman on the first ballot. As a ward of the nation, he was mighty hard to carry at the primaries.

"John Tom and me got together and began to make medicine — how to get up some lawful, genteel swindle which we might work in a quiet way so as not to excite the stupidity of the police or the cupidity of the larger corporations. We had close upon $500 between us, and we pined to make it grow, as all respectable capitalists do.

"So we figured out a proposition which seems to be as honorable as a gold mine prospectus and as profitable as a church raffle. And inside of thirty days you find us swarming into Kansas with a pair of fluent horses and a red camping wagon on the European plan. John Tom is Chief Wish-Heap-Dough, the famous Indian medicine man and Samaritan Sachem of the Seven Tribes. Mr. Peters is business manager and half owner. We needed a third man, so we looked around and found J. Conyngham Binkly leaning against the want column of a newspaper. This Binkly has a disease for Shakespearian rôles, and an hallucination about a 200 nights' run on the New York stage. But he confesses that he never could earn the butter to spread on his William S. rôles, so he is willing to drop to the ordinary baker's kind, and be satisfied with a 200-mile run behind the medicine ponies. Besides Richard III, he could do twenty-seven coon songs and banjo specialties, and was willing to cook, and curry the horses. We carried a fine line of excuses for taking money. One was a magic soap for removing grease spots and quarters from clothes. One was a Sum-wah-tah, the great Indian Remedy made from a prairie herb revealed by the Great Spirit in a dream to his favorite medicine men, the great chiefs McGarrity and Silberstein, bottlers, Chicago. And the other was a frivolous system of pick-

pocketing the Kansasters that had the department stores
reduced to a decimal fraction. Look ye! A pair of silk
garters, a dream book, one dozen clothespins, a gold tooth,
and 'When Knighthood Was in Flower' all wrapped up in
a genuine Japanese silkarina handkerchief and handed to
the handsome lady by Mr. Peters for the trivial sum of
fifty cents, while Professor Binkly entertains us in a three-
minute round with the banjo.

"'Twas an eminent graft we had. We ravaged peacefully through the State, determined to remove all doubt
as to why 'twas called bleeding Kansas. John Tom Little
Bear, in full Indian chief's costume, drew crowds away
from the parchesi sociables and government ownership
conversaziones. While at the football college in the East
he had acquired quantities of rhetoric and the art of calis-
thenics and sophistry in his classes, and when he stood up
in the red wagon and explained to the farmers, eloquent,
about chilblains and hyperæsthesia of the cranium, Jeff
couldn't hand out the Indian Remedy fast enough for 'em.

"One night we was camped on the edge of a little town
out west of Salina. We always camped near a stream, and
put up a little tent. Sometimes we sold out of the Remedy unexpected, and then Chief Wish-Heap-Dough would
have a dream in which the Manitou commanded him to fill
up a few bottles of Sum-wah-tah at the most convenient
place. 'Twas about ten o'clock, and we'd just got in from
a street performance. I was in the tent with the lantern,
figuring up the day's profits. John Tom hadn't taken off
his Indian make-up, and was sitting by the campfire

minding a fine sirloin steak in the pan for the Professor
till he finished his hair-raising scene with the trained
horses.

"All at once out of dark bushes comes a pop like a fire-
cracker, and John Tom gives a grunt and digs out of his
bosom a little bullet that has dented itself against his
collar-bone. John Tom makes a dive in the direction of
the fireworks, and comes back dragging by the collar a
kid about nine or ten years young, in a velveteen suit, with
a little nickel-mounted rifle in his hand about as big as a
fountain-pen.

"'Here, you pappoose,' says John Tom, 'what are you
gunning for with that howitzer? You might hit somebody
in the eye. Come out, Jeff, and mind the steak. Don't
let it burn, while I investigate this demon with the pea
shooter.'

"'Cowardly redskin,' says the kid like he was quoting
from a favorite author. 'Dare to burn me at the stake
and the paleface will sweep you from the prairies like —
like everything. Now, you lemme go, or I'll tell mamma.'

"John Tom plants the kid on a camp-stool, and sits
down by him. 'Now, tell the big chief,' he says, 'why you
try to shoot pellets into your Uncle John's system.
Didn't you know it was loaded?'

"'Are you a Indian?' asks the kid, looking up cute as
you please at John Tom's buckskin and eagle feathers. 'I
am,' says John Tom. 'Well, then, that's why,' answers
the boy, swinging his feet. I nearly let the steak burn
watching the nerve of that youngster.

"'O-ho!' says John Tom, 'I see. You're the Boy Avenger. And you've sworn to rid the continent of the savage redman. Is that about the way of it, son?'

"The kid halfway nodded his head. And then he looked glum. 'Twas indecent to wring his secret from his bosom before a single brave had fallen before his parlor-rifle.

"'Now, tell us where your wigwam is, pappoose,' says John Tom — 'where you live? Your mamma will be worrying about you being out so late. Tell me, and I'll take you home.'

"The kid grins. 'I guess not,' he says. 'I live thousands and thousands of miles over there.' He gyrated his hand toward the horizon. 'I come on the train,' he says, 'by myself. I got off here because the conductor said my ticket had ex-pirated.' He looks at John Tom with sudden suspicion. 'I bet you ain't a Indian,' he says. 'You don't talk like a Indian. You look like one, but all a Indian can say is "heap good" and "paleface die." Say, I bet you are one of them make-believe Indians that sell medicine on the streets. I saw one once in Quincy.'

"'You never mind,' says John Tom, 'whether I'm a cigar-sign or a Tammany cartoon. The question before the council is what's to be done with you. You've run away from home. You've been reading Howells. You've disgraced the profession of boy avengers by trying to shoot a tame Indian, and never saying: "Die, dog of a redskin! You have crossed the path of the Boy Avenger nineteen times too often." What do you mean by it?'

"The kid thought for a minute. 'I guess I made a mistake,' he says. 'I ought to have gone farther west. They find 'em wild out there in the cañons.' He holds out his hand to John Tom, the little rascal. 'Please excuse me, sir,' says he, 'for shooting at you. I hope it didn't hurt you. But you ought to be more careful. When a scout sees a Indian in his war-dress, his rifle must speak.' Little Bear give a big laugh with a whoop at the end of it, and swings the kid ten feet high and sets him on his shoulder, and the runaway fingers the fringe and the eagle feathers and is full of the joy the white man knows when he dangles his heels against an inferior race. It is plain that Little Bear and that kid are chums from that on. The little renegade has already smoked the pipe of peace with the savage; and you can see in his eye that he is figuring on a tomahawk and a pair of moccasins, children's size.

"We have supper in the tent. The youngster looks upon me and the Professor as ordinary braves, only intended as a background to the camp scene. When he is seated on a box of Sum-wah-tah, with the edge of the table sawing his neck, and his mouth full of beefsteak, Little Bear calls for his name. 'Roy,' says the kid, with a sirloiny sound to it. But when the rest of it and his post-office address is referred to, he shakes his head. 'I guess not,' he says. 'You'll send me back. I want to stay with you. I like this camping out. At home, we fellows had a camp in our back yard. They called me Roy, the Red Wolf. I guess that'll do for a name. Gimme another piece of beefsteak, please.'

"We had to keep that kid. We knew there was a hul-labaloo about him somewheres, and that Mamma, and Uncle Harry, and Aunt Jane, and the Chief of Police were hot after finding his trail, but not another word would he tell us. In two days he was the mascot of the Big Medicine outfit, and all of us had a sneaking hope that his owners wouldn't turn up. When the red wagon was doing business he was in it, and passed up the bottles to Mr. Peters as proud and satisfied as a prince that's abjured a two-hundred-dollar crown for a million-dollar parvenuess. Once John Tom asked him something about his papa. 'I ain't got any papa,' he says. 'He runned away and left us. He made my mamma cry. Aunt Lucy says he's a shape.' 'A what?' somebody asks him. 'A shape,' says the kid; 'some kind of a shape — lemme see — oh, yes, a feendenuman shape. I don't know what it means.' John Tom was for putting our brand on him, and dressing him up like a little chief, with wampum and beads, but I vetoes it. 'Somebody's lost that kid, is my view of it, and they may want him. You let me try him with a few stratagems, and see if I can't get a look at his visiting-card.'

"So that night I goes up to Mr. Roy Blank by the camp-fire, and looks at him contemptuous and scornful. 'Snickenwitzel!' says I, like the word made me sick; 'Snickenwitzel! Bah! Before I'd be named Snicken-witzel!'

"'What's the matter with you, Jeff?' says the kid, opening his eyes wide.

"'Snickenwitzel!' I repeats, and I spat the word out. 'I saw a man to-day from your town, and he told me your name. I'm not surprised you was ashamed to tell it. Snickenwitzel! Whew!'

"'Ah, here, now,' says the boy, indignant and wriggling all over, 'what's the matter with you? That ain't my name. It's Conyers. What's the matter with you?'

"'And that's not the worst of it,' I went on quick, keeping him hot and not giving him time to think. 'We thought you was from a nice, well-to-do family. Here's Mr. Little Bear, a chief of the Cherokees, entitled to wear nine otter tails on his Sunday blanket, and Professor Binkly, who plays Shakespeare and the banjo, and me, that's got hundreds of dollars in that black tin box in the wagon, and we've got to be careful about the company we keep. That man tells me your folks live 'way down in little old Hencoop Alley, where there are no sidewalks, and the goats eat off the table with you.'

"That kid was almost crying now. ''Taint so,' he splutters. 'He — he don't know what he's talking about. We live on Poplar Av'noo. I don't 'sociate with goats. What's the matter with you?'

"'Poplar Avenue,' says I, sarcastic. 'Poplar Avenue! That's a street to live on! It only runs two blocks and then falls off a bluff. You can throw a keg of nails the whole length of it. Don't talk to me about Poplar Avenue.'

"'It's — it's miles long,' says the kid. 'Our number's

862 and there's lots of houses after that. What's the matter with — aw, you make me tired, Jeff.'

"'Well, well, now,' says I. 'I guess that man made a mistake. Maybe it was some other boy he was talking about. If I catch him I'll teach him to go around slandering people.' And after supper I goes up town and telegraphs to Mrs. Conyers, 862 Poplar Avenue, Quincy, Ill., that the kid is safe and sassy with us, and will be held for further orders. In two hours an answer comes to hold him tight, and she'll start for him by next train.

"The next train was due at 6 P. M. the next day, and me and John Tom was at the depot with the kid. You might scour the plains in vain for the big Chief Wish-Heap-Dough. In his place is Mr. Little Bear in the human habiliments of the Anglo-Saxon sect; and the leather of his shoes is patented and the loop of his necktie is copyrighted. For these things John Tom had grafted on him at college along with metaphysics and the knockout guard for the low tackle. But for his complexion, which is some yellowish, and the black mop of his straight hair, you might have thought here was an ordinary man out of the city directory that subscribes for magazines and pushes the lawnmower in his shirt-sleeves of evenings.

"Then the train rolled in, and a little woman in a gray dress, with sort of illuminating hair, slides off and looks around quick. And the Boy Avenger sees her, and yells 'Mamma,' and she cries 'O!' and they meet in a clinch, and now the pesky redskins can come forth from their caves on the plains without fear any more of the rifle of

Roy, the Red Wolf.   Mrs. Conyers comes up and thanks
me an'John Tom without the usual extremities you always
look for in a woman.   She says just enough, in a way to
convince, and there is no incidental music by the orchestra.
I made a few illiterate requisitions upon the art of conversation, at which the lady smiles friendly, as if she had
known me a week.   And then Mr. Little Bear adorns the
atmosphere with the various idioms into which education
can fracture the wind of speech.   I could see the kid's
mother didn't quite place John Tom; but it seemed she
was apprised in his dialects, and she played up to his lead
in the science of making three words do the work of one.

"That kid introduced us, with some footnotes and ex-
planations that made things plainer than a week of
rhetoric.   He danced around, and punched us in the back,
and tried to climb John Tom's leg.   'This is John Tom,
mamma,' says he.   'He's a Indian.   He sells medicine
in a red wagon.   I shot him, but he wasn't wild.   The
other one's Jeff.   He's a fakir, too.   Come on and see the
camp where we live, won't you, mamma?'

"It is plain to see that the life of the woman is in that
boy.   She has got him again where her arms can gather
him, and that's enough.   She's ready to do anything to
please him.   She hesitates the eighth of a second and takes
another look at these men.   I imagine she says to herself
about John Tom, 'Seems to be a gentleman, if his hair
don't curl.'   And Mr. Peters she disposes of as follows:
'No ladies' man, but a man who knows a lady.'

"So we all rambled down to the camp as neighborly as

coming from a wake. And there she inspects the wagon, and pats the place with her hand where the kid used to sleep, and dabs around her eyewinkers with her handkerchief. And Professor Binkly gives us 'Trovatore' on one string of the banjo, and is about to slide off into Hamlet's monologue when one of the horses gets tangled in his rope and he must go look after him, and says something about 'foiled again.'

"When it got dark me and John Tom walked back up to the Corn Exchange Hotel, and the four of us had supper there. I think the trouble started at that supper, for then was when Mr. Little Bear made an intellectual balloon ascension. I held on to the tablecloth, and listened to him soar. That redman, if I could judge, had the gift of information. He took language, and did with it all a Roman can do with macaroni. His vocal remarks was all embroidered over with the most scholarly verbs and prefixes. And his syllables was smooth, and fitted nicely to the joints of his idea. I thought I'd heard him talk before, but I hadn't. And it wasn't the size of his words, but the way they come; and 'twasn't his subjects, for he spoke of common things like cathedrals and football and poems and catarrh and souls and freight rates and sculpture. Mrs. Conyers understood his accents, and the elegant sounds went back and forth between 'em. And now and then Jefferson D. Peters would intervene a few shop-worn, senseless words to have the butter passed or another leg of the chicken.

"Yes, John Tom Little Bear appeared to be inveigled

some in his bosom about that Mrs. Conyers.   She was of
the kind that pleases.   She had the good looks and more,
I'll tell you.   You take one of these cloak models in a big
store.   They strike you as being on the impersonal system.
They are adapted for the eye.   What they run to is inches
around and complexion, and the art of fanning the delusion
that the sealskin would look just as well on the lady with
the warts and the pocket-book.   Now, if one of them
models was off duty, and you took it, and it would say
'Charlie' when you pressed it, and sit up at the table, why,
then you would have something similar to Mrs. Conyers.
I could see how John Tom could resist any inclination to
hate that white squaw.

"The lady and the kid stayed at the hotel.   In the
morning, they say, they will start for home.   Me and
Little Bear left at eight o'clock, and sold Indian Remedy
on the courthouse square till nine.   He leaves me and the
Professor to drive down to camp, while he stays up town.
I am not enamored with that plan, for it shows John Tom
is uneasy in his composures, and that leads to firewater,
and sometimes to the green corn dance and costs.   Not
often does Chief Wish-Heap-Dough get busy with the
firewater, but whenever he does there is heap much doing
in the lodges of the palefaces who wear blue and carry the
club.

"At half-past nine Professor Binkly is rolled in his quilt
snoring in blank verse, and I am sitting by the fire listening
to the frogs.   Mr. Little Bear slides into camp and sits
down against a tree.   There is no symptoms of firewater.

"'Jeff,' says he, after a long time, 'a little boy came West to hunt Indians.'

"'Well, then?' says I, for I wasn't thinking as he was.

"'And he bagged one,' says John Tom, 'and 'twas not with a gun, and he never had on a velveteen suit of clothes in his life.' And then I began to catch his smoke.

"'I know it,' says I. 'And I'll bet you his pictures are on valentines, and fool men are his game, red and white.'

"'You win on the red,' says John Tom, calm. 'Jeff, for how many ponies do you think I could buy Mrs. Conyers?'

"'Scandalous talk!' I replies. ''Tis not a paleface custom.' John Tom laughs loud and bites into a cigar. 'No,' he answers; ''tis the savage equivalent for the dollars of the white man's marriage settlement. Oh, I know. There's an eternal wall between the races. If I could do it, Jeff, I'd put a torch to every white college that a redman has ever set foot inside. Why don't you leave us alone,' says he, 'to our own ghost-dances and dog-feasts, and our dingy squaws to cook our grasshopper soup and darn our moccasins?'

"'Now, you sure don't mean disrespect to the perennial blossom entitled education?' says I, scandalized, 'because I wear it in the bosom of my own intellectual shirt-waist. I've had education,' says I, 'and never took any harm from it.'

"'You lasso us,' goes on Little Bear, not noticing my prose insertions, 'and teach us what is beautiful in literature and in life, and how to appreciate what is fine in

men and women. What have you done to me?' says he.
'You've made me a Cherokee Moses. You've taught me
to hate the wigwams and love the white man's ways. I
can look over into the promised land and see Mrs. Conyers, but my place is—on the reservation.'

"Little Bear stands up in his chief's dress, and laughs
again. 'But, white man Jeff,' he goes on, 'the paleface
provides a recourse. 'Tis a temporary one, but it gives
a respite and the name of it is whiskey.' And straight off
he walks up the path to town again. 'Now,' says I in my
mind, 'may the Manitou move him to do only bailable
things this night!' For I perceive that John Tom is
about to avail himself of the white man's solace.

"Maybe it was 10:30, as I sat smoking, when I hear
pit-a-pats on the path, and here comes Mrs. Conyers running, her hair twisted up any way, and a look on her face
that says burglars and mice and the flour's-all-out rolled
in one. 'Oh, Mr. Peters,' she calls out, as they will,
'oh, oh!' I made a quick think, and I spoke the gist of it
out loud. 'Now,' says I, 'we've been brothers, me and
that Indian, but I'll make a good one of him in two
minutes if ——'

"'No, no, she says, wild and cracking her knuckles,
'I haven't seen Mr. Little Bear. 'Tis my — husband.
He's stolen my boy. Oh,' she says, 'just when I had him
back in my arms again! That heartless villain! Every
bitterness life knows,' she says, 'he's made me drink. My
poor little lamb, that ought to be warm in his bed, carried
off by that fiend!'

Zeke sells the "Basket of Toads" to the "Bloated Bondholder." (Herlow's Hotel)

An early illustration by O. Henry, done in pencil on ordinary pasteboard

Morning Visitors

(One of O. Henry's early drawings)

"'How did all this happen?' I ask. 'Let's have the facts.'

"'I was fixing his bed,' she explains, 'and Roy was playing on the hotel porch and he drives up to the steps. I heard Roy scream, and ran out. My husband had him in the buggy then. I begged him for my child. This is what he gave me.' She turns her face to the light. There is a crimson streak running across her cheek and mouth. 'He did that with his whip,' she says.

"'Come back to the hotel,' says I, 'and we'll see what can be done.'

"On the way she tells me some of the wherefores. When he slashed her with the whip he told her he found out she was coming for the kid, and he was on the same train. Mrs. Conyers had been living with her brother, and they'd watched the boy always, as her husband had tried to steal him before. I judge that man was worse than a street railway promoter. It seems he had spent her money and slugged her and killed her canary bird, and told it around that she had cold feet.

"At the hotel we found a mass meeting of five infuriated citizens chewing tobacco and denouncing the outrage. Most of the town was asleep by ten o'clock. I talks the lady some quiet, and tells her I will take the one o'clock train for the next town, forty miles east, for it is likely that the esteemed Mr. Conyers will drive there to take the cars. 'I don't know,' I tells her, 'but what he has legal rights; but if I find him I can give him an illegal left in the eye, and tie him up for a day or two, anyhow, on a disturbal of the peace proposition.'

"Mrs. Conyers goes inside and cries with the landlord's wife, who is fixing some catnip tea that will make everything all right for the poor dear. The landlord comes out on the porch, thumbing his one suspender, and says to me:

"'Ain't had so much excitements in town since Bedford Steegall's wife swallered a spring lizard. I seen him through the winder hit her with the buggy whip, and everything. What's that suit of clothes cost you you got on? 'Pears like we'd have some rain, don't it? Say, doc, that Indian of yorn's on a kind of a whizz to-night, ain't he? He comes along just before you did, and I told him about this here occurrence. He gives a cur'us kind of a hoot, and trotted off. I guess our constable 'll have him in the lock-up 'fore morning.'

"I thought I'd sit on the porch and wait for the one o'clock train. I wasn't feeling saturated with mirth. Here was John Tom on one of his sprees, and this kidnapping business losing sleep for me. But then, I'm always having trouble with other people's troubles. Every few minutes Mrs. Conyers would come out on the porch and look down the road the way the buggy went, like she expected to see that kid coming back on a white pony with a red apple in his hand. Now, wasn't that like a woman? And that brings up cats. 'I saw a mouse go in this hole,' says Mrs. Cat; 'you can go prize up a plank over there if you like; I'll watch this hole.'

"About a quarter to one o'clock the lady comes out

again, restless, crying easy, as females do for their own amusement, and she looks down that road again and listens. 'Now, ma'am,' says I, 'there's no use watching cold wheel-tracks. By this time they're halfway to ——' 'Hush,' she says, holding up her hand. And I do hear something coming 'flip-flap' in the dark; and then there is the awfulest war-whoop ever heard outside of Madison Square Garden at a Buffalo Bill matinée. And up the steps and on to the porch jumps the disrespectable Indian. The lamp in the hall shines on him, and I fail to recognize Mr. J. T. Little Bear, alumnus of the class of '91. What I see is a Cherokee brave, and the warpath is what he has been travelling. Firewater and other things have got him going. His buckskin is hanging in strings, and his feathers are mixed up like a frizzly hen's. The dust of miles is on his moccasins, and the light in his eye is the kind the aborigines wear. But in his arms he brings that kid, his eyes half closed, with his little shoes dangling and one hand fast around the Indian's collar.

"'Pappoose!' says John Tom, and I notice that the flowers of the white man's syntax have left his tongue. He is the original proposition in bear's claws and copper color. 'Me bring,' says he, and he lays the kid in his mother's arms. 'Run fifteen mile,' says John Tom — 'Ugh! Catch white man. Bring pappoose.'

"The little woman is in extremities of gladness. She must wake up that stir-up trouble youngster and hug him and make proclamation that he is his mamma's own precious treasure. I was about to ask questions, but I looked

at Mr. Little Bear, and my eye caught the sight of something in his belt. 'Now go to bed, ma'am,' says I, 'and
this gadabout youngster likewise, for there's no more
danger, and the kidnapping business is not what it was
earlier in the night.'

"I inveigled John Tom down to camp quick, and when
he tumbled over asleep I got that thing out of his belt and
disposed of it where the eye of education can't see it. For
even the football colleges disapprove of the art of scalp-
taking in their curriculums.

"It is ten o'clock next day when John Tom wakes up
and looks around. I am glad to see the nineteenth century in his eye again.

"'What was it, Jeff?' he asks.

"'Heap firewater,' says I.

"John Tom frowns, and thinks a little. 'Combined,'
says he directly, 'with the interesting little physiological
shake-up known as reversion to type. I remember now.
Have they gone yet?'

"'On the 7:30 train,' I answers.

"'Ugh!' says John Tom; 'better so. Paleface, bring
big Chief Wish-Heap-Dough a little bromo-seltzer, and
then he'll take up the redman's burden again.

HELPING THE OTHER FELLOW

[Originally published in *Munsey's Magazine*, December, 1908.]

"But can thim that helps others help thimselves!"
—*Mulvaney.*

THIS is the story that William Trotter told me on the beach at Aguas Frescas while I waited for the gig of the captain of the fruit steamer *Andador*, which was to take me aboard. Reluctantly I was leaving the Land of Always Afternoon. William was remaining, and he favored me with a condensed oral autobiography as we sat on the sands in the shade cast by the Bodega Nacional.

As usual, I became aware that the Man from Bombay had already written the story; but as he had compressed it to an eight-word sentence, I have become an expansionist, and have quoted his phrase above, with apologies to him and best regards to *Terence.*

II

"Don't you ever have a desire to go back to the land of derby hats and starched collars?" I asked him. "You seem to be a handy man and a man of action," I continued, "and I am sure I could find you a comfortable job somewhere in the States."

Ragged, shiftless, barefooted, a confirmed eater of the

53

lotos, William Trotter had pleased me much, and I hated to see him gobbled up by the tropics.

"I've no doubt you could," he said, idly splitting the bark from a section of sugar-cane. "I've no doubt you could do much for me. If every man could do as much for himself as he can for others, every country in the world would be holding millenniums instead of centennials."

There seemed to be pabulum in W. T.'s words. And then another idea came to me.

I had a brother in Chicopee Falls who owned manufactories — cotton, or sugar, or A. A. sheetings, or something in the commercial line. He was vulgarly rich, and therefore reverenced art. The artistic temperament of the family was monopolized at my birth. I knew that Brother James would honor my slightest wish. I would demand from him a position in cotton, sugar, or sheetings for William Trotter — something, say, at two hundred a month or thereabouts. I confided my beliefs and made my large propositions to William. He had pleased me much, and he was ragged.

While we were talking, there was a sound of firing guns — four or five, rattlingly, as if by a squad. The cheerful noise came from the direction of the cuartel, which is a kind of makeshift barracks for the soldiers of the republic.

"Hear that?" said William Trotter. "Let me tell you about it.

"A year ago I landed on this coast with one solitary dollar. I have the same sum in my pocket to-day. I was second cook on a tramp fruiter; and they marooned me here early one morning, without benefit of clergy, just because I poulticed the face of the first mate with cheese omelette at dinner. The fellow had kicked because I'd put horseradish in it instead of cheese.

"When they threw me out of the yawl into three feet of surf, I waded ashore and sat down under a palm-tree. By and by a fine-looking white man with a red face and white clothes, genteel as possible, but somewhat under the influence, came and sat down beside me.

"I had noticed there was a kind of a village back of the beach, and enough scenery to outfit a dozen moving-picture shows. But I thought, of course, it was a cannibal suburb, and I was wondering whether I was to be served with carrots or mushrooms. And, as I say, this dressed-up man sits beside me, and we become friends in the space of a minute or two. For an hour we talked, and he told me all about it.

"It seems that he was a man of parts, conscientious-ness, and plausibility, besides being educated and a wreck to his appetites. He told me all about it. Colleges had turned him out, and distilleries had taken him in. Did I tell you his name? It was Clifford Wain-wright. I didn't exactly catch the cause of his being cast away on that particular stretch of South America; but I reckon it was his own business. I asked him if he'd ever been second cook on a tramp fruiter, and he said no; so that concluded my line of surmises. But he talked like the encyclopedia from 'A — Berlin' to 'Trilo — Zyria.'

And he carried a watch—a silver arrangement with works, and up to date within twenty-four hours, anyhow.

"'I'm pleased to have met you,' says Wainwright. 'I'm a devotee to the great joss Booze; but my ruminating facilities are unrepaired,' says he — or words to that effect. 'And I hate,' says he, 'to see fools trying to run the world.'

"'I never touch a drop,' says I, 'and there are many kinds of fools; and the world runs on its own apex, according to science, with no meddling from me.'

"'I was referring,' says he, 'to the president of this republic. His country is in a desperate condition. Its treasury is empty, it's on the verge of war with Nicamala, and if it wasn't for the hot weather the people would be starting revolutions in every town. Here is a nation,' goes on Wainwright, 'on the brink of destruction. A man of intelligence could rescue it from its impending doom in one day by issuing the necessary edicts and orders. President Gomez knows nothing of statesmanship or policy. Do you know Adam Smith?'

"'Lemme see,' says I. 'There was a one-eared man named Smith in Fort Worth, Texas, but I think his first name was —— '

"'I am referring to the political economist,' says Wainwright.

"'S'mother Smith, then,' says I. 'The one I speak of never was arrested.'

"So Wainwright boils some more with indignation at the insensibility of people who are not corpulent to fill public positions; and then he tells me he is going out to the president's summer palace, which is four miles from Aguas Frescas, to instruct him in the art of running steam-heated republics.

"'Come along with me, Trotter,' says he, 'and I'll show you what brains can do.'

"'Anything in it?' I asks.

"'The satisfaction,' says he, 'of redeeming a country of two hundred thousand population from ruin back to prosperity and peace.'

"'Great,' says I. 'I'll go with you. I'd prefer to eat a live broiled lobster just now; but give me liberty as second choice if I can't be in at the death.'

"Wainwright and me permeates through the town, and he halts at a rum-dispensary.

"'Have you any money?' he asks.

"'I have,' says I, fishing out my silver dollar. 'I always go about with adequate sums of money.'

"'Then we'll drink,' says Wainwright.

"'Not me,' says I. 'Not any demon rum or any of its ramifications for mine. It's one of my non-weaknesses.'

"'It's my failing,' says he. 'What's your particular soft point?'

"'Industry,' says I, promptly. 'I'm hard-working, diligent, industrious, and energetic.'

"'My dear Mr. Trotter,' says he, 'surely I've known you long enough to tell you you are a liar. Every man must have his own particular weakness, and his own particular strength in other things. Now, you will buy me a drink of rum, and we will call on President Gomez.'

III

"Well, sir," Trotter went on, "we walks the four miles out, through a virgin conservatory of palms and ferns and other roof-garden products, to the president's summer White House.   It was blue, and reminded you of what you see on the stage in the third act, which they describe as 'same as the first' on the programs.

"There was more than fifty people waiting outside the iron fence that surrounded the house and grounds.   There was generals and agitators and épergnes in gold-laced uniforms, and citizens in diamonds and Panama hats — all waiting to get an audience with the Royal Five-Card Draw.   And in a kind of a summer-house in front of the mansion we could see a burnt-sienna man eating breakfast out of gold dishes and taking his time.   I judged that the crowd outside had come out for their morning orders and requests, and was afraid to intrude.

"But C. Wainwright wasn't.   The gate was open, and he walked inside and up to the president's table as confident as a man who knows the head waiter in a fifteen-cent restaurant.   And I went with him, because I had only seventy-five cents, and there was nothing else to do.

"The Gomez man rises from his chair, and looks, colored man as he was, like he was about to call out for corporal of the guard, post number one.   But Wainwright says some phrases to him in a peculiarly lubricating manner; and the first thing you know we was all three of us seated at the table, with coffee and rolls and iguana cutlets coming as fast as about ninety peons could rustle 'em.

"And then Wainwright begins to talk; but the president interrupts him.

"'You Yankees,' says he, polite, 'assuredly take the cake for assurance, I assure you' — or words to that effect. He spoke English better than you or me. 'You've had a long walk,' says he, 'but it's nicer in the cool morning to walk than to ride. May I suggest some refreshments?' says he.

"'Rum,' says Wainwright.

"'Gimme a cigar,' says I.

"Well, sir, the two talked an hour, keeping the generals and equities all in their good uniforms waiting outside the fence. And while I smoked, silent, I listened to Clifford Wainwright making a solid republic out of the wreck of one. I didn't follow his arguments with any special collocation of international intelligibility; but he had Mr. Gomez's attention glued and riveted. He takes out a pencil and marks the white linen tablecloth all over with figures and estimates and deductions. He speaks more or less disrespectfully of import and export duties and custom-house receipts and taxes and treaties and budgets and concessions and such truck that politics and government require; and when he gets through the Gomez man hops up and shakes his hand and says he's saved the country and the people.

"'You shall be rewarded,' says the president.

"'Might I suggest another — rum?' says Wainwright.

"'Cigar for me — darker brand,' says I.

"Well, sir, the president sent me and Wainwright back to the town in a victoria hitched to two flea-bitten selling-platers — but the best the country afforded.

"I found out afterward that Wainwright was a regular beachcomber — the smartest man on the whole coast, but kept down by rum. I liked him.

"One day I inveigled him into a walk out a couple of miles from the village, where there was an old grass hut on the bank of a little river. While he was sitting on the grass, talking beautiful of the wisdom of the world that he had learned in books, I took hold of him easy and tied his hands and feet together with leather thongs that I had in my pocket.

"'Lie still,' says I, 'and meditate on the exigencies and irregularities of life till I get back.'

"I went to a shack in Aguas Frescas where a mighty wise girl named Timotea Carrizo lived with her mother. The girl was just about as nice as you ever saw. In the States she would have been called a brunette; but she was better than a brunette — I should say she was what you might term an écru shade. I knew her pretty well. I told her about my friend Wainwright. She gave me a double handful of bark — calisaya, I think it was — and some more herbs that I was to mix with it, and told me what to do. I was to make tea of it and give it to him, and keep him from rum for a certain time. And for two weeks I did it. You know, I liked Wainwright. Both of us was broke; but Timotea sent us goat-meat and plan-

tains and tortillas every day; and at last I got the curse of
drink lifted from Clifford Wainwright. He lost his taste
for it. And in the cool of the evening him and me would
sit on the roof of Timotea's mother's hut, eating harmless
truck like coffee and rice and stewed crabs, and playing
the accordion.

"About that time President Gomez found out that the
advice of C. Wainwright was the stuff he had been looking
for. The country was pulling out of debt, and the treasury had enough boodle in it for him to amuse himself
occasionally with the night-latch. The people were
beginning to take their two-hour siestas again every day
— which was the surest sign of prosperity.

"So down from the regular capital he sends for Clifford Wainwright and makes him his private secretary at
twenty thousand Peru dollars a year. Yes, sir — so
much. Wainwright was on the water-wagon — thanks
to me and Timotea — and he was soon in clover with the
government gang. Don't forget what done it — calisaya
bark with them other herbs mixed — make a tea of it,
and give a cupful every two hours. Try it yourself. It
takes away the desire.

"As I said, a man can do a lot more for another party
than he can for himself. Wainwright, with his brains,
got a whole country out of trouble and on its feet; but
what could he do for himself? And without any special
brains, but with some nerve and common sense, I put him
on his feet because I never had the weakness that he did
— nothing but a cigar for mine, thanks. And ——"

Trotter paused. I looked at his tattered clothes and at his deeply sunburnt, hard, thoughtful face.

"Didn't Cartright ever offer to do anything for you?" I asked.

"Wainwright," corrected Trotter. "Yes, he offered me some pretty good jobs. But I'd have had to leave Aguas Frescas; so I didn't take any of 'em up. Say, I didn't tell you much about that girl — Timotea. We rather hit it off together. She was as good as you find 'em anywhere — Spanish, mostly, with just a twist of lemon-peel on top. What if they did live in a grass hut and went bare-armed?

"A month ago," went on Trotter, "she went away. I don't know where to. But ——"

"You'd better come back to the States," I insisted. "I can promise you positively that my brother will give you a position in cotton, sugar, or sheetings — I am not certain which."

"I think she went back with her mother," said Trotter, "to the village in the mountains that they come from. Tell me, what would this job you speak of pay?"

"Why," said I, hesitating over commerce, "I should say fifty or a hundred dollars a month—maybe two hundred."

"Ain't it funny," said Trotter, digging his toes in the sand, "what a chump a man is when it comes to paddling his own canoe? I don't know. Of course, I'm not making a living here. I'm on the bum. But — well, I wish you could have seen that Timotea. Every man has his own weak spot."

The gig from the *Andador* was coming ashore to take out the captain, purser, and myself, the lone passenger.

"I'll guarantee," said I confidently, "that my brother will pay you seventy-five dollars a month."

"All right, then," said William Trotter. "I'll ——"

But a soft voice called across the blazing sands. A girl, faintly lemon-tinted, stood in the Calle Real and called. She was bare-armed — but what of that?

"It's her!" said William Trotter, looking. "She's come back! I'm obliged; but I can't take the job. Thanks, just the same. Ain't it funny how we can't do nothing for ourselves, but we can do wonders for the other fellow? You was about to get me with your financial proposition; but we've all got our weak points. Timotea's mine. And, say!" Trotter had turned to leave, but he retraced the step or two that he had taken. "I like to have left you without saying good-bye," said he. "It kind of rattles you when they go away unexpected for a month and come back the same way. Shake hands. So long! Say, do you remember them gunshots we heard a while ago up at the cuartel? Well, I knew what they was, but I didn't mention it. It was Clifford Wainwright being shot by a squad of soldiers against a stone wall for giving away secrets of state to that Nicamala republic. Oh, yes, it was rum that did it. He backslided and got his. I guess we all have our weak points, and can't do much toward helping ourselves. Mine's waiting for me. I'd have liked to have that job with your brother, but — we've all got our weak points. So long!"

IV

A big black Carib carried me on his back through the surf to the ship's boat. On the way the purser handed me a letter that he had brought for me at the last moment from the post-office in Aguas Frescas. It was from my brother. He requested me to meet him at the St. Charles Hotel in New Orleans and accept a position with his house — in either cotton, sugar, or sheetings, and with five thousand dollars a year as my salary.

When I arrived at the Crescent City I hurried away—far away from the St. Charles to a dim *chambre garnie* in Bienville Street. And there, looking down from my attic window from time to time at the old, yellow, absinthe house across the street, I wrote this story to buy my bread and butter.

"Can thim that helps others help thimselves?"

Can the horse run?
Yes, the horse can run.
I don't think.

From The Rolling Stone

Will you go in?
Oh, yes! I will go in.

From The Rolling Stone

THE MARIONETTES

[Originally published in *The Black Cat* for April, 1902.]

THE policeman was standing at the corner of Twenty-fourth Street and a prodigiously dark alley near where the elevated railroad crosses the street. The time was two o'clock in the morning; the outlook a stretch of cold, drizzling, unsociable blackness until the dawn.

A man, wearing a long overcoat, with his hat tilted down in front, and carrying something in one hand, walked softly but rapidly out of the black alley. The policeman accosted him civilly, but with the assured air that is linked with conscious authority. The hour, the alley's musty reputation, the pedestrian's haste, the burden he carried — these easily combined into the "suspicious circumstances" that required illumination at the officer's hands.

The "suspect" halted readily and tilted back his hat, exposing, in the flicker of the electric lights, an emotionless, smooth countenance with a rather long nose and steady dark eyes. Thrusting his gloved hand into a side pocket of his overcoat, he drew out a card and handed it to the policeman. Holding it to catch the uncertain light, the officer read the name "Charles Spencer James, M. D." The street and number of the address were of a neighborhood so solid and respectable as to subdue even curiosity.

The policeman's downward glance at the article carried
in the doctor's hand — a handsome medicine case of black
leather, with small silver mountings — further endorsed
the guarantee of the card.

"All right, doctor," said the officer, stepping aside, with
an air of bulky affability. "Orders are to be extra careful. Good many burglars and hold-ups lately. Bad
night to be out. Not so cold, but — clammy."

With a formal inclination of his head, and a word or two
corroborative of the officer's estimate of the weather, Doctor James continued his somewhat rapid progress. Three
times that night had a patrolman accepted his professional card and the sight of his paragon of a medicine case
as vouchers for his honesty of person and purpose. Had
any one of those officers seen fit, on the morrow, to test
the evidence of that card he would have found it borne out
by the doctor's name on a handsome door-plate, his presence, calm and well dressed, in his well-equipped office —
provided it were not too early, Doctor James being a late
riser — and the testimony of the neighborhood to his good
citizenship, his devotion to his family, and his success as a
practitioner the two years he had lived among them.

Therefore, it would have much surprised any one of
those zealous guardians of the peace could they have
taken a peep into that immaculate medicine case. Upon
opening it, the first article to be seen would have been an
elegant set of the latest conceived tools used by the "box
man," as the ingenious safe burglar now denominates himself. Specially designed and constructed were the imple-

ments — the short but powerful "jimmy," the collection
of curiously fashioned keys, the blued drills and punches
of the finest temper — capable of eating their way into
chilled steel as a mouse eats into a cheese, and the clamps
that fasten like a leech to the polished door of a safe and
pull out the combination knob as a dentist extracts a
tooth. In a little pouch in the inner side of the "medicine"
case was a four-ounce vial of nitroglycerine, now half
empty. Underneath the tools was a mass of crumpled
banknotes and a few handfuls of gold coin, the money,
altogether, amounting to eight hundred and thirty dollars.

To a very limited circle of friends Doctor James was
known as "The Swell 'Greek.'" Half of the mysterious
term was a tribute to his cool and gentlemanlike manners;
the other half denoted, in the argot of the brotherhood, the
leader, the planner, the one who, by the power and pres-
tige of his address and position, secured the information
upon which they based their plans and desperate enterprises.

Of this elect circle the other members were Skitsie
Morgan and Gum Decker, expert "box men," and Leo-
pold Pretzfelder, a jeweller downtown, who manipulated
the "sparklers" and other ornaments collected by the
working trio. All good and loyal men, as loose-tongued as
Memnon and as fickle as the North Star.

That night's work had not been considered by the firm
to have yielded more than a moderate repayal for their
pains. An old-style two-story side-bolt safe in the dingy
office of a very wealthy old-style dry-goods firm on a

Saturday night should have excreted more than twenty-five hundred dollars.   But that was all they found, and they had divided it, the three of them, into equal shares upon the spot, as was their custom.   Ten or twelve thousand was what they expected.   But one of the proprietors had proved to be just a trifle too old-style.   Just after dark he had carried home in a shirt box most of the funds on hand.

Doctor James proceeded up Twenty-fourth Street, which was, to all appearance, depopulated.   Even the theatrical folk, who affect this district as a place of residence, were long since abed.   The drizzle had accumulated upon the street; puddles of it among the stones received the fire of the arc lights, and returned it, shattered into a myriad liquid spangles.   A captious wind, shower-soaked and chilling, coughed from the laryngeal flues between the houses.

As the practitioner's foot struck even with the corner of a tall brick residence of more pretension than its fellows the front door popped open, and a bawling negress clattered down the steps to the pavement.   Some medley of words came from her mouth, addressed, like as not, to herself — the recourse of her race when alone and beset by evil.   She looked to be one of that old vassal class of the South — voluble, familiar, loyal, irrepressible; her person pictured it — fat, neat, aproned, kerchiefed.

This sudden apparition, spewed from the silent house, reached the bottom of the steps as Doctor James came opposite.   Her brain transferring its energies from sound to sight, she ceased her clamor and fixed her pop-eyes upon the case the doctor carried.

"Bress de Lawd!" was the benison the sight drew from her. "Is you a doctor, suh?"

"Yes, I am a physician," said Doctor James, pausing.

"Den fo' God's sake come and see Mister Chandler, suh. He done had a fit or sump'n. He layin' jist like he wuz dead. Miss Amy sont me to git a doctor. Lawd knows whar old Cindy'd a skeared one up from, if you, suh, hadn't come along. Ef old Mars' knowed one ten-hundredth part of dese doin's dey'd be shootin' gwine on, suh — pistol shootin' — leb'm feet marked off on de ground, and ev'ybody a-duellin'. And dat po' lamb, Miss Amy ——"

"Lead the way," said Doctor James, setting his foot upon the step, "if you want me as a doctor. As an auditor I'm not open to engagements."

The negress preceded him into the house and up a flight of thickly carpeted stairs. Twice they came to dimly lighted branching hallways. At the second one the now panting conductress turned down a hall, stopping at a door and opening it.

"I done brought de doctor, Miss Amy."

Doctor James entered the room, and bowed slightly to a young lady standing by the side of a bed. He set his medicine case upon a chair, removed his overcoat, throwing it over the case and the back of the chair, and advanced with quiet self-possession to the bedside.

There lay a man, sprawling as he had fallen — a man

dressed richly in the prevailing mode, with only his shoes removed; lying relaxed, and as still as the dead.

There emanated from Doctor James an aura of calm force and reserve strength that was as manna in the desert to the weak and desolate among his patrons. Always had women, especially, been attracted by something in his sick-room manner. It was not the indulgent suavity of the fashionable healer, but a manner of poise, of sureness, of ability to overcome fate, of deference and protection and devotion. There was an exploring magnetism in his steadfast, luminous brown eyes; a latent authority in the impassive, even priestly, tranquillity of his smooth countenance that outwardly fitted him for the part of confidant and consoler. Sometimes, at his first professional visit, women would tell him where they hid their diamonds at night from the burglars.

With the ease of much practice, Doctor James's unroving eyes estimated the order and quality of the room's furnishings. The appointments were rich and costly. The same glance had secured cognizance of the lady's appearance. She was small and scarcely past twenty. Her face possessed the title to a winsome prettiness, now obscured by (you would say) rather a fixed melancholy than the more violent imprint of a sudden sorrow. Upon her forehead, above one eyebrow, was a livid bruise, suffered, the physician's eye told him, within the past six hours.

Doctor James's fingers went to the man's wrist. His almost vocal eyes questioned the lady.

"I am Mrs. Chandler," she responded, speaking with

the plaintive Southern slur and intonation. "My husband was taken suddenly ill about ten minutes before you came. He has had attacks of heart trouble before — some of them were very bad." His clothed state and the late hour seemed to prompt her to further explanation. "He had been out late; to — a supper, I believe."

Doctor James now turned his attention to his patient. In whichever of his "professions" he happened to be engaged he was wont to honor the "case" or the "job" with his whole interest.

The sick man appeared to be about thirty. His countenance bore a look of boldness and dissipation, but was not without a symmetry of feature and the fine lines drawn by a taste and indulgence in humor that gave the redeeming touch. There was an odor of spilled wine about his clothes.

The physician laid back his outer garments, and then, with a penknife, slit the shirt-front from collar to waist. The obstacles cleared, he laid his ear to the heart and listened intently.

"Mitral regurgitation?" he said, softly, when he rose. The words ended with the rising inflection of uncertainty. Again he listened long; and this time he said, "Mitral insufficiency," with the accent of an assured diagnosis.

"Madam," he began, in the reassuring tones that had so often allayed anxiety, "there is a probability——" As he slowly turned his head to face the lady, he saw her fall, white and swooning, into the arms of the old negress.

"Po' lamb! po' lamb! Has dey done killed Aunt

Cindy's own blessed child?   May de Lawd 'stroy wid his
wrath dem what stole her away; what break dat angel
heart; what left ——"

"Lift her feet," said Doctor James, assisting to support
the drooping form.   "Where is her room?   She must be
put to bed."

"In here, suh."   The woman nodded her kerchiefed
head toward a door.   "Dat's Miss Amy's room."

They carried her in there, and laid her on the bed.
Her pulse was faint, but regular.   She passed from the
swoon, without recovering consciousness, into a profound slumber.

"She is quite exhausted," said the physician.   "Sleep
is a good remedy.   When she wakes, give her a toddy —
with an egg in it, if she can take it.   How did she get
that bruise upon her forehead?"

"She done got a lick there, suh.   De po' lamb fell —
No, suh" — the old woman's racial mutability swept her
into a sudden flare of indignation — "old Cindy ain't
gwineter lie for dat debble.   He done it, suh.   May de
Lawd wither de hand what — dar now!   Cindy promise
her sweet lamb she ain't gwine tell.   Miss Amy got hurt,
suh, on de head."

Doctor James stepped to a stand where a handsome
lamp burned, and turned the flame low.

"Stay here with your mistress," he ordered, "and keep
quiet so she will sleep.   If she wakes, give her the toddy.
If she grows any weaker, let me know.   There is something strange about it."

"Dar's mo' strange t'ings dan dat 'round here," began the negress, but the physician hushed her in a seldom-employed peremptory, concentrated voice with which he had often allayed hysteria itself. He returned to the other room, closing the door softly behind him. The man on the bed had not moved, but his eyes were open. His lips seemed to form words. Doctor James bent his head to listen. "The money! the money!" was what they were whispering.

"Can you understand what I say?" asked the doctor, speaking low, but distinctly.

The head nodded slightly.

"I am a physician, sent for by your wife. You are Mr. Chandler, I am told. You are quite ill. You must not excite or distress yourself at all."

The patient's eyes seemed to beckon to him. The doctor stooped to catch the same faint words.

"The money — the twenty thousand dollars."

"Where is this money? — in the bank?"

The eyes expressed a negative. "Tell her" — the whisper was growing fainter — "the twenty thousand dollars — her money" — his eyes wandered about the room.

"You have placed this money somewhere?" — Doctor James's voice was toiling like a siren's to conjure the secret from the man's failing intelligence — "Is it in this room?"

He thought he saw a fluttering assent in the dimming eyes. The pulse under his fingers was as fine and small as a silk thread.

There arose in Doctor James's brain and heart the instincts of his other profession. Promptly, as he acted in everything, he decided to learn the whereabouts of this money, and at the calculated and certain cost of a human life.

Drawing from his pocket a little pad of prescription blanks, he scribbled upon one of them a formula suited, according to the best practice, to the needs of the sufferer. Going to the door of the inner room, he softly called the old woman, gave her the prescription, and bade her take it to some drug store and fetch the medicine.

When she had gone, muttering to herself, the doctor stepped to the bedside of the lady. She still slept soundly; her pulse was a little stronger; her forehead was cool, save where the inflammation of the bruise extended, and a slight moisture covered it. Unless disturbed, she would yet sleep for hours. He found the key in the door, and locked it after him when he returned.

Doctor James looked at his watch. He could call half an hour his own, since before that time the old woman could scarcely return from her mission. Then he sought and found water in a pitcher and a glass tumbler. Opening his medicine case he took out the vial containing the nitroglycerine — "the oil," as his brethren of the brace-and-bit term it.

One drop of the faint yellow, thickish liquid he let fall in the tumbler. He took out his silver hypodermic syringe case, and screwed the needle into its place. Carefully measuring each modicum of water in the graduated glass barrel of the syringe, he diluted the one drop with nearly half a tumbler of water.

Two hours earlier that night Doctor James had, with that syringe, injected the undiluted liquid into a hole drilled in the lock of a safe, and had destroyed, with one dull explosion, the machinery that controlled the movement of the bolts. He now purposed, with the same means, to shiver the prime machinery of a human being — to rend its heart — and each shock was for the sake of the money to follow.

The same means, but in a different guise. Whereas, that was the giant in its rude, primary dynamic strength, this was the courtier, whose no less deadly arms were concealed by velvet and lace. For the liquid in the tumbler and in the syringe that the physican carefully filled was now a solution of glonoin, the most powerful heart stimulant known to medical science. Two ounces had riven the solid door of the iron safe; with one fiftieth part of a minim he was now about to still forever the intricate mechanism of a human life.

But not immediately. It was not so intended. First there would be a quick increase of vitality; a powerful impetus given to every organ and faculty. The heart would respond bravely to the fatal spur; the blood in the veins return more rapidly to its source.

But, as Doctor James well knew, over-stimulation in this form of heart disease means death, as sure as by a rifle shot. When the clogged arteries should suffer congestion from the increased flow of blood pumped into them by the power of the burglar's "oil," they would rapidly become "no thoroughfare," and the fountain of life would cease to flow.

The physician bared the chest of the unconscious Chandler. Easily and skilfully he injected, subcutaneously, the contents of the syringe into the muscles of the region over the heart. True to his neat habits in both professions, he next carefully dried his needle and re-inserted the fine wire that threaded it when not in use.

In three minutes Chandler opened his eyes, and spoke, in a voice faint but audible, inquiring who attended upon him. Doctor James again explained his presence there.

"Where is my wife?" asked the patient.

"She is asleep — from exhaustion and worry," said the doctor. "I would not awaken her, unless ——"

"It isn't — necessary." Chandler spoke with spaces between his words caused by his short breath that some demon was driving too fast. "She wouldn't — thank you to disturb her — on my — account."

Doctor James drew a chair to the bedside. Conversation must not be squandered.

"A few minutes ago," he began, in the grave, candid tones of his other profession, "you were trying to tell me something regarding some money. I do not seek your confidence, but it is my duty to advise you that anxiety and worry will work against your recovery. If you have any communication to make about this — to relieve your mind about this — twenty thousand dollars, I think was the amount you mentioned — you would better do so."

Chandler could not turn his head, but he rolled his eyes in the direction of the speaker.

"Did I — say where this — money is?"

"No," answered the physician. "I only inferred, from your scarcely intelligible words, that you felt a solicitude concerning its safety. If it is in this room ——"

Doctor James paused. Did he only seem to perceive a flicker of understanding, a gleam of suspicion upon the ironical features of his patient? Had he seemed too eager? Had he said too much? Chandler's next words restored his confidence.

"Where — should it be," he gasped, "but in — the safe — there?"

With his eyes he indicated a corner of the room, where now, for the first time, the doctor perceived a small iron safe, half-concealed by the trailing end of a window curtain.

Rising, he took the sick man's wrist. His pulse was beating in great throbs, with ominous intervals between.

"Lift your arm," said Doctor James.

"You know — I can't move, Doctor."

The physician stepped swiftly to the hall door, opened it, and listened. All was still. Without further circumvention he went to the safe, and examined it. Of a primitive make and simple design, it afforded little more security than protection against light-fingered servants. To his skill it was a mere toy, a thing of straw and pasteboard. The money was as good as in his hands. With his clamps he could draw the knob, punch the tumblers and open the door in two minutes. Perhaps, in another way, he might open it in one.

Kneeling upon the floor, he laid his ear to the combination plate, and slowly turned the knob. As he had surmised, it was locked at only a "day com." — upon one number. His keen ear caught the faint warning click as the tumbler was disturbed; he used the clue — the handle turned. He swung the door wide open.

The interior of the safe was bare — not even a scrap of paper rested within the hollow iron cube.

Doctor James rose to his feet and walked back to the bed.

A thick dew had formed upon the dying man's brow, but there was a mocking, grim smile on his lips and in his eyes.

"I never — saw it before," he said, painfully, "medicine and — burglary wedded! Do you — make the — combination pay — dear Doctor?"

Than that situation afforded, there was never a more rigorous test of Doctor James's greatness. Trapped by the diabolic humor of his victim into a position both ridiculous and unsafe, he maintained his dignity as well as his presence of mind. Taking out his watch, he waited for the man to die.

"You were — just a shade — too — anxious — about that money. But it never was — in any danger — from you, dear Doctor. It's safe. Perfectly safe. It's all — in the hands — of the bookmakers. Twenty — thousand — Amy's money. I played it at the races — lost every — cent of it. I've been a pretty bad boy, Burglar —

excuse me — Doctor, but I've been a square sport. I don't think — I ever met — such an — eighteen-carat rascal as you are, Doctor — excuse me — Burglar, in all my rounds. Is it contrary — to the ethics — of your — gang, Burglar, to give a victim — excuse me — patient, a drink of water?"

Doctor James brought him a drink. He could scarcely swallow it. The reaction from the powerful drug was coming in regular, intensifying waves. But his moribund fancy must have one more grating fling.

"Gambler — drunkard — spendthrift — I've been those, but — a doctor-burglar!"

The physician indulged himself to but one reply to the other's caustic taunts. Bending low to catch Chandler's fast crystallizing gaze, he pointed to the sleeping lady's door with a gesture so stern and significant that the prostrate man half-lifted his head, with his remaining strength, to see. He saw nothing; but he caught the cold words of the doctor — the last sounds he was to hear:

"I never yet struck a woman."

It were vain to attempt to con such men. There is no curriculum that can reckon with them in its ken. They are offshoots from the types whereof men say, "He will do this," or "He will do that." We only know that they exist; and that we can observe them, and tell one another of their bare performances, as children watch and speak of the marionettes.

Yet it were a droll study in egoism to consider these two — one an assassin and a robber, standing above his victim; the other baser in his offences, if a lesser law-breaker, lying, abhorred, in the house of the wife he had persecuted, spoiled, and smitten, one a tiger, the other a dog-wolf — to consider each of them sickening at the foulness of the other; and each flourishing out of the mire of his manifest guilt his own immaculate standard — of conduct, if not of honor.

The one retort of Doctor James must have struck home to the other's remaining shreds of shame and manhood, for it proved the *coup de grâce*.   A deep blush suffused his face — an ignominious *rosa mortis;* the respiration ceased, and, with scarcely a tremor, Chandler expired.

Close following upon his last breath came the negress, bringing the medicine.   With a hand gently pressing upon the closed eyelids, Doctor James told her of the end. Not grief, but a hereditary *rapprochement* with death in the abstract, moved her to a dismal, watery snuffling, accompanied by her usual jeremiad.

"Dar now!   It's in de Lawd's hands.   He am de jedge ob de transgressor, and de suppo't of dem in distress.   He gwine hab suppo't us now.   Cindy done paid out de last quarter fer dis bottle of physic, and it nebber come to no use."

"Do I understand," asked Doctor James, "that Mrs. Chandler has no money?"

"Money, suh?   You know what make Miss Amy fall down, and so weak?   Stahvation, suh.   Nothin' to eat in dis house but some crumbly crackers in three days.   Dat angel sell her finger rings and watch mont's ago.   Dis

Here we have Kate and John.
Will Kate fight John or rail
at him?

Oh, no! for Kate loves John.
He bought her a nice ring.

From The Rolling Stone

Did he go up?
Oh, yes! he did go up.

From The Rolling Stone

fine house, suh, wid de red cyarpets and shiny bureaus, it's all hired; and de man talkin' scan'lous about de rent. Dat debble — 'scuse me, Lawd — he done in Yo' hands fer jedgment, now — he made way wid everything."

The physician's silence encouraged her to continue. The history that he gleaned from Cindy's disordered monologue was an old one, of illusion, wilfulness, disaster, cruelty and pride. Standing out from the blurred panorama of her gabble were little clear pictures — an ideal home in the far South; a quickly repented marriage; an unhappy season, full of wrongs and abuse, and, of late, an inheritance of money that promised deliverance; its seizure and waste by the dog-wolf during a two months' absence, and his return in the midst of a scandalous carouse. Unobtruded, but visible between every line, ran a pure white thread through the smudged warp of the story — the simple, all-enduring, sublime love of the old negress, following her mistress unswervingly through everything to the end.

When at last she paused, the physician spoke, asking if the house contained whiskey or liquor of any sort. There was, the old woman informed him, half a bottle of brandy left in the sideboard by the dog-wolf.

"Prepare a toddy as I told you," said Doctor James. "Wake your mistress; have her drink it, and tell her what has happened."

Some ten minutes afterward, Mrs. Chandler entered, supported by old Cindy's arm. She appeared to be a little stronger since her sleep and the stimulant she had taken.   Doctor James had covered, with a sheet, the form upon the bed.

The lady turned her mournful eyes once, with a half-frightened look, toward it, and pressed closer to her loyal protector.   Her eyes were dry and bright.   Sorrow seemed to have done its utmost with her.   The fount of tears was dried; feeling itself paralyzed.

Doctor James was standing near the table, his overcoat donned, his hat and medicine case in his hand. His face was calm and impassive — practice had inured him to the sight of human suffering.   His lambent brown eyes alone expressed a discreet professional sympathy.

He spoke kindly and briefly, stating that, as the hour was late, and assistance, no doubt, difficult to procure, he would himself send the proper persons to attend to the necessary finalities.

"One matter, in conclusion," said the doctor, pointing to the safe with its still wide-open door.   "Your husband, Mrs. Chandler, toward the end, felt that he could not live; and directed me to open that safe, giving me the number upon which the combination is set.   In case you may need to use it, you will remember that the number is forty-one. Turn several times to the right; then to the left once; stop at forty-one.   He would not permit me to waken you, though he knew the end was near.

"In that safe he said he had placed a sum of money — not large — but enough to enable you to carry out his last request.   That was that you should return to your old home, and, in after days, when time shall have made it easier, forgive his many sins against you."

He pointed to the table, where lay an orderly pile of banknotes, surmounted by two stacks of gold coins.

"The money is there — as he described it — eight hundred and thirty dollars. I beg to leave my card with you, in case I can be of any service later on."

So, he had thought of her — and kindly — at the last! So late! And yet the lie fanned into life one last spark of tenderness where she had thought all was turned to ashes and dust. She cried aloud "Rob! Rob!" She turned, and, upon the ready bosom of her true servitor, diluted her grief in relieving tears. It is well to think, also, that in the years to follow, the murderer's falsehood shone like a little star above the grave of love, comforting her, and gaining the forgiveness that is good in itself, whether asked for or no.

Hushed and soothed upon the dark bosom, like a child, by a crooning, babbling sympathy, at last she raised her head — but the doctor was gone.

THE MARQUIS AND MISS SALLY

[Originally published in *Everybody's Magazine*, June, 1903.]

WITHOUT knowing it, Old Bill Bascom had the honor of being overtaken by fate the same day with the Marquis of Borodale.

The Marquis lived in Regent Square, London. Old Bill lived on Limping Doe Creek, Hardeman County, Texas. The cataclysm that engulfed the Marquis took the form of a bursting bubble known as the Central and South American Mahogany and Caoutchouc Monopoly. Old Bill's Nemesis was in the no less perilous shape of a band of civilized Indian cattle thieves from the Territory who ran off his entire herd of four hundred head, and shot old Bill dead as he trailed after them. To even up the consequences of the two catastrophes, the Marquis, as soon as he found that all he possessed would pay only fifteen shillings on the pound of his indebtedness, shot himself.

Old Bill left a family of six motherless sons and daughters, who found themselves without even a red steer left to eat, or a red cent to buy one with.

The Marquis left one son, a young man, who had come to the States and established a large and well-stocked ranch in the Panhandle of Texas. When this young man

learned the news he mounted his pony and rode to town.
There he placed everything he owned except his horse,
saddle, Winchester, and fifteen dollars in his pockets, in
the hands of his lawyers, with instructions to sell and forward the proceeds to London to be applied upon the pay-
ment of his father's debts.   Then he mounted his pony
and rode southward.

One day, arriving about the same time, but by different
trails, two young chaps rode up to the Diamond-Cross
ranch, on the Little Piedra, and asked for work.   Both
were dressed neatly and sprucely in cowboy costume.
One was a straight-set fellow, with delicate, handsome
features, short, brown hair, and smooth face, sunburned to
a golden brown.   The other applicant was stouter and
broad-shouldered, with fresh, red complexion, somewhat
freckled, reddish, curling hair, and a rather plain face,
made attractive by laughing eyes and a pleasant mouth.

The superintendent of the Diamond-Cross was of the
opinion that he could give them work.   In fact, word had
reached him that morning that the camp cook — a most
important member of the outfit — had straddled his
broncho and departed, being unable to withstand the fire
of fun and practical jokes of which he was, ex officio, the
legitimate target.

"Can either of you cook?" asked the superintendent.

"I can," said the reddish-haired fellow, promptly.
"I've cooked in camp quite a lot.   I'm willing to take the
job until you've got something else to offer."

"Now, that's the way I like to hear a man talk," said

the superintendent, approvingly. "I'll give you a note to Saunders, and he'll put you to work."

Thus the names of John Bascom and Charles Norwood were added to the pay-roll of the Diamond-Cross. The two left for the round-up camp immediately after dinner. Their directions were simple, but sufficient: "Keep down the arroyo for fifteen miles till you get there." Both being strangers from afar, young, spirited, and thus thrown together by chance for a long ride, it is likely that the comradeship that afterward existed so strongly between them began that afternoon as they meandered along the little valley of the Canada Verda.

They reached their destination just after sunset. The main camp of the round-up was comfortably located on the bank of a long water-hole, under a fine mott of timber. A number of small A tents pitched upon grassy spots and the big wall tent for provisions showed that the camp was intended to be occupied for a considerable length of time.

The round-up had ridden in but a few moments before, hungry and tired, to a supperless camp. The boys were engaged in an emulous display of anathemas supposed to fit the case of the absconding cook. While they were unsaddling and hobbling their ponies, the newcomers rode in and inquired for Pink Saunders. The boss of the round-up came forth and was given the superintendent's note.

Pink Saunders, though a boss during working hours, was a humorist in camp, where everybody, from cook to superintendent, is equal.   After reading the note he waved his hand toward the camp and shouted, ceremoniously, at the top of his voice, "Gentlemen, allow me to present to you the Marquis and Miss Sally."

At the words both the new arrivals betrayed confusion. The newly employed cook started, with a surprised look on his face, but, immediately recollecting that "Miss Sally" is the generic name for the male cook in every west Texas cow camp, he recovered his composure with a grin at his own expense.

His companion showed little less discomposure, even turning angrily, with a bitten lip, and reaching for his saddle pommel, as if to remount his pony; but "Miss Sally" touched his arm and said, laughingly, "Come now, Marquis; that was quite a compliment from Saunders. It's that distinguished air of yours and aristocratic nose that made him call you that."

He began to unsaddle, and the Marquis, restored to equanimity, followed his example. Rolling up his sleeves, Miss Sally sprang for the grub wagon, shouting:

"I'm the new cook b'thunder! Some of you chaps rustle a little wood for a fire, and I'll guarantee you a hot square meal inside of thirty minutes." Miss Sally's energy and good-humor, as he ransacked the grub wagon for coffee, flour, and bacon, won the good opinion of the camp instantly.

And also, in days following, the Marquis, after becoming better acquainted, proved to be a cheerful, pleasant fellow, always a little reserved, and taking no part in the rough camp frolics; but the boys gradually came to respect this reserve — which fitted the title Saunders had given him — and even to like him for it. Saunders had assigned him to a place holding the herd during the cuttings. He proved to be a skilful rider and as good with the lariat or in the branding pen as most of them.

The Marquis and Miss Sally grew to be quite close comrades. After supper was over, and everything cleaned up, you would generally find them together, Miss Sally smoking his brier-root pipe, and the Marquis plaiting a quirt or scraping rawhide for a new pair of hobbles.

The superintendent did not forget his promise to keep an eye on the cook. Several times, when visiting the camp, he held long talks with him. He seemed to have taken a fancy to Miss Sally. One afternoon he rode up, on his way back to the ranch from a tour of the camps, and said to him:

"There'll be a man here in the morning to take your place. As soon as he shows up you come to the ranch. I want you to take charge of the ranch accounts and correspondence. I want somebody that I can depend upon to keep things straight when I'm away. The wages 'll be all right. The Diamond-Cross 'll hold its end up with a man who'll look after its interests."

"All right," said Miss Sally, as quietly as if he had expected the notice all along. "Any objections to my bringing my wife down to the ranch?"

"You married?" said the superintendent, frowning a little. "You didn't mention it when we were talking."

"Because I'm not," said the cook. "But I'd like to be.
Thought I'd wait till I got a job under roof. I couldn't
ask her to live in a cow camp."

"Right," agreed the superintendent. "A camp isn't
quite the place for a married man — but — well, there's
plenty of room at the house, and if you suit us as well as I
think you will you can afford it. You write to her to
come on."

"All right," said Miss Sally again, "I'll ride in as soon
as I am relieved to-morrow."

It was a rather chilly night, and after supper the cow-
punchers were lounging about a big fire of dried mesquite
chunks.

Their usual exchange of jokes and repartee had dwin-
dled amost to silence, but silence in a cow camp generally
betokens the brewing of mischief.

Miss Sally and the Marquis were seated upon a log,
discussing the relative merits of the lengthened or short-
ened stirrup in long-distance riding. The Marquis arose
presently and went to a tree near by to examine some strips
of rawhide he was seasoning for making a lariat. Just
as he left a little puff of wind blew some scraps of tobacco
from a cigarette that Dry-Creek Smithers was rolling, into
Miss Sally's eyes. While the cook was rubbing at them,
with tears flowing, "Phonograph" Davis — so called on
account of his strident voice — arose and began a speech.

"Fellers and citizens! I desire to perpound a inter-
rogatory. What is the most grievous spectacle what
the human mind can contemplate?"

A volley of answers responded to his question.

"A busted flush!"

"A Maverick when you ain't got your branding iron!"

"Yourself!"

"The hole in the end of some other feller's gun!"

"Shet up, you ignoramuses," said old Taller, the fat cow-puncher. "Phony knows what it is. He's waitin' for to tell us."

"No, fellers and citizens," continued Phonograph. "Them spectacles you've e-numerated air shore grievious, and way up yonder close to the so-lution, but they ain't it. The most grievious spectacle air that" — he pointed to Miss Sally, who was still rubbing his streaming eyes — "a trustin' and a in-veegled female a-weepin' tears on account of her heart bein' busted by a false deceiver. Air we men or air we catamounts to gaze upon the blightin' of our Miss Sally's affections by a a-risto-crat, which has come among us with his superior beauty and his glitterin' title to give the weeps to the lovely critter we air bound to pertect? Air we goin' to act like men, or air we goin' to keep on eatin' soggy chuck from her cryin' so plentiful over the bread-pan?"

"It's a gallopin' shame," said Dry-Creek, with a sniffle. 'It ain't human. I've noticed the varmint a-palaverin' round her frequent. And him a Marquis! Ain't that a title, Phony?

"It's somethin' like a king," the Brushy Creek Kid hastened to explain, "only lower in the deck. Guess it comes in between the Jack and the ten-spot."

"Don't miscontruct me," went on Phonograph, "as undervaluatin' the a-ristocrats. Some of 'em air proper people and can travel right along with the Watson boys. I've herded some with 'em myself. I've viewed the elephant with the Mayor of Fort Worth, and I've listened to the owl with the gen'ral passenger agent of the Katy, and they can keep up with the percession from where you laid the chunk. But when a Marquis monkeys with the innocent affections of a cook-lady, may I inquire what the case seems to call for?"

"The leathers," shouted Dry-Creek Smithers.

"You hearn 'er, Charity!" was the Kid's form of corroboration.

"We've got your company," assented the cow-punchers, in chorus.

Before the Marquis realized their intention, two of them seized him by each arm and led him up to the log. Phonograph Davis, self-appointed to carry out the sentence, stood ready, with a pair of stout leather leggings in his hands.

It was the first time they had ever laid hands on the Marquis during their somewhat rude sports.

"What are you up to?" he asked, indignantly, with flashing eyes

"Go easy, Marquis," whispered Rube Fellows, one of the boys that held him. "It's all in fun. Take it good-natured and they'll let you off light. They're only goin' to stretch you over the log and tan you eight or ten times with the leggin's. 'Twon't hurt much."

The Marquis, with an exclamation of anger, his white teeth gleaming, suddenly exhibited a surprising strength. He wrenched with his arms so violently that the four men were swayed and dragged many yards from the log. A cry of anger escaped him, and then Miss Sally, his eyes cleared of the tobacco, saw, and he immediately mixed with the struggling group.

But at that moment a loud "Hallo!" rang in their ears, and a buckboard drawn by a team of galloping mustangs spun into the campfire's circle of light. Every man turned to look, and what they saw drove from their minds all thoughts of carrying out Phonograph Davis's rather time-worn contribution to the evening's amusement. Bigger game than the Marquis was at hand, and his captors released him and stood staring at the approaching victim.

The buckboard and team belonged to Sam Holly, a cattleman from the Big Muddy. Sam was driving, and with him was a stout, smooth-faced man, wearing a frock coat and a high silk hat. That was the county judge, Mr. Dave Hackett, candidate for reëlection. Sam was escorting him about the county, among the camps, to shake up the sovereign voters.

The men got out, hitched the team to a mesquite, and walked toward the fire.

Instantly every man in camp, except the Marquis, Miss Sally, and Pink Saunders, who had to play host, uttered a frightful yell of assumed terror and fled on all sides into the darkness.

"Heavens alive!" exclaimed Hackett, "are we as ugly as that? How do you do, Mr. Saunders? Glad to see you again. What are you doing to my hat, Holly?"

"I was afraid of this hat," said Sam Holly, meditatively. He had taken the hat from Hackett's head and was holding it in his hand, looking dubiously around at the shadows beyond the firelight where now absolute stillness reigned. "What do you think, Saunders?"

Pink grinned.

"Better elevate it some," he said, in the tone of one giving disinterested advice. "The light ain't none too good. I wouldn't want it on my head."

Holly stepped upon the hub of a hind wheel of the grub wagon and hung the hat upon a limb of a live-oak. Scarcely had his foot touched the ground when the crash of a dozen six-shooters split the air, and the hat fell to the ground riddled with bullets.

A hissing noise was heard as if from a score of rattlesnakes, and now the cow-punchers emerged on all sides from the darkness, stepping high, with ludicrously exaggerated caution, and "hist" - ing to one another to observe the utmost prudence in approaching. They formed a solemn, wide circle about the hat, gazing at it in manifest alarm, and seized every few moments by little stampedes of panicky flight.

"It's the varmint," said one in awed tones, "that flits up and down in the low grounds at night, saying, 'Willie-wallo!'"

"It's the venemous Kypootum," proclaimed another. "It stings after it's dead, and hollers after it's buried."

"It's the chief of the hairy tribe," said Phonograph Davis. "But it's stone dead, now, boys."

"Don't you believe it," demurred Dry-Creek. "It's only 'possumin'.' It's the dreaded Highgollacum fantod from the forest. There's only one way to destroy its life."

He led forward Old Taller, the 240-pound cow-puncher. Old Taller placed the hat upright on the ground and sol- ‹ ʒ sat upon it, crushing it as flat as a pancake.

Hackett had viewed these proceedings with wide-open eyes. Sam Holly saw that his anger was rising and said to him:

"Here's where you win or lose, Judge. There are sixty votes on the Diamond Cross. The boys are trying your mettle. Take it as a joke, and I don't think you'll regret it." And Hackett saw the point and rose to the occasion.

Advancing to where the slayers of the wild beast were standing above its remains and declaring it to be at last defunct, he said, with deep earnestness:

"Boys, I must thank you for this gallant rescue. While driving through the arroyo that cruel monster that you have so fearlessly and repeatedly slaughtered sprang upon us from the tree tops. To you I shall consider that I owe my life, and also, I hope, reëlection to the office for which I am again a candidate. Allow me to hand you my card."

The cow-punchers, always so sober-faced while engaged in their monkey-shines, relaxed into a grin of approval.

But Phonograph Davis, his appetite for fun not yet appeased, had something more up his sleeve.

"Pardner," he said, addressing Hackett with grave severity, "many a camp would be down on you for turnin' loose a pernicious varmint like that in it; but, bein' as we all escaped without loss of life, we'll overlook it. You can play square with us if you'll do it."

"How's that?" asket Hackett suspiciously.

"You're authorized to perform the sacred rights and lefts of mattermony, air you not?"

"Well, yes," replied Hackett. "A marriage cere conducted by me would be legal."

"A wrong air to be righted in this here camp," said Phonography, virtuously. "A a-ristocrat have slighted a 'umble but beautchoos female wat's pinin' for his affections. It's the jooty of the camp to drag forth the haughty descendant of a hundred — or maybe a hundred and twenty-five — earls, even so at the p'int of a riat, and jine him to the weepin' lady. Fellows! round up Miss Sally and the Marquis, there's goin' to be a weddin'."

This whim of Phonograph's was received with whoops of appreciation. The cow-punchers started to apprehend the principals of the proposed ceremony.

"Kindly prompt me," said Hackett, wiping his forehead, though the night was cool, "how far this thing is to be carried. And might I expect any further portions of my raiment to be mistaken for wild animals and killed?"

"The boys are livelier than usual to-night," said Saunders. "The ones they are talking about marrying are two of the boys — a herd rider and the cook. It's another joke.   You and Sam will have to sleep here to-night anyway; p'rhaps you'd better see 'em through with it. Maybe they'll quiet down after that."

The matchmakers found Miss Sally seated on the tongue of the grub wagon, calmly smoking his pipe.   The Marquis was leaning idly against one of the trees under which the supply tent was pitched.

Into this tent they were both hustled, and Phonograph, as master of ceremonies, gave orders for the preparations.

"You, Dry-Creek and Jimmy, and Ben and Taller — hump yourselves to the wildwood and rustle flowers for the blow-out — mesquite 'll do — and get that Spanish dagger blossom at the corner of the horse corral for the bride to pack.   You, Limpy, get out that red and yaller blanket of your'n for Miss Sally's skyirt.   Marquis, you'll do 'thout fixin'; nobody don't ever look at the groom."

During their absurd preparation, the two principals were left alone for a few moments in the tent.   The Marquis suddenly showed wild perturbation.

"This foolishness must not go on," he said, turning to Miss Sally a face white in the light of the lantern hanging to the ridge-pole.

"Why not?" said the cook, with an amused smile. "It's fun for the boys; and they've always let you off pretty light in their frolics.   I don't mind it."

"But you don't understand," persisted the Marquis, pleadingly.   "That man is county judge, and his acts are binding.   I can't — oh, you don't know ——"

See Tom and the dog.
Will Tom hurt the dog?
Oh, no! Tom will not hurt
   the dog.
Tom will give the dog a bite
   to eat.

From The Rolling Stone

See him do it.
Can John find the ball?
Is it in the cup?
No, it is not in it:
Neither is John.

From The Rolling Stone

The cook stepped forward and took the Marquis's hands.

"Sally Bascom," he said, "I KNOW!"

"You know!" faltered the Marquis, trembling. "And you — want to —— "

"More than I ever wanted anything. Will you — here come the boys!"

The cow-punchers crowded in, laden with armfuls of decorations.

"Perfifious coyote!" said Phonograph, sternly, addressing the Marquis. "Air you willing to patch up the damage you've did this ere slab-sided but trustin' bunch o' calico by single-footin' easy to the altar, or will we have to rope ye, and drag you thar?"

The Marquis pushed back his hat, and leaned jauntily against some high-piled sacks of beans. His cheeks were flushed, and his eyes were shining.

"Go on with the rat killin'," said he.

A little while after a procession approached the tree under which Hackett, Holly, and Saunders were sitting smoking.

Limpy Walker was in the lead, extracting a doleful tune from his concertina. Next came the bride and groom. The cook wore the gorgeous Navajo blanket tied around his waist and carried in one hand the waxen-white Spanish dagger blossom as large as a peck-measure and weighing fifteen pounds. His hat was ornamented with mesquite branches and yellow ratama blooms. A resurrected mosquito bar served as a veil. After them stumbled Phonograph Davis, in the character of the bride's father, weeping into a saddle blanket with sobs that could be heard a mile away. The cow-punchers followed by twos, loudly commenting upon the bride's appearance, in a supposed imitation of the audiences at fashionable weddings.

Hackett rose as the procession halted before him, and after a little lecture upon matrimony, asked:

"What are your names?"

"Sally and Charles," answered the cook.

"Join hands, Charles and Sally."

Perhaps there never was a stranger wedding. For, wedding it was, though only two of those present knew it.

When the ceremony was over, the cow-punchers gave one yell of congratulation and immediately abandoned their foolery for the night. Blankets were unrolled and sleep became the paramount question.

The cook (divested of his decorations) and the Marquis lingered for a moment in the shadow of the grub wagon. The Marquis leaned her head against his shoulder.

"I didn't know what else to do," she was saying. "Father was gone, and we kids had to rustle. I had helped him so much with the cattle that I thought I'd turn cowboy. There wasn't anything else I could make a living at. I wasn't much stuck on it though, after I got here, and I'd have left only ——"

"Only what?"

"You know. Tell me something. When did you first — what made you ——"

"Oh, it was as soon as we struck the camp, when Saunders bawled out 'The Marquis and Miss Sally!' I saw how rattled you got at the name, and I had my sus ——"

"Cheeky!" whispered the Marquis. "And why should you think that I thought he was calling me 'Miss Sally'?"

"Because," answered the cook, calmly, "I was the Marquis. My father was the Marquis of Borodale. But you'll excuse that, won't you, Sally? It really isn't my fault, you know."

A FOG IN SANTONE

[Published in *The Cosmopolitan*, October, 1912. Probably written in 1904, or shortly after O. Henry's first successes in New York.]

THE drug clerk looks sharply at the white face half concealed by the high-turned overcoat collar.

"I would rather not supply you," he said doubtfully. "I sold you a dozen morphine tablets less than an hour ago."

The customer smiles wanly. "The fault is in your crooked streets. I didn't intend to call upon you twice, but I guess I got tangled up. Excuse me."

He draws his collar higher, and moves out, slowly. He stops under an electric light at the corner, and juggles absorbedly with three or four little pasteboard boxes. "Thirty-six," he announces to himself. "More than plenty." For a gray mist had swept upon Santone that night, an opaque terror that laid a hand to the throat of each of the city's guests. It was computed that three thousand invalids were hibernating in the town. They had come from far and wide, for here, among these contracted river-sliced streets, the goddess Ozone has elected to linger.

Purest atmosphere, sir, on earth! You might think from the river winding through our town that we are mala-

100

rial, but, no, sir! Repeated experiments made both by
the Government and local experts show that our air contains nothing deleterious — nothing but ozone, sir, pure
ozone. Litmus paper tests made all along the river show—
but you can read it all in the prospectuses; or the San-
tonian will recite it for you, word by word.

We may achieve climate, but weather is thrust upon
us. Santone, then, cannot be blamed for this cold gray
fog that came and kissed the lips of the three thousand,
and then delivered them to the cross. That night the
tubercles, whose ravages hope holds in check, multi-
plied. The writhing fingers of the pale mist did not go
thence bloodless. Many of the wooers of ozone capitu-
lated with the enemy that night, turning their faces to
the wall in that dumb, isolated apathy that so terrifies
their watchers. On the red stream of Hemorrhagia a few
souls drifted away, leaving behind pathetic heaps, white
and chill as the fog itself. Two or three came to view this
atmospheric wraith as the ghost of impossible joys, sent
to whisper to them of the egregious folly it is to inhale
breath into the lungs, only to exhale it again, and these
used whatever came handy to their relief, pistols, gas or
the beneficent muriate.

The purchaser of the morphia wanders into the fog, and
at length, finds himself upon a little iron bridge, one of the
score or more in the heart of the city, under which the
small tortuous river flows. He leans on the rail and
gasps, for here the mist has concentrated, lying like a foot-
pad to garrote such of the Three Thousand as creep that

way. The iron bridge guys rattle to the strain of his
cough, a mocking phthiscal rattle, seeming to say to him:
"Clickety-clack! just a little rusty cold, sir — but not
from our river. Litmus paper all along the banks and
nothing but ozone. Clacket-y-clack!"

The Memphis man at last recovers sufficiently to be
aware of another overcoated man ten feet away, leaning
on the rail, and just coming out of a paroxysm. There is
a freemasonry among the Three Thousand that does
away with formalities and introductions. A cough is
your card; a hemorrhage a letter of credit. The Memphis
man, being nearer recovered, speaks first.

"Goodall.   Memphis — pulmonary   tuberculosis —
guess last stages." The Three Thousand economize on
words. Words are breath and they need breath to write
checks for the doctors.

"Hurd," gasps the other. "Hurd; of T'leder.
T'leder, Ah-hia. Catarrhal bronkeetis. Name's Dennis,
too — doctor says. Says I'll live four weeks if I — take
care of myself. Got your walking papers yet?"

"My doctor," says Goodall of Memphis, a little boast-
ingly, "gives me three months."

"Oh," remarks the man from Toledo, filling up great
gaps in his conversation with wheezes, "damn the dif-
ference. What's months! Expect to — cut mine down
to one week — and die in a hack — a four wheeler, not a
cough. Be considerable moanin' of the bars when I put
out to sea. I've patronized 'em pretty freely since I
struck my — present gait. Say, Goodall of Memphis —

if your doctor has set your pegs so close — why don't you
— get on a big spree and go — to the devil quick and easy
— like I'm doing?"

"A spree," says Goodall, as one who entertains a new
idea, "I never did such a thing. I was thinking of another way, but ——"

"Come on," invites the Ohioan, "and have some drinks.
I've been at it — for two days, but the inf — ernal stuff
won't bite like it used to. Goodall of Memphis, what's
your respiration?"

"Twenty-four."

"Daily — temperature?"

"Hundred and four."

"You can do it in two days. It'll take me a — week.
Tank up, friend Goodall — have all the fun you can; then
— off you go, in the middle of a jag, and s-s-save trouble
and expense. I'm a s-son of a gun if this ain't a health
resort — for your whiskers! A Lake Erie fog'd get lost
here in two minutes."

"You said something about a drink," says Goodall.

A few minutes later they line up at a glittering bar, and
hang upon the arm rest. The bartender, blond, heavy,
well-groomed, sets out their drinks, instantly perceiving
that he serves two of the Three Thousand. He observes
that one is a middle-aged man, well-dressed, with a lined
and sunken face; the other a mere boy who is chiefly eyes
and overcoat. Disguising well the tedium begotten by
many repetitions, the server of drinks begins to chant the
sanitary saga of Santone. "Rather a moist night, gentle-

men, for our town. A little fog from our river, but noth-ing to hurt. Repeated Tests."

"Damn your litmus papers," gasps Toledo — "without any — personal offense intended."

"We've heard of 'em before. Let 'em turn red, white and blue. What we want is a repeated test of that — whiskey. Come again. I paid for the last round, Goodall of Memphis."

The bottle oscillates from one to the other, continues to do so, and is not removed from the counter. The bar-tender sees two emaciated invalids dispose of enough Kentucky Belle to floor a dozen cowboys, without displaying any emotion save a sad and contempla-tive interest in the peregrinations of the bottle. So he is moved to manifest a solicitude as to the conse-quences.

"Not on your Uncle Mark Hanna," responds Toledo, "will we get drunk. We've been — vaccinated with whiskey — and — cod liver oil. What would send you to the police station — only gives us a thirst. S-s-set out another bottle."

It is slow work trying to meet death by that route. Some quicker way must be found. They leave the saloon and plunge again into the mist. The sidewalks are mere flanges at the base of the houses; the street a cold ravine, the fog filling it like a freshet. Not far away is the Mexi-can quarter. Conducted as if by wires along the heavy air comes a guitar's tinkle, and the demoralizing voice of some señorita singing:

"En las tardes sombrillos del invierro
En el prado a Marar me reclino
Y maldigo mi fausto destino—
Una vida la mas infeliz."

The words of it they do not understand—neither Toledo nor Memphis, but words are the least important things in life. The music tears the breasts of the seekers after Nepenthe, inciting Toledo to remark:

"Those kids of mine—I wonder—by God, Mr. Goodall of Memphis, we had too little of that whiskey! No slow music in mine, if you please. It makes you disremember to forget."

Hurd of Toledo, here pulls out his watch, and says:

"I'm a son of a gun! Got an engagement for a hack ride out to San Pedro Springs at eleven. Forgot it. A fellow from Noo York, and me, and the Castillo sisters at Rhinegelder's Garden. That Noo York chap's a lucky dog—got one whole lung—good for a year yet. Plenty of money, too. He pays for everything. I can't afford —to miss the jamboree. Sorry you ain't going along. Good-by, Goodall of Memphis."

He rounds the corner and shuffles away, casting off thus easily the ties of acquaintanceship as the moribund do, the season of dissolution being man's supreme hour of egoism and selfishness. But he turns and calls back through the fog to the other: "I say, Goodall of Memphis! If you get there before I do, tell 'em Hurd's a-comin' too. Hurd, of T'leder, Ah-hia."

Thus Goodall's tempter deserts him. That youth, uncomplaining and uncaring, takes a spell at coughing, and, recovered, wanders desultorily on down the street, the name of which he neither knows nor recks. At a certain point he perceives swinging doors, and hears, filtering between them a noise of wind and string instruments. Two men enter from the street as he arrives, and he follows them in. There is a kind of ante-chamber, plentifully set with palms and cactuses and oleanders. At little marble-topped tables some people sit, while soft-shod attendants bring the beer. All is orderly, clean, melancholy, gay, of the German method of pleasure. At his right is the foot of a stairway. A man there holds out his hand. Goodall extends his, full of silver, the man selects therefrom a coin. Goodall goes upstairs and sees there two galleries extending along the sides of a concert hall which he now perceives to lie below and beyond the anteroom he first entered. These galleries are divided into boxes or stalls, which bestow with the aid of hanging lace curtains, a certain privacy upon their occupants.

Passing with aimless feet down the aisle contiguous to these saucy and discreet compartments, he is half checked by the sight in one of them of a young woman, alone and seated in an attitude of reflection. This young woman becomes aware of his approach. A smile from her brings him to a standstill, and her subsequent invitation draws him, though hesitating, to the other chair in the box, a little table between them.

Goodall is only nineteen. There are some whom, when the terrible god Phthisis wishes to destroy he first makes beautiful; and the boy is one of these. His face is wax, and an awful pulchritude is born of the menacing flame in his cheeks. His eyes reflect an unearthly vista engendered by the certainty of his doom. As it is forbidden man to guess accurately concerning his fate, it is inevitable that he shall tremble at the slightest lifting of the veil.

The young woman is well-dressed, and exhibits a beauty of distinctly feminine and tender sort; an Eve-like comeliness that scarcely seems predestined to fade.

It is immaterial, the steps by which the two mount to a certain plane of good understanding; they are short and few, as befits the occasion.

A button against the wall of the partition is frequently disturbed and a waiter comes and goes at signal.

Pensive beauty would nothing of wine; two thick plaits of her blond hair hang almost to the floor; she is a lineal descendant of the Lorelei. So the waiter brings the brew; effervescent, icy, greenish golden. The orchestra on the stage is playing "Oh, Rachel." The youngsters have exchanged a good bit of information. She calls him, "Walter" and he calls her "Miss Rosa."

Goodall's tongue is loosened and he has told her everything about himself, about his home in Tennessee, the old pillared mansion under the oaks, the stables, the hunting; the friends he has; down to the chickens, and the box bushes bordering the walks. About his coming South for the climate, hoping to escape the hereditary foe of his family. All about his three months on a ranch; the deer hunts, the rattlers, and the rollicking in the cow camps.

Then of his advent to Santone, where he had indirectly learned, from a great specialist that his life's calendar probably contains but two more leaves. And then of this death-white, choking night which has come and strangled his fortitude and sent him out to seek a port amid its depressing billows.

"My weekly letter from home failed to come," he told her, "and I was pretty blue. I knew I had to go before long and I was tired of waiting. I went out and bought morphine at every drug store where they would sell me a few tablets. I got thirty-six quarter grains, and was going back to my room and take them, but I met a queer fellow on a bridge, who had a new idea."

Goodall fillips a little pasteboard box upon the table. "I put 'em all together in there."

Miss Rosa, being a woman, must raise the lid, and gave a slight shiver at the innocent looking triturates. "Horrid things! but those little, white bits — they could never kill one!"

Indeed they could. Walter knew better. Nine grains of morphia! Why, half the amount might.

Miss Rosa demands to know about Mr. Hurd, of Toledo, and is told. She laughs like a delighted child. "What a funny fellow! But tell me more about your home and your sisters, Walter. I know enough about Texas and tarantulas and cowboys."

The theme is dear, just now, to his mood, and he lays before her the simple details of a true home; the little ties and endearments that so fill the exile's heart. Of his sisters, one, Alice, furnishes him a theme he loves to dwell upon.

"She is like you, Miss Rosa," he says. "Maybe not quite so pretty, but just as nice, and good, and ——"

"There! Walter," says Miss Rosa sharply, "now talk about something else."

But a shadow falls upon the wall outside, preceding a big, softly treading man, finely dressed, who pauses a second before the curtains and then passes on. Presently comes the waiter with a message: "Mr. Rolfe says ——"

"Tell Rolfe I'm engaged."

"I don't know why it is," says Goodall, of Memphis, "but I don't feel as bad as I did. An hour ago I wanted to die, but since I've met you, Miss Rosa, I'd like so much to live. '

The young woman whirls around the table, lays an arm behind his neck and kisses him on the cheek.

"You must, dear boy," she says. "I know what was the matter. It was the miserable foggy weather that has lowered your spirit and mine too — a little. But look, now."

With a little spring she has drawn back the curtains. A window is in the wall opposite, and lo! the mist is cleared away. The indulgent moon is out again, revoyaging the plumbless sky. Roof and parapet and spire are softly pearl enamelled. Twice, thrice the retrieved river flashes back, between the houses, the light of the firmament. A tonic day will dawn, sweet and prosperous.

"Talk of death when the world is so beautiful!" says Miss Rosa, laying her hand on his shoulder. "Do something to please me, Walter. Go home to your rest and say: 'I mean to get better,' and do it."

"If you ask it," says the boy, with a smile, "I will."

The waiter brings full glasses. Did they ring? No; but it is well. He may leave them. A farewell glass. Miss Rosa says: "To your better health, Walter." He says: "To our next meeting."

His eyes look no longer into the void, but gaze upon the antithesis of death. His foot is set in an undiscovered country to-night. He is obedient, ready to go. "Good night," she says.

"I never kissed a girl before," he confesses, "except my sisters."

"You didn't this time," she laughs, "I kissed you — good night."

"When shall I see you again," he persists.

"You promised me to go home," she frowns, "and get well. Perhaps we shall meet again soon. Good night." He hesitates, his hat in hand. She smiles broadly and kisses him once more upon the forehead. She watches him far down the aisle, then sits again at the table.

The shadow falls once more against the wall. This time the big, softly stepping man parts the curtains and looks in. Miss Rosa's eyes meet his and for half a minute they remain thus, silent, fighting a battle with that king of weapons. Presently the big man drops the curtains and passes on.

The orchestra ceases playing suddenly, and an important voice can be heard loudly talking in one of the boxes farther down the aisle. No doubt some citizen entertains there some visitor to the town, and Miss Rosa leans back in her chair and smiles at some of the words she catches:

"Purest atmosphere — in the world — litmus paper all long — nothing hurtful — our city — nothing but pure ozone."

The waiter returns for the tray and glasses. As he enters, the girl crushes a little empty pasteboard box in her hand and throws it in a corner. She is stirring something in her glass with her hatpin.

"Why, Miss Rosa," says the waiter with the civil familiarity he uses — "putting salt in your beer this early in the night!"

THE FRIENDLY CALL

[Published in "Monthly Magazine Section," July, 1910.]

WHEN I used to sell hardware in the West, I often "made" a little town called Saltillo, in Colorado. I was always certain of securing a small or a large order from Simms Bell, who kept a general store there. Bell was one of those six-foot, low-voiced products, formed from a union of the West and the South. I liked him. To look at him you would think he should be robbing stage coaches or juggling gold mines with both hands; but he would sell you a paper of tacks or a spool of thread, with ten times more patience and courtesy than any saleslady in a city department store.

I had a twofold object in my last visit to Saltillo. One was to sell a bill of goods; the other to advise Bell of a chance that I knew of by which I was certain he could make a small fortune.

In Mountain City, a town on the Union Pacific, five times larger than Saltillo, a mercantile firm was about to go to the wall. It had a lively and growing custom, but was on the edge of dissolution and ruin. Mismanagement and the gambling habits of one of the partners explained it. The condition of the firm was not yet public property. I had my knowledge of it from a private source. I knew

PORTER & DALTON.
DEALERS IN DRUGS

Greensboro, N C ___May 26___ 1884

To whom it may concern.

We have known the bearer Mr W S. Porter intimately, both as druggist and citizen. His character here was above reproach, and as a Druggist we invariably found him careful painstaking and accurate.

We feel sure that he will acceptably fill any position he is willing to accept.

R H Chegety M. D.,
Wm E Logan M D
W. P. Beall, M.D.,
Jas. K. Hall M D - Ex Pres Med Asso N C

This and the letter on the opposite page, were the credentials that the boy Will Porter brought along from North Carolina to Texas.

Greensboro N.C.
May 26th 1884

To all whom it May Concern:
I J N Nelson Clerk of the Superior Court.
do hereby Certify that I have been intimately
acquainted with W S Porter for more than
ten years. When I first became acquainted
with him he was Clerking for his Uncle W.C.
Porter at his Drug Store and remained
with him up to the time he left for the
State of Texas. And he is undoubtedly a young
Man of good Moral Character and reputed
to be a No one druggist and a very
popular young Man among his Many friends

J. N. Nelson Cfk

I fully endorse the above —
Mii. U. Steiner
Register of Deeds

J D White P.M.
Greensboro N.C.

"A young man of good moral character and an A No. 1
Druggist."

that, if the ready cash were offered, the stock and good will could be bought for about one fourth their value.

On arriving in Saltillo I went to Bell's store. He nodded to me, smiled his broad, lingering smile, went on leisurely selling some candy to a little girl, then came around the counter and shook hands.

"Well," he said (his invariable preliminary jocosity at every call I made), "I suppose you are out here making kodak pictures of the mountains. It's the wrong time of the year to buy any hardware, of course."

I told Bell about the bargain in Mountain City. If he wanted to take advantage of it, I would rather have missed a sale than have him overstocked in Saltillo.

"It sounds good," he said, with enthusiasm. "I'd like to branch out and do a bigger business, and I'm obliged to you for mentioning it. But — well, you come and stay at my house to-night and I'll think about it."

It was then after sundown and time for the larger stores in Saltillo to close. The clerks in Bell's put away their books, whirled the combination of the safe, put on their coats and hats and left for their homes. Bell padlocked the big, double wooden front doors, and we stood, for a moment, breathing the keen, fresh mountain air coming across the foothills.

A big man walked down the street and stopped in front of the high porch of the store. His long, black moustache, black eyebrows, and curly black hair contrasted queerly with his light, pink complexion, which belonged, by rights, to a blonde. He was about forty, and wore a white vest, white hat, a watch chain made of five-dollar gold pieces linked together, and a rather well-fitting two-piece gray suit of the cut that college boys of eighteen are wont to affect. He glanced at me distrustfully, and then at Bell with coldness and, I thought, something of enmity in his expression.

"Well," asked Bell, as if he were addressing a stranger, "did you fix up that matter?"

"Did I!" the man answered, in a resentful tone. "What do you suppose I've been here two weeks for? The business is to be settled to-night. Does that suit you, or have you got something to kick about?"

"It's all right," said Bell. "I knew you'd do it."

"Of course, you did," said the magnificent stranger. "Haven't I done it before?"

"You have," admitted Bell. "And so have I. How do you find it at the hotel?"

"Rocky grub. But I ain't kicking. Say — can you give me any pointers about managing that — affair? It's my first deal in that line of business, you know."

"No, I can't," answered Bell, after some thought. "I've tried all kinds of ways. You'll have to try some of your own."

"Tried soft soap?"

"Barrels of it."

"Tried a saddle girth with a buckle on the end of it?"

"Never none. Started to once; and here's what I got."

Bill held out his right hand. Even in the deepening twilight, I could see on the back of it a long, white scar, that might have been made by a claw or a knife or some sharp-edged tool.

"Oh, well," said the florid man, carelessly, "I'll know what to do later on."

He walked away without another word. When he had gone ten steps he turned and called to Bell:

"You keep well out of the way when the goods are delivered, so there won't be any hitch in the business."

"All right," anwered Bell, "I'll attend to my end of the line."

This talk was scarcely clear in its meaning to me; but as it did not concern me, I did not let it weigh upon my mind. But the singularity of the other man's appearance lingered with me for a while; and as we walked toward Bell's house I remarked to him:

"Your customer seems to be a surly kind of fellow — not one that you'd like to be snowed in with in a camp on a hunting trip."

"He is that," assented Bell, heartily. "He reminds me of a rattlesnake that's been poisoned by the bite of a tarantula."

"He doesn't look like a citizen of Saltillo," I went on.

"No," said Bell, "he lives in Sacramento. He's down here on a little business trip. His name is George Ringo, and he's been my best friend — in fact the only friend I ever had — for twenty years."

I was too surprised to make any further comment.

Bell lived in a comfortable, plain, square, two-story white house on the edge of the little town. I waited in the parlor — a room depressingly genteel — furnished with red plush, straw matting, looped-up lace curtains, and a glass case large enough to contain a mummy, full of mineral specimens.

While I waited, I heard, upstairs, that unmistakable sound instantly recognized the world over — a bickering woman's voice, rising as her anger and fury grew. I could hear, between the gusts, the temperate rumble of Bell's tones, striving to oil the troubled waters.

The storm subsided soon; but not before I had heard the woman say, in a lower, concentrated tone, rather more carrying than her high-pitched railings: "This is the last time. I tell you — the last time. Oh, you *will* understand."

The household seemed to consist of only Bell and his wife and a servant or two. I was introduced to Mrs. Bell at supper.

At first sight she seemed to be a handsome woman, but I soon perceived that her charm had been spoiled. An uncontrolled petulance, I thought, an emotional egotism, an absence of poise and a habitual dissatisfaction had marred her womanhood. During the meal, she showed that false gayety, spurious kindliness and reactionary softness that mark the woman addicted to tantrums. Withal, she was a woman who might be attractive to many men.

After supper, Bell and I took our chairs outside, set them on the grass in the moonlight and smoked. The full moon is a witch. In her light, truthful men dig up for you nuggets of purer gold; while liars squeeze out brighter colors from the tubes of their invention. I saw Bell's broad, slow smile come out upon his face and linger there.

"I reckon you think George and me are a funny kind of friends," he said. "The fact is we never did take much interest in each other's company. But his idea and mine, of what a friend should be, was always synonymous and we lived up to it, strict, all these years. Now, I'll give you an idea of what our idea is.

"A man don't need but one friend. The fellow who drinks your liquor and hangs around you, slapping you on the back and taking up your time, telling you how much he likes you, ain't a friend, even if you did play marbles at school and fish in the same creek with him. As long as you don't need a friend one of that kind may answer. But a friend, to my mind, is one you can deal with on a strict reciprocity basis like me and George have always done.

"A good many years ago, him and me was connected in a number of ways. We put our capital together and run a line of freight wagons in New Mexico, and we mined some and gambled a few. And then, we got into trouble of one or two kinds; and I reckon that got us on a better understandable basis than anything else did, unless it was the fact that we never had much personal use for each other's ways. George is the vainest man I ever see, and the biggest brag. He could blow the biggest geyser in the Yosemite valley back into its hole with one whisper. I am a quiet man, and fond of studiousness and thought. The more we used to see each other, personally, the less we seemed to like to be together.   If he ever had slapped me on the back and snivelled over me like I've seen men do to what they called their friends, I know I'd have had a rough-and-tumble with him on the spot.   Same way with George.   He hated my ways as bad as I did his.   When we were mining, we lived in separate tents, so as not to intrude our obnoxiousness on each other.

"But after a long time, we begun to know each of us could depend on the other when we were in a pinch, up to his last dollar, word of honor or perjury, bullet, or drop of blood we had in the world.   We never even spoke of it to each other, because that would have spoiled it.   But we tried it out, time after time, until we came to know.   I've grabbed my hat and jumped a freight and rode 200 miles to identify him when he was about to be hung by mistake, in Idaho, for a train robber.   Once, I laid sick of typhoid in a tent in Texas, without a dollar or a change of clothes, and sent for George in Boise City.   He came on the next train.   The first thing he did before speaking to me, was to hang up a little looking glass on the side of the tent and curl his moustache and rub some hair dye on his head. His hair is naturally a light reddish.   Then he gave me the most scientific cussing I ever had, and took off his coat.

"'If you wasn't a Moses-meek little Mary's lamb, you wouldn't have been took down this way,' says he. 'Haven't you got gumption enough not to drink swamp water or fall down and scream whenever you have a little colic or feel a mosquito bite you?'   He made me a little mad.

"'You've got the bedside manners of a Piute medicine man,' says I. 'And I wish you'd go away and let me die a natural death. I'm sorry I sent for you.'

"'I've a mind to,' says George, 'for nobody cares whether you live or die. But now I've been tricked into coming, I might as well stay until this little attack of indigestion or nettle rash or whatever it is, passes away.'

"Two weeks afterward, when I was beginning to get around again, the doctor laughed and said he was sure that my friend's keeping me mad all the time did more than his drugs to cure me.

"So that's the way George and me was friends. There wasn't any sentiment about it — it was just give and take, and each of us knew that the other was ready for the call at any time.

"I remember, once, I played a sort of joke on George, just to try him. I felt a little mean about it afterward, because I never ought to have doubted he'd do it.

"We was both living in a little town in the San Luis valley, running some flocks of sheep and a few cattle. We were partners, but, as usual, we didn't live together. I had an old aunt, out from the East, visiting for the summer, so I rented a little cottage. She soon had a couple of cows and some pigs and chickens to make the place look like home. George lived alone in a little cabin half a mile out of town.

"One day a calf that we had, died. That night I broke its bones, dumped it into a coarse sack and tied it up with wire. I put on an old shirt, tore a sleeve 'most out of it, and the collar half off, tangled up my hair, put some red ink on my hands and spashed some of it over my shirt and face. I must have looked like I'd been having the fight of my life. I put the sack in a wagon and drove out to George's cabin. When I hallooed, he came out in a yellow dressing-gown, a Turkish cap and patent leather shoes. George always was a great dresser.

"I dumped the bundle to the ground.

"'Sh-sh!' says I, kind of wild in my way. 'Take that and bury it, George, out somewhere behind your house — bury it just like it is. And don ——'

"'Don't get excited,' says George. 'And for the Lord's sake go and wash your hands and face and put on a clean shirt.'

"And he lights his pipe, while I drive away at a gallop. The next morning he drops around to our cottage, where my aunt was fiddling with her flowers and truck in the front yard. He bends himself and bows and makes compliments as he could do, when so disposed, and begs a rose bush from her, saying he had turned up a little land back of his cabin, and wanted to plant something on it by way of usefulness and ornament. So my aunt, flattered, pulls up one of her biggest by the roots and gives it to him. Afterward I see it growing where he planted it, in a place where the grass had been cleared off and the dirt levelled. But neither George nor me ever spoke of it to each other again."

The moon rose higher, possibly drawing water from the

sea, pixies from their dells and certainly more confidences from Simms Bell, the friend of a friend.

"There come a time, not long afterward," he went on, "when I was able to do a good turn for George Ringo. George had made a little pile of money in beeves and he was up in Denver, and he showed up when I saw him, wearing deer-skin vests, yellow shoes, clothes like the awnings in front of drug stores, and his hair dyed so blue that it looked black in the dark. He wrote me to come up there, quick — that he needed me, and to bring the best outfit of clothes I had. I had 'em on when I got the letter, so I left on the next train. George was ——"

Bell stopped for half a minute, listening intently.

"I thought I heard a team coming down the road," he explained. George was at a summer resort on a lake near Denver and was putting on as many airs as he knew how. He had rented a little two-room cottage, and had a Chihauhau dog and a hammock and eight different kinds of walking sticks.

"'Simms,' he says to me, 'there's a widow woman here that's pestering the soul out of me with her intentions. I can't get out of her way. It ain't that she ain't handsome and agreeable, in a sort of style, but her attentions is serious, and I ain't ready for to marry nobody and settle down. I can't go to no festivity nor sit on the hotel piazza or mix in any of the society round-ups, but what she cuts me out of the herd and puts her daily brand on me. I like this here place,' goes on George, 'and I'm making a hit here in the most censorious circles, so I don't want to have to run away from it. So I sent for you.'

"'What do you want me to do?' I asks George.

"'Why,' says he, 'I want you to head her off. I want you to cut me out. I want you to come to the rescue. Suppose you seen a wildcat about for to eat me, what would you do?'

"'Go for it,' says I.

"'Correct,' says George. 'Then go for this Mrs. De Clinton the same.'

"'How am I to do it?' I asks. 'By force and awfulness or in some gentler and less lurid manner?'

"'Court her,' George says, 'get her off my trail. Feed her. Take her out in boats. Hang around her and stick to her. Get her mashed on you if you can. Some women are pretty big fools. Who knows but what she might take a fancy to you.'

"'Had you ever thought,' I asks, 'of repressing your fatal fascinations in her presence; of squeezing a harsh note in the melody of your siren voice, of veiling your beauty — in other words, of giving her the bounce yourself?'

"George sees no essence of sarcasm in my remark. He twists his moustache and looks at the points of his shoes.

"'Well, Simms,' he said, 'you know how I am about the ladies. I can't hurt none of their feelings. I'm, by nature, polite and esteemful of their intents and purposes. This Mrs. De Clinton don't appear to be the suitable sort for me. Besides, I ain't a marrying man by all means.'

"'All right,' said I, 'I'll do the best I can in the case.'

"So I bought a new outfit of clothes and a book on etiquette and made a dead set for Mrs. De Clinton. She was a fine-looking woman, cheerful and gay. At first, I almost had to hobble her to keep her from loping around at George's heels; but finally I got her so she seemed glad to go riding with me and sailing on the lake; and she seemed real hurt on the mornings when I forgot to send her a bunch of flowers. Still, I didn't like the way she looked at George, sometimes, out of the corner of her eye. George was having a fine time now, going with the whole bunch just as he pleased. Yes'm," continued Bell, "she certainly was a fine-looking woman at that time. She's changed some since, as you might have noticed at the supper table."

"What!" I exclaimed.

"I married Mrs. De Clinton," went on Bell. "One evening while we were up at the lake. When I told George about it, he opened his mouth and I thought he was going to break our traditions and say something grateful, but he swallowed it back.

"'All right,' says he, playing with his dog. 'I hope you won't have too much trouble. Myself, I'm not never going to marry.'

"That was three years ago," said Bell. "We came here to live. For a year we got along medium fine. And then everything changed. For two years I've been having something that rhymes first-class with my name. You heard the row upstairs this evening? That was a merry welcome compared to the usual average. She's tired of me and of this little town life and she rages all day, like a panther in a cage. I stood it until two weeks ago and then I had to send out The Call. I located George in Sacramento. He started the day he got my wire."

Mrs. Bell came out of the house swiftly toward us. Some strong excitement or anxiety seemed to possess her, but she smiled a faint hostess smile, and tried to keep her voice calm.

"The dew is falling," she said, "and it's growing rather late. Wouldn't you gentlemen rather come into the house?"

Bell took some cigars from his pocket and answered: "It's most too fine a night to turn in yet. I think Mr. Ames and I will walk out along the road a mile or so and have another smoke. I want to talk with him about some goods that I want to buy."

"Up the road or down the road?" asked Mrs. Bell.

"Down," said Bell.

I thought she breathed a sigh of relief.

When we had gone a hundred yards and the house became concealed by trees, Bell guided me into the thick grove that lined the road and back through them toward the house again. We stopped within twenty yards of the house, concealed by the dark shadows. I wondered at this maneuver. And then I heard in the distance coming down the road beyond the house, the regular hoofbeats of a team of horses. Bell held his watch in a ray of moon-light.

"On time, within a minute," he said. "That's George's way."

The team slowed up as it drew near the house and stopped in a patch of black shadows. We saw the figure of a woman carrying a heavy valise move swiftly from the other side of the house, and hurry to the waiting vehicle. Then it rolled away briskly in the direction from which it had come.

I looked at Bell inquiringly, I suppose. I certainly asked him no question.

"She's running away with George," said Bell, simply. "He's kept me posted about the progress of the scheme all along. She'll get a divorce in six months and then George will marry her. He never helps anybody halfway. It's all arranged between them."

I began to wonder what friendship was, after all.

When we went into the house, Bell began to talk easily on other subjects; and I took his cue. By and by the big chance to buy out the business in Mountain City came back to my mind and I began to urge it upon him. Now that he was free, it would be easier for him to make the move; and he was sure of a splendid bargain.

Bell was silent for some minutes, but when I looked at him I fancied that he was thinking of something else — that he was not considering the project.

"Why, no, Mr. Ames," he said, after a while, "I can't make that deal. I'm awful thankful to you, though, for telling me about it. But I've got to stay here. I can't go to Mountain City."

"Why?" I asked.

"Missis Bell," he replied "won't live in Mountain City. She hates the place and wouldn't go there. I've got to keep right on here in Saltillo."

"Mrs. Bell!" I exclaimed, too puzzled to conjecture what he meant.

"I ought to explain," said Bell. "I know George and I know Mrs. Bell. He's impatient in his ways. He can't stand things that fret him, long, like I can. Six months, I give them — six months of married life, and there'll be another disunion. Mrs. Bell will come back to me. There's no other place for her to go. I've got to stay here and wait. At the end of six months, I'll have to grab a satchel and catch the first train. For George will be sending out The Call."

A DINNER AT ——— *

[The story referred to in this skit appears in "The Trimmed Lamp" under the same title—"The Badge of Policeman O'Roon."]

THE ADVENTURES OF AN AUTHOR WITH HIS OWN HERO

ALL that day — in fact from the moment of his creation — Van Sweller had conducted himself fairly well in my eyes. Of course I had had to make many concessions; but in return he had been no less considerate. Once or twice we had had sharp, brief contentions over certain points of behavior; but, prevailingly, give and take had been our rule.

His morning toilet provoked our first tilt. Van Sweller went about it confidently.

"The usual thing, I suppose, old chap," he said, with a smile and a yawn. "I ring for a b. and s., and then I have my tub. I splash a good deal in the water, of course. You are aware that there are two ways in which I can receive Tommy Carmichael when he looks in to have a chat about polo. I can talk to him through the bathroom door, or I can be picking at a grilled bone which my man has brought in. Which would you prefer?"

* See advertising column, "Where to Dine Well," in the daily newspapers.

127

I smiled with diabolic satisfaction at his coming discomfiture.

"Neither," I said. "You will make your appearance on the scene when a gentleman should — after you are fully dressed, which indubitably private function shall take place behind closed doors. And I will feel indebted to you if, after you do appear, your deportment and manners are such that it will not be necessary to inform the public, in order to appease its apprehension, that you have taken a bath."

Van Sweller slightly elevated his brows.

"Oh, very well," he said, a trifle piqued. "I rather imagine it concerns you more than it does me. Cut the 'tub' by all means, if you think best. But it has been the usual thing, you know."

This was my victory; but after Van Sweller emerged from his apartments in the "Beaujolie" I was vanquished in a dozen small but well-contested skirmishes. I allowed him a cigar; but routed him on the question of naming its brand. But he worsted me when I objected to giving him a "coat unmistakably English in its cut." I allowed him to "stroll down Broadway," and even permitted "passers by" (God knows there's nowhere to pass but by) to "turn their heads and gaze with evident admiration at his erect figure." I demeaned myself, and, as a barber, gave him a "smooth, dark face with its keen, frank eye, and firm jaw."

Later on he looked in at the club and saw Freddy Vavasour, polo team captain, dawdling over grilled bone No.1.

PAGE FROM

THE PlUNKVILLE PATRiOT,

VOL. XXXI·   PLUNKVILLE TEX APRIL   O2Ti 1895   NO IXL.

THe PLUnKViLle PaTRiOt,

ρ o Published nearlÿ evȩry Friday. o o

COL. ARISTO₁LE JORDAN,

Editor & **MAYOR !**

Office after Feb. 1st; Back of Grimes' slaughter pen, two doors north of Caney Creek.

Subscripṭioɳ per ᴙ ear ᵔ ᵔ ᵔ ᵔ $₁.00
"   ,ᵔ .6 moS ᵔ ;   .200

writeUp for candidates 50 per linea.
Obituary poetry ᵔ 10c ".

R. R. timetable.

N. bound arr. Plunkville 7.15 AM
" leaves ." ᵔ 7.15ℳ."

Spring has come.

Bob Taylor and Sue Billings were married at 11 a. M yesterday.

The affair took place in M·x church S by S. W. The building was decorated with evergreens and roses, over the pulpit was an immense bell made of of hyacinths ᴣd old band-box. The groom was ᴙd f f f ᴣ Pete Schieffer BillWilliams and a₁ eyed man from 'Pikeville they called cut y· Mrs pendergrast played a dead march on the organ as the gand didas take walk up the ile"

ṭhis ṭhroir ᴣhis wnluⱱ ᵃ co pȩq sig box pleats and was the sinecure ofall ᴣyes. Bob had on his usual ᴢants & and his qrotherᴣams , Prince abert The happy couple had a feed at old man Billinges, and then flagged the 7.15 freight for a three days bridle trip

Bob is rather triflinᴣ ,and the chances are that old Billings will gains son in stead of losing a daugher. Vax Po'iscum !

PATRONIZE THE ELITE SALOOM

Cold gear always on tap.

Back door opened on 3 taps Sund-ᴙys.

VICTORY!!

PeRCHe" ON THe BAnneR of

MAYOB JORDAN

And good Government!

PERKINS HOG-PEN SQUASHED

By a haqeas corpus & an Axe.

perkins Maker A Bold resistence!!

The HOG takes a Hand to the proce-ding.

1900 People on the Ground.

(Special report by US for the Patriot.).

Plunkvile, Adril 17th—Wednesday began about- daylight, and people on horseback and all kinds to vehicles began to come in town. The day had been advertised as 1ᴣ one when we, , as Mayorshould forcibuy remove the disgusting hog-pen of judge Per-cins' that fronts along our priaci al street—Belle Meade Avenue.

About 8 oc'lock we walked down the Avenue" unofficially, as simple Col. jcrdan! and thaᵔᵔ uf the aeid₁ There were about 300 country people on the groround eatng apples and pop-corn and liberally patroniz-ing the lemonade and gold.brick sta-nds. We netted over $1 ᴣ by selling privileges for same.

After a high breakfast of a bottle of beer and a piece of lemon pei, we swung Indian clvbs for 10 minutes and then washed our face and careful-ly read over the Marquis of queens-bury's rules .

At five minute to 8 we sallied afh on our omision carrying a copy of the Revised Statutes, a pair of brassknu-cks, an axe and about 7 cocxtails.

When we got to Belle Meade Aven-ue a cheer went up from at least 1900 people. All the- stores aero closed and the whole town was there to see the fun . The hog pen was still there enclosing a large, supercilious hog,

in decidedly bad odor, about 14 han-ds high.

Judge Perkins sat on the edge of the pen baretoomed ; with a long. sin-gle barreled shot gun in his hand . He was breathing hard, and his bla tors were working viciously.

As we walked up in front of the Judge there was an intense silence.

We Hd the Revised Statues on a peanut stand, shifted ano axe round, and kept an eye on the Jud'ges gun. "Judge perkins," we said in a loud voice, "by the authority invested in us by the Commonwealth of Plunk-vile and the power of the Press, we commanp you to remove, takeaway, absquatulate and disperso ,yourself piece and dignity of the State and Texas until death youdo part, so help you God !"

"Go to h—!" says the Judge.

We were about to spito n ovr hands but caused findinᴣ our mouth too def. when a little flea dog from the coun-ty section the hogs' tail protruding through the pen, bit off about 2 Inches of same. The hog gave a squeal that so startled the J udge that he pulled the trigger and his gun dropeeaed tahi ing ollbia left great toe and killing a chil naman and a poodle, belonginig to Mrs, ᴣol. Dogget. We sprang for-ward with our axe and quickly sma-shed the boards of the pea. The hog saw the opening and remaking "Wooi" in deep baritone voice, shot ᴣhrough the hole.

An eye witness tells us that Judge Perkins was standing on one foot ab-outto smash us in the bock of the head wyth his gun barrel when 400lbs of deep brunette hog, with a Maud s escape movement passed between his legs . ,

Mrs Col. Dogget struck the Judge just as he struck the sipewalk, and while she was jabbing him with her parasol we demolished the rest of the pen.

The hog upset the lemonade and beer stands, pied the flying Jenny and the High School graduating class, and

then struck up Caney creek in a noth westerly direction.

We were escorted at once to the Elete by x crowd of cheering citizens who had witnessed the downfall of Monopoly and Despotism in Plunk-vile. Pete Dollinger made a speech nominating us ᴣfion Govenor ᴣn 1896, but this we consider a little prema-ture.

Judge Perkins will be out again ᴣn about three weeks.

IN MEMORIAM.

We received a telegram just befor going to press, announcing the death of our mother in Branchtown, Ga. She was the best woman in the world, and the only being who has loved and taken any interest in us. She was very poor, and we have for ten years sent her all our slender income beyond our actual needs.

We know that we are uneducated, and not a genius, having had to work hard since were ten years of age, but we have made a big bluff and have al-ways succeeded in keeping her in comfort, and, thank God, she always

don us for dragging in our personal affairs, but we feel lonely, and we have veŷ little to encourage us now the world.

She always kept each copy of this poor little paper, and read it as ff is were a fountain of the brightest wis-dom, and laid them away reverently. thinking her bod one of the world's geniuses.

We shall continue in our line of duty, but a little sadly, for the only hand that has ever pressed ours with love is gone, and the only lips that ever whispered words of praise are silent.

Widows !

Send your name, hight, weight, reach inches around biceps and forearm for $4.75. and receive by return mail a picture of your last husband, free !
Mrs. Jiuba, Spiritual Medium, New York.

O. Henry himself always went over the type of this page (a feature of *The Rolling Stone*) and carefully made the right kind of typographical errors,

THE ROLLING STONE

VOL. II. NO. 2.   AUSTIN AND SAN ANTONIO, TEXAS, SATURDAY, JANUARY 26, 1895.   PRICE FIVE CENTS.

WHERE IT STARTED.

Adam . . This apple sauce is not as good as I have eaten.
Eve . . Well, there's one consolation; you can't say your mother ever made any better.

"DON'T give it a weigh," said the grocer, when he said 24 pounds of sugar for a dollar.

Deacons' Pilgrim's Progress

— Life

CULTURE IN CHICAGO.

Mrs. Lakeside—"Mr. Links is such a refined man. His manners are perfect."
Mrs. Ribbes—"Indeed, in what way?"
Mrs. Lakeside—"Why, when he dines here he always brings his own toothpick with him."

ONLY AMATEURS.

Edith—"Oh, dear, I don't see how I am to go on the stage before all those Austin people in these clothes."
Violet—"It's hard, I'm sure. I'll see the stage manager for you, and try to get him to let you take off the skirt and cloak."

INCONSISTENCY.

Call a pretty girl a witch,
And she'll do her best to charm you;
Tell an old maid she's a witch,
And she certainly will harm you;
Thus you see how hard it is
To please them all.

Call a pretty maiden "you,"
And she'll archly smile upon you.
Call an ancient one a "gal"
And she'll grab so sure and run you.
The same name will not fit
Them all at all.

If you tell your girl a "house,"
She will think it cute and pretty;
If before an ancient spinster
You cap "rats" you have our pity.
Thus you see you need not try
To please them all.

COMMERCIAL ÆSTHETICS.

IS the editor in?"

A pale young man with elongated hair and spectacles, stood the doorway of the ROLLING STONE office.

The youth with inky fingers, who sat in the editor's chair looked up quickly.

"The real, sure-enough editor has gone to the telegraph office," he said, "to verify explanation of a joke, to a London paper, too. During his absence I sometimes pass on his jokes submitted in person. That roll of paper under your arm, now, you want to have printed. Have I called the turn?"

"It is true, I have a little story here that I dashed off in an idle hour," said the young man, hesitatingly, "but I wanted to see the editor, himself."

"Oh, it's all right," said the youth. "I know what the office needs just the same as the editor. Is there anything in your story about the Court leaning against a statue of Parian marble, while Lurline, sweeping, with snow-white hands the trembling strings of an ancient harp filling with her exquisite voice the vast halls of the castle with the lovely strains of Mendelssohn's 'Lieder ohne Worte?'"

"Well," said the visitor, "I must confess that in one chapter there is a scene resembling your description, but—"

"And in another place," continued the inky-headed youth, "does Lurline gaze from the window of the castle at the crimson tempers of sunset that are flung upon the distant peaks, and then at the gray and darkening valley, and, thinking of the brave, true heart of honest Hans, the hunter, fall upon a velvet ottoman and weep as if her heart would break?"

"The heroine," said the young man, moistening his lips, "does thus lose sea, thoughts, and naturally weeps, but—"

"Excuse me," said the youth, "for appearing inquisitive, but do the next chapter does the baffled count, foiled at every turn, leave the room, and pausing at the door, hiss between his clenched teeth: 'Beware how you press the path of a Strabensmith,' but Lurline bending her head against the broad breast of Hans, the hunter and gazing up at his face, murmurs these anguished words of Heine's:

'Go but forlicht mein kind,
Vas ist der matter here?'"

"Oh, no," said the young man, "you are quite mistaken. The Count falls from the summit of the Matterhorn and is badly hurt. Lurline, of course, is terrified to Hans, but—"

"Same thing," said the youth, reviving. "Now, see here, it's quite a little step over to the Matterhorn. Do you happen, to say anything in your little story about the Racket Store, or the Schradale Wood Yard, or the Blue Rain Saloon here in Austin?"

"No."

"Don't you give the Travis County Clerk a send-off, when the Court buys his marriage license, or put Edmund White on the back when he robbers are captured by Hans?"

"No indeed. The scene is laid on the Rhine, and—"

"Can't help it, business is business. You should have Lurline drink Lone Star beer at the wedding, and get her trousseau at Scarbrough & Hicks."

"But the story you're afraid of such things. As I said, the scene is laid—"

"See here, Mr.," said the youth rising, "I see the editor coming up the alley now. He looks like he has had about four beers, and unless you can work that story in about a minute, or so to bring in a reading notice for four grocery stores, a restaurant, or two and a steam laundry in Austin, you got in the waste basket. I'm going to set type now. So long."

"I think I will revise this story and return later," said the pale young man as he stopped out the door, just as the breathing of the editor became audible as he climbed a brick pile in the alley.

IN a Light House by the Sea," is what the opera company sang to a forty dollar audience in Galveston.

KIND TO DUMB BRUTES.

Justice—"I see in the paper that the S. P. C. A. at their meeting went into the committee of the whole. What does that mean?"
Jack—"Committee of the hole? Oh, that means that some of them were detailed to see that the kittywas properly fed."

A TRAGEDY IN ONE ACT.

(Scene—A grocery store.)

[Merchant is discovered sitting behind his counter playing checkers with his clerk.]

[The advertising solicitor of the ROLLING STONE enters apparently in a hurry.]

Merchant—It's my move, Bill. Wait a minute. Anything you want, sir?

Solicitor—Like to see you a few minutes, sir, if you are not too busy.

[Kewkunt crowns one of the clerk's kings and comes forward.]

Merchant—Well?

Solicitor—I want to talk to you a little about advertising. We are going to get out a big edition next week of 500 copies. We—

Merchant—Copies of what?

Solicitor—The ROLLING STONE.

Merchant—I don't advertise. Jup, Bill, you moved that man.

Bill—No, I didn't.

Merchant (turning to solicitor)—Oh, what was it you wanted; a whetstone?

Solicitor—I want you to advertise in my paper. The rates are low, and our circulation constantly increasing. We have—

[Telephone rings.]

Merchant—Excuse me a minute.

[Goes to telephone.]

Merchant—Hello! No, we have no Hamburg edging. Got some good oolish and clothespins, though. 'Goodbye.

Merchant—Now, Bill, it's my move, remember. I've got three kings, and you haven't got but two.

[She faces at checker board.]

Solicitor—Excuse me just a minute; I—

Merchant (rising)—Oh, be busy; you want some soapstone. We haven't got any, but—

Solicitor—The ROLLING STONE, you mean.

AT THE INAUGURAL BALL.

Clara—"Charlie came very near proposing tonight. I was so agitated. I was all in a tremble."
Lillie—"Yes; I heard him say he was going to shake you."

NEARLY CAUGHT.

Wholesale Merchant—"What is this item in your Austin expense bill, Mr. Roads, 'Incidental, $100'"
Mr. Roads—"Oh—ah—er—that's Inside details. Had some jaw teeth filled while there. (By George, he nearly got on to that little supper at the Driskill.)"

I want you to advertise your business in the paper.

Merchant—Oh, advertise my business. What do you charge?

Solicitor—Dollar an inch; 10 per cent discount.

Merchant—Don't want any; cost too much.

Solicitor (with deadly calm)—Say, it won't cost you a cent to get an ad. in for your business. Obituary notices are free. Good day. Come around and see us.

[Goes out.]

Merchant takes off his vest and catches three of the clerk's men in one jump.

A front page of *The Rolling Stone.*

"Dear old boy," began Van Sweller; but in an instant I had seized him by the collar and dragged him aside with the scantiest courtesy.

"For heaven's sake talk like a man," I said, sternly. "Do you think it is manly to use those mushy and inane forms of address? That man is neither dear nor old nor a boy."

To my surprise Van Sweller turned upon me a look of frank pleasure.

"I am glad to hear you say that," he said, heartily. "I used those words because I have been forced to say them so often. They really are contemptible. Thanks for correcting me, dear old boy."

Still I must admit that Van Sweller's conduct in the park that morning was almost without flaw. The courage, the dash, the modesty, the skill, and fidelity that he displayed atoned for everything.

This is the way the story runs.

Van Sweller has been a gentleman member of the "Rugged Riders," the company that made a war with a foreign country famous. Among his comrades was Lawrence O'Roon, a man whom Van Sweller liked. A strange thing — and a hazardous one in fiction — was that Van Sweller and O'Roon resembled each other mightily in face, form, and general appearance. After the war Van Sweller pulled wires, and O'Roon was made a mounted policeman.

Now, one night in New York there are commemorations and libations by old comrades, and in the morning, Mounted Policeman O'Roon, unused to potent liquids — another premise hazardous in fiction — finds the earth bucking and bounding like a bronco, with no stirrup into which he may insert foot and save his honor and his badge.

Noblesse oblige? Surely. So out along the driveways and bridle paths trots Hudson Van Sweller in the uniform of his incapacitated comrade, as like unto him as one French pea is unto a *petit pois*.

It is, of course, jolly larks for Van Sweller, who has wealth and social position enough for him to masquerade safely even as a police commissioner doing his duty, if he wished to do so. But society, not given to scanning the countenances of mounted policemen, sees nothing unusual in the officer on the beat.

And then comes the runaway.

That is a fine scene — the swaying victoria, the impetuous, daft horses plunging through the line of scattering vehicles, the driver stupidly holding his broken reins, and the ivory-white face of Amy Ffolliott, as she clings desperately with each slender hand. Fear has come and gone: it has left her expression pensive and just a little pleading, for life is not so bitter.

And then the clatter and swoop of Mounted Policeman Van Sweller! Oh, it was — but the story has not yet been printed. When it is you shall learn how he sent his bay like a bullet after the imperilled victoria. A Crichton, a Crœsus, and a Centaur in one, he hurls the invincible combination into the chase.

When the story is printed you will admire the breathless scene where Van Sweller checks the headlong team.

And then he looks into Amy Ffolliott's eyes and sees two
things — the possibilities of a happiness he has long sought,
and a nascent promise of it. He is unknown to her; but
he stands in her sight illuminated by the hero's potent
glory, she his and he hers by all the golden, fond, unreason-
able laws of love and light literature.

Ay, that is a rich moment. And it will stir you to find
Van Sweller in that fruitful nick of time thinking of his
comrade O'Roon, who is cursing his gyrating bed and in-
capable legs in an unsteady room in a West Side hotel while
Van Sweller holds his badge and his honor.

Van Sweller hears Miss Ffolliott's voice thrillingly asking
the name of her preserver. If Hudson Van Sweller, in
policeman's uniform, has saved the life of palpitating
beauty in the park—where is Mounted Policeman O'Roon,
in whose territory the deed is done? How quickly by a
word can the hero reveal himself, thus discarding his
masquerade of ineligibility and doubling the romance!
But there is his friend!

Van Sweller touches his cap. "It's nothing, Miss,"
he says, sturdily; "that's what we are paid for — to do
our duty." And away he rides. But the story does not
end there.

As I have said, Van Sweller carried off the park scene
to my decided satisfaction. Even to me he was a hero
when he foreswore, for the sake of his friend, the romantic
promise of his adventure. It was later in the day,
amongst the more exacting conventions that encompass
the society hero, when we had our liveliest disagreement.

At noon he went to O'Roon's room and found him far enough recovered to return to his post, which he at once did.

At about six o'clock in the afternoon Van Sweller fingered his watch, and flashed at me a brief look full of such shrewd cunning that I suspected him at once.

"Time to dress for dinner, old man," he said, with exaggerated carelessness.

"Very well," I answered, without giving him a clew to my suspicions; "I will go with you to your rooms and see that you do the thing properly. I suppose that every author must be a valet to his own hero."

He affected cheerful acceptance of my somewhat officious proposal to accompany him. I could see that he was annoyed by it, and that fact fastened deeper in my mind the conviction that he was meditating some act of treachery.

When he had reached his apartments he said to me, with a too patronizing air: "There are, as you perhaps know, quite a number of little distinguishing touches to be had out of the dressing process. Some writers rely almost wholly upon them. I suppose that I am to ring for my man, and that he is to enter noiselessly, with an expressionless countenance."

"He may enter," I said, with decision, "and only enter. Valets do not usually enter a room shouting college songs or with St. Vitus's dance in their faces; so the contrary may be assumed without fatuous or gratuitous asseveration."

"I must ask you to pardon me," continued Van Sweller, gracefully, "for annoying you with questions, but some of your methods are a little new to me. Shall I don a full-dress suit with an immaculate white tie — or is there another tradition to be upset?"

"You will wear," I replied, "evening dress, such as a gentleman wears. If it is full, your tailor should be responsible for its bagginess. And I will leave it to whatever erudition you are supposed to possess whether a white tie is rendered any whiter by being immaculate. And I will leave it to the consciences of you and your man whether a tie that is not white, and therefore not immaculate, could possibly form any part of a gentleman's evening dress. If not, then the perfect tie is included and understood in the term 'dress,' and its expressed addition predicates either a redundancy of speech or the spectacle of a man wearing two ties at once."

With this mild but deserved rebuke I left Van Sweller in his dressing-room, and waited for him in his library.

About an hour later his valet came out, and I heard him telephone for an electric cab. Then out came Van Sweller, smiling, but with that sly, secretive design in his eye that was puzzling me.

"I believe," he said easily, as he smoothed a glove, "that I will drop in at ——* for dinner."

I sprang up, angrily, at his words. This, then, was the paltry trick he had been scheming to play upon me. I

---

*See advertising column, "Where to Dine Well," in the daily newspapers.

faced him with a look so grim that even his patrician poise
was flustered.

"You will never do so," I exclaimed, "with my permission. What kind of a return is this," I continued, hotly,
"for the favors I have granted you? I gave you a 'Van'
to your name when I might have called you 'Perkins' or
'Simpson.' I have humbled myself so far as to brag of
your polo ponies, your automobiles, and the iron muscles
that you acquired when you were stroke-oar of your
'varsity eight,' or 'eleven,' whichever it is. I created you
for the hero of this story; and I will not submit to having
you queer it. I have tried to make you a typical young
New York gentleman of the highest social station and
breeding. You have no reason to complain of my treatment to you. Amy Ffolliott, the girl you are to win, is a
prize for any man to be thankful for, and cannot be
equalled for beauty — provided the story is illustrated
by the right artist. I do not understand why you should
try to spoil everything. I had thought you were a gentleman."

"What it is you are objecting to, old man?" asked Van
Sweller, in a surprised tone.

"To your dining at ——,*" I answered. "The pleasure
would be yours, no doubt, but the responsibility would fall
upon me. You intend deliberately to make me out a tout
for a restaurant. Where you dine to-night has not the
slightest connection with the thread of our story. You

---

*See advertising column, "Where to Dine Well," in the daily news-
papers.

know very well that the plot requires that you be in front of the Alhambra Opera House at 11:30 where you are to rescue Miss Ffolliott a second time as the fire engine crashes into her cab.   Until that time your movements are immaterial to the reader.   Why can't you dine out of sight somewhere, as many a hero does, instead of insisting upon an inapposite and vulgar exhibition of yourself?"

"My dear fellow," said Van Sweller, politely, but with a stubborn tightening of his lips, "I'm sorry it doesn't please you, but there's no help for it.   Even a character in a story has rights that an author cannot ignore.   The hero of a story of New York social life must dine at ———* at least once during its action."

"'Must,'" I echoed, disdainfully; "why 'must'?   Who demands it?"

"The magazine editors," answered Van Sweller, giving me a glance of significant warning.

"But why?" I persisted.

"To please subscribers around Kankakee, Ill.," said Van Sweller, without hesitation.

"How do you know these things?" I inquired, with sudden suspicion.   "You never came into existence until this morning.   You are only a character in fiction, any-way.   I, myself, created you.   How is it possible for you to know anything?"

"Pardon me for referring to it," said Van Sweller, with

———
*See advertising column, "Where to Dine Well," in the daily news-papers.

a sympathetic smile, "but I have been the hero of hundreds of stories of this kind."

I felt a slow flush creeping into my face.

"I thought . . ." I stammered; "I was hoping
. . . that is . . . Oh, well, of course an absolutely
original conception in fiction is impossible in these
days."

"Metropolitan types," continued Van Sweller, kindly,
"do not offer a hold for much originality. I've sauntered
through every story in pretty much the same way. Now
and then the women writers have made me cut some rather
strange capers, for a gentleman; but the men generally
pass me along from one to another without much change.
But never yet, in any story, have I failed to dine at ——.*"

"You will fail this time," I said, emphatically.

"Perhaps so," admitted Van Sweller, looking out of the
window into the street below, "but if so it will be for the
first time. The authors all send me there. I fancy that
many of them would have liked to accompany me, but
for the little matter of the expense."

"I say I will be touting for no restaurant," I repeated,
loudly. "You are subject to my will, and I declare that
you shall not appear of record this evening until the time
arrives for you to rescue Miss Ffolliott again. If the
reading public cannot conceive that you have dined during
that interval at some one of the thousands of establishments provided for that purpose that do not receive

*See advertising column, "Where to Dine Well," in the daily news-
papers.

literary advertisement it may suppose, for aught I care, that you have gone fasting."

"Thank you," said Van Sweller, rather coolly, "you are hardly courteous. But take care! it is at your own risk that you attempt to disregard a fundamental principle in metropolitan fiction — one that is dear alike to author and reader. I shall, of course attend to my duty when it comes time to rescue your heroine; but I warn you that it will be your loss if you fail to send me to-night to dine at ———.*"

"I will take the consequences if there are to be any, I replied. "I am not yet come to be sandwich man for an eating-house."

I walked over to a table where I had left my cane and gloves. I heard the whirr of the alarm in the cab below and I turned quickly. Van Sweller was gone.

I rushed down the stairs and out to the curb. An empty hansom was just passing. I hailed the driver excitedly.

"See that auto cab halfway down the block?" I shouted. "Follow it. Don't lose sight of it for an instant, and I will give you two dollars!"

If I only had been one of the characters in my story instead of myself I could easily have offered $10 or $25 or even $100. But $2 was all I felt justified in expending, with fiction at its present rates.

The cab driver, instead of lashing his animal into a

---

*See advertising column, "Where to Dine Well," in the daily newspapers.

foam, proceeded at a deliberate trot that suggested a by-the-hour arrangement.

But I suspected Van Sweller's design; and when we lost sight of his cab I ordered my driver to proceed at once to ——.*

I found Van Sweller at a table under a palm, just glancing over the menu, with a hopeful waiter hovering at his elbow.

"Come with me," I said, inexorably. "You will not give me the slip again. Under my eye you shall remain until 11:30."

Van Sweller countermanded the order for his dinner, and arose to accompany me. He could scarcely do less. A fictitious character is but poorly equipped for resisting a hungry but live author who comes to drag him forth from a restaurant. All he said was: "You were just in time; but I think you are making a mistake. You cannot afford to ignore the wishes of the great reading public."

I took Van Sweller to my own rooms — to my room. He had never seen anything like it before.

"Sit on that trunk," I said to him, "while I observe whether the landlady is stalking us. If she is not, I will get things at a delicatessen store below, and cook something for you in a pan over the gas jet. It will not be so bad. Of course nothing of this will appear in the story."

"Jove! old man!" said Van Sweller, looking about him with interest, "this is a jolly little closet you live in! Where the devil do you sleep? — Oh, that pulls down! And

---

*See advertising column, "Where] to Dine Well," in the daily news-papers.

I say — what is this under the corner of the carpet? — Oh, a frying pan! I see — clever idea! Fancy cooking over the gas! What larks it will be!"

"Think of anything you could eat?" I asked; "try a chop, or what?"

"Anything," said Van Sweller, enthusiastically, "except a grilled bone."

Two weeks afterward the postman brought me a large, fat envelope. I opened it, and took out something that I had seen before, and this typewritten letter from a magazine that encourages society fiction:

Your short story, "The Badge of Policeman O'Roon," is herewith returned.

We are sorry that it has been unfavorably passed upon; but it seems to lack in some of the essential requirements of our publication.

The story is splendidly constructed; its style is strong and inimitable, and its action and character-drawing deserve the highest praise. As a story *per se* it has merit beyond anything that we have read for some time. But, as we have said, it fails to come up to some of the standards we have set.

Could you not re-write the story, and inject into it the social atmosphere, and return it to us for further consideration? It is suggested to you that you have the hero, Van Sweller, drop in for luncheon or dinner once or twice at——* or at the ——* which will be in line with the changes desired.

Very truly yours,
THE EDITORS.

———

*See advertising column, "Where to Dine Well," in the daily newspapers.

SOUND AND FURY

[O. Henry wrote this for *Ainslee's Magazine*, where it appeared in March, 1903.]

PERSONS OF THE DRAMA

Mr. Penne . . . . *An Author*
Miss Lore . . . . *An Amanuensis*

SCENE — *Workroom of* Mr. Penne's *popular novel factory.*

Mr. Penne — Good morning, Miss Lore. Glad to see you so prompt. We should finish that June installment for the *Epoch* to-day. Leverett is crowding me for it. Are you quite ready? We will resume where we left off yesterday. (*Dictates.*) "Kate, with a sigh, rose from his knees, and ——"

Miss Lore — Excuse me; you mean "rose from *her* knees," instead of "his," don't you?

Mr. Penne — Er — no — "his," if you please. It is the love scene in the garden. (*Dictates.*) "Rose from his knees where, blushing with youth's bewitching coyness, she had rested for a moment after Cortland had declared his love. The hour was one of supreme and tender joy. When Kate — scene that Cortland never ——"

Miss Lore — Excuse me; but wouldn't it be more grammatical to say "when Kate *saw*," instead of "seen"?

140

Mr. Penne — The context will explain. (*Dictates.*) "When Kate — scene that Cortland never forgot — came tripping across the lawn it seemed to him the fairest sight that earth had ever offered to his gaze."

Miss Lore — Oh!

Mr. Penne (*dictates*) — "Kate had abandoned herself to the joy of her new-found love so completely, that no shadow of her former grief was cast upon it. Cortland, with his arm firmly entwined about her waist, knew nothing of her sighs ——"

Miss Lore — Goodness! If he couldn't tell her size with his arm around ——

Mr. Penne (*frowning*) — "Of her sighs and tears of the previous night."

Miss Lore — Oh!

Mr. Penne (*dictates*) — "To Cortland the chief charm of this girl was her look of innocence and unworldliness. Never had nun ——"

Miss Lore — How about changing that to "never had any?"

Mr. Penne (*emphatically*) — "Never had nun in cloistered cell a face more sweet and pure."

Miss Lore — Oh!

Mr. Penne (*dictates*) — "But now Kate must hasten back to the house lest her absence be discovered. After a fond farewell she turned and sped lightly away. Cortland's gaze followed her. He watched her rise ——"

Miss Lore — Excuse me, Mr. Penne; but how could he watch her eyes while her back was turned toward him?

Mr. Penne (*with extreme politeness*) — Possibly you would gather my meaning more intelligently if you would wait for the conclusion of the sentence. (*Dictates.*) "Watched her rise as gracefully as a fawn as she mounted the eastern terrace."

Miss Lore — Oh!

Mr. Penne (*dictates*) — "And yet Cortland's position was so far above that of this rustic maiden that he dreaded to consider the social upheaval that would ensue should he marry her. In no uncertain tones the traditional voices of his caste and world cried out loudly to him to let her go. What should follow ——"

Miss Lore (*looking up with a start*) — I'm sure I can't say, Mr. Penne. Unless (*with a giggle*) you would want to add "Gallegher."

Mr. Penne (*coldly*) — Pardon me. I was not seeking to impose upon you the task of a collaborator. Kindly consider the question a part of the text.

Miss Lore — Oh!

Mr. Penne (*dictates*)—"On one side was love and Kate; on the other side his heritage of social position and family pride. Would love win? Love, that the poets tell us will last forever! (*Perceives that* Miss Lore *looks fatigued, and looks at his watch.*) That's a good long stretch. Perhaps we'd better knock off a bit.

(Miss Lore *does not reply.*)

Mr. Penne — I said, Miss Lore, we've been at it quite a long time — wouldn't you like to knock off for a while?

Miss Lore — Oh! Were you addressing me before? I put what you said down. I thought it belonged in the story. It seemed to fit in all right. Oh, no; I'm not tired.

Mr. Penne — Very well, then, we will continue. (*Dictates.*) "In spite of these qualms and doubts, Cortland was a happy man. That night at the club he silently toasted Kate's bright eyes in a bumper of the rarest vintage. Afterward he set out for a stroll with, as Kate on ——"

Miss Lore — Excuse me, Mr. Penne, for venturing a suggestion; but don't you think you might state that in a less coarse manner?

Mr. Penne (*astounded*) — Wh-wh — I'm afraid I fail to understand you.

Miss Lore — His condition. Why not say he was "full" or "intoxicated?" It would sound much more elegant than the way you express it.

Mr. Penne (*still darkly wandering*) — Will you kindly point out, Miss Lore, where I have intimated that Cortland was "full," if you prefer that word?

Miss Lore (*calmly consulting her stenographic notes*) — It is right here, word for word. (*Reads.*) "Afterward he set out for a stroll with a skate on."

Mr. Penne (*with peculiar emphasis*) — Ah! And now will you kindly take down the expurgated phrase? (*Dictates.*) "Afterward he set out for a stroll with, as Kate on one occasion had fancifully told him, her spirit leaning upon his arm."

Miss Lore — Oh!

MR. PENNE (*dictates*) — Chapter thirty-four. Heading — "What Kate Found in the Garden."   "That fragrant summer morning brought gracious tasks to all.   The bees were at the honeysuckle blossoms on the porch.   Kate, singing a little song, was training the riotous branches of her favorite woodbine. The sun, himself, had rows——."

MISS LORE — Shall I say "had risen"?

MR. PENNE (*very slowly and with desperate deliberation*) — "The — sun — himself — had — rows — of — blushing — pinks — and — hollyhocks — and — hyacinths — waiting — that — he — might — dry — their — dew-drenched — cups."

MISS LORE — Oh!

MR. PENNE (*dictates*) — "The earliest trolley, scattering the birds from its pathway like some marauding cat, brought Cortland over from Oldport. He had forgotten his fair ——"

MISS LORE — Hm!   Wonder how he got the conductor to ——

MR. PENNE (*very loudly*) — "Forgotten his fair and roseate visions of the night in the practical light of the sober morn."

MISS LORE — Oh!

MR. PENNE (*dictates*) — "He greeted her with his usual smile and manner. 'See the waves,' he cried, pointing to the heaving waters of the sea, 'ever wooing and returning to the rockbound shore.' "'Ready to break,' Kate said, with ——"

MISS LORE — My!   One evening he has his arm around

her, and the next morning he's ready to break her head! Just like a man!

Mr. Penne (*with suspicious calmness*) — There are times, Miss Lore, when a man becomes so far exasperated that even a woman —— But suppose we finish the sentence. (*Dictates.*) "'Ready to break,' Kate said, with the thrilling look of a soul-awakened woman, 'into foam and spray, destroying themselves upon the shore they love so well.'"

Miss Lore — Oh!

Mr. Penne (*dictates*) — "Cortland, in Kate's presence heard faintly the voice of caution. Thirty years had not cooled his ardor. It was in his power to bestow great gifts upon this girl. He still retained the beliefs that he had at twenty." (*To* Miss Lore, *wearily*) I think that will be enough for the present.

Miss Lore (*wisely*) — Well, if he had the twenty that he believed he had, it might buy her a rather nice one.

Mr. Penne (*faintly*) — The last sentence was my own. We will discontinue for the day, Miss Lore.

Miss Lore — Shall I come again to-morrow?

Mr. Penne (*helpless under the spell*) — If you will be so good.

(*Exit* Miss Lore.)

ASBESTOS CURTAIN.

TICTOCQ

[These two farcical stories about Tictocq appeared in *The Rolling Stone*. They are reprinted here with all of their local references because, written hurriedly and for neighborly reading, they nevertheless have an interest for the admirer of O. Henry. They were written in 1894.]

THE GREAT FRENCH DETECTIVE, IN AUSTIN

A Successful Political Intrigue

CHAPTER I

IT IS not generally known that Tictocq, the famous French detective, was in Austin last week. He registered at the Avenue Hotel under an assumed name, and his quiet and reserved manners singled him out at once for one not to be singled out.

No one knows why he came to Austin, but to one or two he vouchsafed the information that his mission was an important one from the French Government.

One report is that the French Minister of State has discovered an old statute among the laws of the empire, resulting from a treaty between the Emperor Charlemagne and Governor Roberts which expressly provides for the north gate of the Capitol grounds being kept open, but this is merely a conjecture.

Last Wednesday afternoon a well-dressed gentleman knocked at the door of Tictocq's room in the hotel.

The detective opened the door.

"Monsieur Tictocq, I believe," said the gentleman.

"You will see on the register that I sign my name Q. X. Jones," said Tictocq, "and gentlemen would understand that I wish to be known as such. If you do not like being referred to as no gentleman, I will give you satisfaction any time after July 1st, and fight Steve O'Donnell, John McDonald, and Ignatius Donnelly in the meantime if you desire."

"I do not mind it in the least," said the gentleman. "In fact, I am accustomed to it. I am Chairman of the Democratic Executive Committee, Platform No. 2, and I have a friend in trouble. I knew you were Tictocq from your resemblance to yourself."

"Entrez vous," said the detective.

The gentleman entered and was handed a chair.

"I am a man of few words," said Tictocq. "I will help your friend if possible. Our countries are great friends. We have given you Lafayette and French fried potatoes. You have given us California champagne and — taken back Ward McAllister. State your case."

"I will be very brief," said the visitor. "In room No. 76 in this hotel is stopping a prominent Populist Candidate. He is alone. Last night some one stole his socks. They cannot be found. If they are not recovered, his party will attribute their loss to the Democracy. They will make great capital of the burglary, although I am sure it was not a political move at all.   The socks must be recovered.   You are the only man that can do it."

Tictocq bowed.

"Am I to have carte blanche to question every person connected with the hotel?"

"The proprietor has already been spoken to.   Everything and everybody is at your service."

Tictocq consulted his watch.

"Come to this room to-morrow afternoon at 6 o'clock with the landlord, the Populist Candidate, and any other witnessess elected from both parties, and I will return the socks."

"Bien, Monsieur; schlafen sie wohl."

"Au revoir."

The Chairman of the Democratic Executive Committee, Platform No. 2, bowed courteously and withdrew.

.   .   .   .

Tictocq sent for the bell boy.

"Did you go to room 76 last night?"

"Yes, sir."

"Who was there?"

"An old hayseed what come on the 7:25."

"What did he want?"

"The bouncer."

"What for?"

"To put the light out."

"Did you take anything while in the room?"

"No, he didn't ask me."

" What is your name?"

"Jim."

"You can go."

CHAPTER II

The drawing-rooms of one of the most magnificent private residences in Austin are a blaze of lights. Carriages line the streets in front, and from gate to doorway is spread a velvet carpet, on which the delicate feet of the guests may tread.

The occasion is the entrée into society of one of the fairest buds in the City of the Violet Crown. The rooms are filled with the culture, the beauty, the youth and fashion of society. Austin society is acknowledged to be the wittiest, the most select, and the highest bred to be found southwest of Kansas City.

Mrs. Rutabaga St. Vitus, the hostess, is accustomed to draw around her a circle of talent, and beauty, rarely equalled anywhere. Her evenings come nearer approaching the dignity of a salon than any occasion, except, perhaps, a Tony Faust and Marguerite reception at the Iron Front.

Miss St. Vitus, whose advent into society's maze was heralded by such an auspicious display of hospitality, is a slender brunette, with large, lustrous eyes, a winning smile, and a charming ingénue manner. She wears a china silk, cut princesse, with diamond ornaments, and a couple of towels inserted in the back to conceal prominence of shoulder blades. She is chatting easily and naturally on a plush covered tête-à-tête with Harold St. Clair, the agent for a Minneapolis pants company. Her friend and school-mate, Elsie Hicks, who married three drummers in one day, a week or two before, and won a wager of two dozen bottles of Budweiser from the handsome and talented young hack-driver, Bum Smithers, is promenading in and out the low French windows with Ethelbert Windup, the popular young candidate for hide inspector, whose name is familiar to every one who reads police court reports.

Somewhere, concealed by shrubbery, a band is playing, and during the pauses in conversation, onions can be smelt frying in the kitchen.

Happy laughter rings out from ruby lips, handsome faces grow tender as they bend over white necks and droop-ing heads; timid eyes convey things that lips dare not speak, and beneath silken bodice and broadcloth, hearts beat time to the sweet notes of "Love's Young Dream."

"And where have you been for some time past, you recreant cavalier?" says Miss St. Vitus to Harold St. Clair. "Have you been worshipping at another shrine? Are you recreant to your whilom friends? Speak, Sir Knight, and defend yourself."

"Oh, come off," says Harold, in his deep, musical bari-tone; "I've been having a devil of a time fitting pants on a lot of bow-legged jays from the cotton-patch. Got knobs on their legs, some of 'em big as gourds, and all expect a fit. Did you ever try to measure a bow-legged — I mean — can't you imagine what a jam-swizzled time I have getting pants to fit 'em? Business dull too, nobody wants 'em over three dollars."

"You witty boy," says Miss St. Vitus. "Just as full of bon mots and clever sayings as ever. What do you take now?"

"Oh, beer."

"Give me your arm and let's go into the drawing-room and draw a cork. I'm chewing a little cotton myself."

Arm in arm, the handsome couple pass across the room, the cynosure of all eyes. Luderic Hetherington, the rising and gifted night-watchman at the Lone Star slaughter house, and Mabel Grubb, the daughter of the millionaire owner of the Humped-backed Camel saloon, are standing under the oleanders as they go by.

"She is very beautiful," says Luderic.

"Rats," says Mabel.

A keen observer would have noted all this time the figure of a solitary man who seemed to avoid the company, but by adroit changing of his position, and perfectly cool and self-possessed manner, avoided drawing any especial attention to himself.

The lion of the evening is Herr Professor Ludwig von Bum, the pianist.

He had been found drinking beer in a saloon on East Pecan Street by Colonel St. Vitus about a week before, and according to the Austin custom in such cases, was invited home by the colonel, and the next day accepted into society, with large music classes at his service.

Professor von Bum is playing the lovely symphony in G minor from Beethoven's "Songs Without Music." The grand chords fill the room with exquisite harmony.

He plays the extremely difficult passages in the obligato home run in a masterly manner, and when he finishes with that grand te deum with arpeggios on the side, there is that complete hush in the room that is dearer to the artist's heart than the loudest applause.

The professor looks around.

The room is empty.

Empty with the exception of Tictocq, the great French detective, who springs from behind a mass of tropical plants to his side.

The professor rises in alarm.

"Hush," says Tictocq: "Make no noise at all. You have already made enough."

Footsteps are heard outside.

"Be quick," says Tictocq: "give me those socks. There is not a moment to spare."

"Vas sagst du?"

"Ah, he confesses," says Tictocq. "No socks will do but those you carried off from the Populist Candidate's room."

The company is returning, no longer hearing the music.

Tictocq hesitates not. He seizes the professor, throws him upon the floor, tears off his shoes and socks, and escapes with the latter through the open window into the garden.

CHAPTER III

Tictocq's room in the Avenue Hotel.

A knock is heard at the door.

Tictocq opens it and looks at his watch.

"Ah," he says, "it is just six. Entrez, Messieurs."

The messieurs entrez. There are seven of them; the Populist Candidate who is there by invitation, not knowing for what purpose; the chairman of the Democratic Executive Committee, platform No. 2, the hotel proprietor, and three or four Democrats and Populists, as near as could be found out.

"I don't know," begins the Populist Candidate, "what in the h ——"

"Excuse me," says Tictocq, firmly. "You will oblige me by keeping silent until I make my report. I have been employed in this case, and I have unravelled it. For the honor of France I request that I be heard with attention."

"Certainly," says the chairman; "we will be pleased to listen."

Tictocq stands in the centre of the room. The electric light burns brightly above him. He seems the incarnation of alertness, vigor, cleverness, and cunning.

The company seat themselves in chairs along the wall.

"When informed of the robbery," begins Tictocq, "I first questioned the bell boy. He knew nothing. I went to the police headquarters. They knew nothing. I invited one of them to the bar to drink. He said there used to be a little colored boy in the Tenth Ward who stole things and kept them for recovery by the police, but failed to be at the place agreed upon for arrest one time, and had been sent to jail.

"I then began to think. I reasoned. No man, said I, would carry a Populist's socks in his pocket without wrapping them up. He would not want to do so in the hotel. He would want a paper. Where would he get one? At the *Statesman* office, of course. I went there. A young man with his hair combed down on his forehead sat behind the desk. I knew he was writing society items, for a young lady's slipper, a piece of cake, a fan, a half emptied bottle of cocktail, a bunch of roses, and a police whistle lay on the desk before him.

"Can you tell me if a man purchased a paper here in the last three months?" I said.

"Yes," he replied; "we sold one last night."

"Can you describe the man?"

"Accurately. He had blue whiskers, a wart between his shoulder blades, a touch of colic, and an occupation tax on his breath."

"Which way did he go?"

"Out."

"I then went ——"

"Wait a minute," said the Populist Candidate, rising; "I don't see why in the h ——"

"Once more I must beg that you will be silent," said Tictocq, rather sharply. "You should not interrupt me in the midst of my report."

"I made one false arrest," continued Tictocq. "I was passing two finely dressed gentlemen on the street, when one of them remarked that he had 'stole his socks.' I handcuffed him and dragged him to a lighted store, when his companion explained to me that he was somewhat intoxicated and his tongue was not entirely manageable.

He had been speaking of some business transaction, and what he intended to say was that he had 'sold his stocks.'

"I then released him.

"An hour afterward I passed a saloon, and saw this Professor von Bum drinking beer at a table. I knew him in Paris. I said 'here is my man.' He worshipped Wagner, lived on limburger cheese, beer, and credit, and would have stolen anybody's socks. I shadowed him to the reception at Colonel St. Vitus's, and in an opportune moment I seized him and tore the socks from his feet. There they are."

With a dramatic gesture, Tictocq threw a pair of dingy socks upon the table, folded his arms, and threw back his head.

With a loud cry of rage, the Populist Candidate sprang once more to his feet.

"Gol darn it! I WILL say what I want to. I ——"

The two other Populists in the room gazed at him coldly and sternly.

"Is this tale true?" they demanded of the Candidate.

"No, by gosh, it ain't!" he replied, pointing a trembling finger at the Democratic Chairman. "There stands the man who has concocted the whole scheme. It is an infernal, unfair political trick to lose votes for our party. How far has this thing gone?" he added, turning savagely to the detective.

"All the newspapers have my written report on the matter, and the *Statesman* will have it in plate matter next week," said Tictocq, complacently.

"All is lost!" said the Populists, turning toward the door.

"For God's sake, my friends," pleaded the Candidate, following them; "listen to me; I swear before high heaven that I never wore a pair of socks in my life. It is all a devilish campaign lie."

The Populists turn their backs.

"The damage is already done," they said. "The people have heard the story. You have yet time to withdraw decently before the race."

All left the room except Tictocq and the Democrats.

"Let's all go down and open a bottle of fizz on the Finance Committee," said the Chairman of the Executive Committee, Platform No. 2.

TRACKED TO DOOM

OR

THE MYSTERY OF THE RUE DE PEYCHAUD

'TIS midnight in Paris.

A myriad of lamps that line the Champs Elysées and the Rouge et Noir, cast their reflection in the dark waters of the Seine as it flows gloomily past the Place Vendôme and the black walls of the Convent Notadam.

The great French capital is astir.

It is the hour when crime and vice and wickedness reign.

Hundreds of fiacres drive madly through the streets conveying women, flashing with jewels and as beautiful as dreams, from opera and concert, and the little bijou supper rooms of the Café Tout le Temps are filled with laughing groups, while bon mots, persiflage and repartee fly upon the air — the jewels of thought and conversation.

Luxury and poverty brush each other in the streets. The homeless gamin, begging a sou with which to purchase a bed, and the spendthrift roué, scattering golden louis d'or, tread the same pavement.

When other cities sleep, Paris has just begun her wild revelry.

157

The first scene of our story is a cellar beneath the Rue de Peychaud.

The room is filled with smoke of pipes, and is stifling with the reeking breath of its inmates. A single flaring gas jet dimly lights the scene, which is one Rembrandt or Moreland and Keisel would have loved to paint.

A garçon is selling absinthe to such of the motley crowd as have a few sous, dealing it out in niggardly portions in broken teacups.

Leaning against the bar is Carnaignole Cusheau — generally known as the Gray Wolf.

He is the worst man in Paris.

He is more than four feet ten in height, and his sharp, ferocious looking face and the mass of long, tangled gray hair that covers his face and head, have earned for him the name he bears.

His striped blouse is wide open at the neck and falls outside of his dingy leather trousers. The handle of a deadly looking knife protrudes from his belt. One stroke of its blade would open a box of the finest French sardines.

"Voilà, Gray Wolf," cries Couteau, the bartender. "How many victims to-day? There is no blood upon your hands. Has the Gray Wolf forgotten how to bite?"

"Sacre Bleu, Mille Tonnerre, by George," hisses the Gray Wolf. "Monsieur Couteau, you are bold indeed to speak to me thus.

"By Ventre St. Gris! I have not even dined to-day. Spoils indeed. There is no living in Paris now. But one rich American have I garroted in a fortnight."

"Bah! those Democrats. They have ruined the country. With their income tax and their free trade, they have destroyed the millionaire business. Carrambo! Diable! D — n it!"

"Hist!" suddenly says Chamounix the rag-picker, who is worth 20,000,000 francs, "some one comes!"

The cellar door opened and a man crept softly down the rickety steps. The crowd watches him with silent awe.

He went to the bar, laid his card on the counter, bought a drink of absinthe, and then drawing from his pocket a little mirror, set it up on the counter and proceeded to don a false beard and hair and paint his face into wrinkles, until he closely resembled an old man seventy-one years of age.

He then went into a dark corner and watched the crowd of people with sharp, ferret-like eyes.

Gray Wolf slipped cautiously to the bar and examined the card left by the newcomer.

"Holy Saint Bridget!" he exclaims. "It is Tictocq, the detective."

Ten minutes later a beautiful woman enters the cellar.

Tenderly nurtured, and accustomed to every luxury that money could procure, she had, when a young vivandière at the Convent of Saint Susan de la Montarde, run away with the Gray Wolf, fascinated by his many crimes and the knowledge that his business never allowed him to scrape his feet in the hall or snore.

"Parbleu, Marie," snarls the Gray Wolf. "Que

voulez vous?   Avez-vous le beau cheval de mon frère, ou le joli chien de votre père?"

"No, no, Gray Wolf," shouts the motley group of assassins; rogues and pickpockets, even their hardened hearts appalled at his fearful words. "Mon Dieu! You cannot be so cruel!"

"Tiens!" shouts the Gray Wolf, now maddened to desperation, and drawing his gleaming knife. "Voilà! Canaille! Tout le monde, carte blanche enbonpoint sauve que peut entre nous revenez nous a nous moutous!"

The horrified sans-culottes shrink back in terror as the Gray Wolf seizes Maria by the hair and cuts her into twenty-nine pieces, each exactly the same size.

As he stands with reeking hands above the corpse, amid a deep silence, the old, gray-bearded man who has been watching the scene springs forward, tears off his false beard and locks, and Tictocq, the famous French detective, stands before them.

Spellbound and immovable, the denizens of the cellar gaze at the greatest modern detective as he goes about the customary duties of his office.

He first measures the distance from the murdered woman to a point on the wall, then he takes down the name of the bartender and the day of the month and the year. Then drawing from his pocket a powerful microscope, he examines a little of the blood that stands upon the floor in little pools.

"Mon Dieu!" he mutters, "it is as I feared — human blood."

Selected Articles from "The Plunkville Patriot"

Prospects are brighter. The grand jury adjourned yesterday seven black & White Kittens given away at at this office to the next subscriber.

—Uncle Han Bascom's new Barn is a Daizy.

Business in Plunkville is Booming.

—We notice a new tace behind the counte rat Schlemmer bro,.it is that o lour poplar Sheriff Bob Hoskins.

☞ Ye Editor returns thanks to Jim Walsh anp Teddy Potts for a fine mess of fish and to Ant Sallie Grimes for a slice of Light Bread.

Why will you suffer?

Jimtown, PA., Oct'r 1st ,94.
GENTS: I suffered from botts end disinclination for work for sixty-four years, and as I am a District Judge I tried several Drs. in our neighborhood, but without success. One day I was confined to my bed 36 hours with pains for a week back. I tried ninety-eight bottles of your Git Up & Git Prophylactic, and got up next morning feeling perfectly well. Since then I have worked over forty men with good results.
May heaven bless you and your gall.
ANDREW J. QUEER,
Dist. Judge Cell No. 1409.

Massage treatment and fried oysters at the Red Front tizot

Go to the Misfit Parlors for a shave or a divorce.

ESTRAY NOTICE

Mrs. Col Ratherford, who has been visiting her brother, Dr. Buntington for a few months, writes that she has both teate now tall, black legs, about 15 hands high, one ear gootled, was last seen about 12 o'clock at night near Herbert's Bend; thought to arrived at her home St. Louis. be in that neighborhood.

Estrayed from my place a bay colt,

Our capitol 5's were stolen by a local burglar, and we use $ marks un-

fourth time Miss Susie has been before the Mayor on such charges. It she is not more care full she will lose herp lace in Society.

The oyster supper given by the ladies of the Dorking Society la't night over Sharp and Bledsoe's bucketshop was an immense success.

The total recipes was $37.28. Everybody enjoyed the proceedings to the uttermost.

The gra'y-bed was a source of much amusement. Lige Peterson paid ten cts, and got out a horned frog and an old liver pad. The young folks played games to their heart's content. —"thimqle," ",Copenhagin," ane "Steam out Arrive d last Night." were the order of the day. Some one proposed to play drop the handkercheil. but after much inquiry and merriment it was found that everybody had forgot to bring one, so the played Pillow instead. Dr. Skaggs the venerable Pastor, seemed to enter into the fun as heartily as the youngest, & when Sam Brockman suggested that he had kissed Sally Yates some 17 or eighteen times more than the rujes the of game allowed, he playfuly knocked out 3 of Sam,s front teeth and jammed him on top of the stove, laughing merrily all while.

Mrs Deacon Hughes reported astrong smell of whisky while the Deacon & parson Skaggs were teaching the girls of the senior Bible class to play Puss in the corner, bet the Reporter of the PATRIOT saw nothiog of the kind.

Elder Samson' whow as blindfolded during one of the games, stuck his hand in the hot steam from a teakitile and said something that the Reporter could not catch, but immediately afterwards 9 of the ladies went home. Deacon Hughes secured a red table cloth about this time and did a skirt dance while Tom Elderkin beat time on the stove aith Parson Skaggs' cane

Then the rest of the ladys left, and the boys broke up some blue and white china plates ond qad quite a lively time with the gate reciepts.

Next Tuesday the Dorking Society will give a shadow Dance & Lunch over Peter's Livery Stable for the behefit of the Skating Rink.

Use Kuticura for scratched tickets

in a white demi train of surah silk corded with gassametay trimmings: cut bias after the ceremony. The happy co uple rep aired to the palatal residence of the bride,s fathar—Col. Gripe, and when an elegant collection had been spread and fasted till they were full to the neck. They then took the 6-30 to Hog Prairi where the groome hasa prominet position in busiuess circles, —in other words.the cotton seed ring

Henry Pond, who has been on the jury for 3 days, broke his leg while going up the steps of the Star saloon.

probed be. not find them woods with a winch. Sheriff's posse will pro sure of oeing lynched if h hard to catch, but the dogs I ly set on his trail. Owing to the ity of our jail, it may become ne to hang him anyhon.

We are authorized to annon Patrick O. Hoolihan for alderm of the 4th ward. Votes wanted. particulars see small bills on elec day.

GRAND MONOHIPPIC AGGREGATION!
OPEBA HOUSE
FRIDAY OCT'R the 27th.

KATAMORBA! — QUEEN OF THE REPTILE WORLD.

Matinee Free. For Prohibitionists.
The greatest Snake Charmer living· Handles the cobra-di-capello, anaconda, Rattlesnake & Viper without gloves. All kinds of snakes successfully controlled. See recommendations from Keely Institute and Georgetown Republican.

—Full Orchestra of 6 Rajahs from Farther India.—

LITTLE ELSIE,
The child Wonder, recites one of Ella Wheeler Wilcox's Poems while sitting on a cake of REAL ICE!
LIVING PICTURES | THE GREATEST LIVING
Lady Godiva, the only BAREBACKED | ACROBATS,
Lady Rider, on her Arabian | Chas. Collerson, Joon H. Raggles
steed, Anthony Cornstalk. | and Roger M. Quills, do the split,
balancing on high fence. To wind!
Platforms at once.

SPECIAL ATTRACTION.
County-officers race. The ticket com ming around Hornsby's Bend. Tha great show carries more canvass t any other aggregation in the except ten Texas State Govern and their henchmen just befor election.
One ticket admits to Al Grand procession.

The editor of *The Rolling Stone* collected old, quaint cuts of which this page from "The Plunkville Patriot" shows several specimens.

THE ROLLING STONE

VOL. II. NO. 3.   AUSTIN AND SAN ANTONIO, TEXAS, SATURDAY, FEBRUARY 2, 1895.   PRICE FIVE CENTS.

LOTTERY COMPANY

DEPARTMENT CLERK . "Mr. Legislator, if you want to save money for the State, why don't you stop that leak instead of cutting down my salary?"

ARISTOCRACY VS. HASH.

THE snake reporter of the ROLLING STONE was wandering up the avenue last night on his way home from the Y M C A rooms when he was approached by a gaunt, hungry-looking man with wild eyes and disheveled hair. He accosted the reporter in a hollow, weak voice.

"Can you tell me, sir, where I can find in this town a family of some kind?"

"I don't understand exactly."

"Let me tell you how it is," said the stranger, inserting his fore finger in the reporter's button hole and badly damaging his chrysanthemum. "I am a Representative from the Legislature, and I and my family are houseless, homeless and shelterless. We have not tasted food for over a week. I brought my family with me, as I have indignation and could not get around much with the boys. Some days ago I started out to find a boarding house, as I cannot afford to put up at a hotel. I found a nice aristocratic-looking place that suited me, and went in and asked for the two proprietress. A very stately lady with a Roman nose came in the room. She had one hand laid across her chest—across her waist, and the other held a lace handkerchief. I told her I wanted board for myself and family, and she condescended to take us. I asked for her terms, and she said $200 per week.

"I told two dollars to my pocket and I gave her that for a fine wagon that I broke when I fell over the table when she spoke."

"You appear surprised," says she. "You will please remember that I am the widow of Governor Riddle of Georgia, sir family is very highly connected, I give you board as a favor; I do not consider money any equivalent for the advantage of my society, I—"

"Well, I got out of there, and I went to some other places. The next lady was a cousin of General Mahone of Virginia, and wanted four dollars an hour for a back room with a pink mosia and a Burean granite bed in it. The next one was an aunt of Davy Crockett, and asked eight dollars a day for a room furnished in imitation of the Alamo, with prunes for breakfast and one hour's conversation with her for dinner. Another one said she was a descendant of Benedict Arnold on her father's side and Captain Kidd on the other.

"She took more after Captain Kidd.

"She only had one meal and prayers a day, and counted her society worth $150 a week.

"I found nine widows of Supreme Judges, twelve relatives of governors and generals and twenty-two ruins left by various happy colonels, professors and majors, who valued their aristocratic society worth from $50 to $200 per week, with wash-boand hash and dried apples on the side. I admire people of fine descent but my stomach yearns for pork and beans instead of culture. Am I not right?"

"Your words," said the reporter, "convince me that you have suffered what you have said."

"Thanks. You see how it is. I am not wealthy; I have only my per diem and my per question, and I cannot afford to pay for high lineage and windy ancestors. A little corned-beef goes farther with me than a coronet, and when I am cold a comb-of-arms does not warm me."

"I greatly fear," said the reporter, with a playful kindness, "that you have run against a high-toned town. Most all the first class boarding houses here are run by ladies who do not do so to make a living; they want to get the atmosh on Hatty Green."

"I am not dangerous," said the Representative, as he showed a dark article, thinking it was a glove. "I want to find a boarding house where the proprietress was an orphan found in a livery stable, whose father was a dago from East Austin, and whose grandfather was never placed on the map. I want a scrubby, ornery, low-down, snuff-dipping, back-woodsy, pieball gang, who never heard of finger-bowls or Ward McAllister, but who can get up 4 mess of hot cornbread and Irish stew at regular market quotations.

"Is there such a place in Austin?"

The snake reporter sadly shook his head. "I do not know," he said, "but I will shake you for the beer."

*   *   *

[46 minutes later the slate in the Blue Ruin Saloon bore two additional characters.]

10.

HAD THE DROP ON HIM.

Last night about 8 o'clock, a man was seen standing on the walk in front of the Capitol with both hands raised high above his head. A ROLLING STONE reporter happened to see him and went over to investigate. The gentleman proved to be a member of the House from one of the western counties.

"What's the matter?" asked the reporter

"Don't flash power drop on me. Look out, m' free, you'll get shot in minute. Beaner hol' up your hands.

"I don't see anyone," said the reporter

"I see 'm. Called 'm a tar las night 'n a poker game. Bold ho'd lay f' me to day. Goaner goa'n big as er maxims. Goin' ter shoot 'n minute. Beaner run. See 'm up in window?"

"You might as well put your hands down," said the reporter That fellow with a gun is a heanie figure on the Alamo tenement.

"Tat so. You don't know how much you've relieved me. Been standing here half hour. Mush 'bliged, stranger, you've shaved m' life. Goin' home now. G'bye."

The relieved representative took a zig zag course northward and the reporter left in his vest pocket conveniently for blood mock, and also turned his face homeward.

AND IN A HURRY, TOO.

"What time did Mr Spooner leave last night?" asked Mrs Tompkins at the breakfast table.

"He went some time ago," said the old man, glaring proudly at the watch, which was one number larger than a ten.

A LUNAR EPISODE.

THE scene was one of supernatural weirdness. Tall, fantastic mountains reared their seamed peaks over a dreary waste of igneous rocks and burned-out lava beds. Deep lakes of black water stood motionless or gave under freezing, honey-combed crags, from which ever and anon dropped crumbled masses with a sullen plunge. Vegetation there was none. Bitter cold reigned, and ridges of black and shapeless rocks cut the horizon on all sides. An extinct volcano loomed against a purple sky, black as night and as old as the world.

The firmament was studded with immense stars that shone with a wan and spectral light. Orion's belt hung high above. Aldebaran faintly shone many millions of miles away, and the earth glimpsed like a raw crack moon with a lurid, blood-like glow On a lofty mountain that hung toppling above, sat lone black man about a dwelling built of stone. From its solitary window came a bright light that gleamed upon the mistshaven rocks.

The door opened, and two men emerged, looked in a deadly struggle.

They snapped and twisted upon the edge of a precipice, now one gaining the advantage, and now another.

Along with the advantage, the setting of the vast space, the flow of space,

At length one prevailed. He seized his opponent, and raising him high above his head, hurled him into space.

The tumultuous combatant shot through the air like a stone from a catapult in the direction of the luminous earth.

"That's three of 'em this week," said the Man in the Moon, as he lit a cigarette and turned back into the home. "Those New York World interviewers are going to make the third if they keep this thing up much longer."

THE RIGHT MAN

Biggs—"I see they have a new scavenger on our street. Wonder what has become of the old one?"

Griggs—"Oh, he's been selected by Hopper & Co. to write the society novel in their Black and Blue series."

CHICAGO FORESIGHT

Miss Linke—"How could you be so unwise as to reject Mr. Wheeler's suit? He is regarded as one of the biggest catches in the west."

Miss Porque—"Yes, but he only pays $2129.95 income tax."

THE ROLLING STONE One Year and half a dozen of Hill's best Cabinet Photographs for $2 00! Do you want photos of your wife, baby, brother, sister, or yourself, free? If not, let the cook have some taken.

A front page of The Rolling Stone.

He then enters rapidly in a memorandum book the result of his investigations, and leaves the cellar.

Tictocq bends his rapid steps in the direction of the headquarters of the Paris gendarmerie, but suddenly pausing, he strikes his hand upon his brow with a gesture of impatience.

"Mille tonnerre," he mutters. "I should have asked the name of that man with the knife in his hand."

.　　.　　.　　　.　　　.　　　.　　　.

It is reception night at the palace of the Duchess Valerie du Bellairs.

The apartments are flooded with a mellow light from paraffine candles in solid silver candelabra.

The company is the most aristocratic and wealthy in Paris.

Three or four brass bands are playing behind a portière between the coal shed, and also behind time. Footmen in gay-laced livery bring in beer noiselessly and carry out apple-peelings dropped by the guests.

Valerie, seventh Duchess du Bellairs, leans back on a solid gold ottoman on eiderdown cushions, surrounded by the wittiest, the bravest, and the handsomest courtiers in the capital.

"Ah, madame," said the Prince Champvilliers, of Palais Royale, corner of Seventy-third Street, "as Montesquiaux says, 'Rien de plus bon tutti frutti' — Youth seems your inheritance. You are to-night the most beautiful, the wittiest in your own salon. I can scarce believe my own senses, when I remember that thirty-one years ago you ——"

"Saw it off!" says the Duchess peremptorily.

The Prince bows low, and drawing a jewelled dagger, stabs himself to the heart.

"The displeasure of your grace is worse than death," he says, as he takes his overcoat and hat from a corner of the mantelpiece and leaves the room.

"Voilà," says Bèebè Françillon, fanning herself languidly. "That is the way with men. Flatter them, and they kiss your hand. Loose but a moment the silken leash that holds them captive through their vanity and self-opinionativeness, and the son-of-a-gun gets on his ear at once. The devil go with him, I say."

"Ah, mon Princesse," sighs the Count Pumpernickel, stooping and whispering with eloquent eyes into her ear. "You are too hard upon us. Balzac says, 'All women are not to themselves what no one else is to another.' Do you not agree with him?"

"Cheese it!" says the Princess. "Philosophy palls upon me. I'll shake you."

"Hosses?" says the Count.

Arm and arm they go out to the salon au Beurre.

Armande de Fleury, the young pianissimo danseuse from the Folies Bergère is about to sing.

She slightly clears her throat and lays a voluptuous cud of chewing gum upon the piano as the first notes of the accompaniment ring through the salon.

As she prepares to sing, the Duchess du Bellairs grasps

the arm of her ottoman in a vice-like grip, and she watches with an expression of almost anguished suspense.

She scarcely breathes.

Then, as Armande de Fleury, before uttering a note, reels, wavers, turns white as snow and falls dead upon the floor, the Duchess breathes a sigh of relief.

The Duchess had poisoned her.

Then the guests crowd about the piano, gazing with bated breath, and shuddering as they look upon the music rack and observe that the song that Armande came so near singing is "Sweet Marie."

Twenty minutes later a dark and muffled figure was seen to emerge from a recess in the mullioned wall of the Arc de Triomphe and pass rapidly northward.

It was no other than Tictocq, the detective.

The network of evidence was fast being drawn about the murderer of Marie Cusheau.

.   .   .   .

It is midnight on the steeple of the Cathedral of Notadam.

It is also the same time at other given points in the vicinity.

The spire of the Cathedral is 20,000 feet above the pavement, and a casual observer, by making a rapid mathematical calculation, would have readily perceived that this Cathedral is, at least, double the height of others that measure only 10,000 feet.

At the summit of the spire there is a little wooden

platform on which there is room for but one man to stand.

Crouching on this precarious footing, which swayed, dizzily with every breeze that blew, was a man closely muffled, and disguised as a wholesale grocer.

Old François Beongfallong, the great astronomer, who is studying the sidereal spheres from his attic window in the Rue de Bologny, shudders as he turns his telescope upon the solitary figure upon the spire.

"Sacrè Bleu!" he hisses between his new celluloid teeth. "It is Tictocq, the detective. I wonder whom he is following now?"

While Tictocq is watching with lynx-like eyes the hill of Montmartre, he suddenly hears a heavy breathing beside him, and turning, gazes into the ferocious eyes of the Gray Wolf.

Carnaignole Cusheau had put on his W. U. Tel. Co. climbers and climbed the steeple.

"Parbleu, monsieur," says Tictocq. "To whom am I indebted for the honor of this visit?"

The Gray Wolf smiled softly and depreciatingly.

"You are Tictocq, the detective?" he said.

"I am."

"Then listen. I am the murderer of Marie Cusheau. She was my wife and she had cold feet and ate onions. What was I to do? Yet life is sweet to me. I do not wish to be guillotined. I have heard that you are on my track. Is it true that the case is in your hands?"

"It is."

"Thank le bon Dieu, then, I am saved."

The Gray Wolf carefully adjusts the climbers on his feet and descends the spire.

Tictocq takes out his notebook and writes in it.

"At last," he says, "I have a clue."

.   .   .   .   .   .

Monsieur le Compte Carnaignole Cusheau, once known as the Gray Wolf, stands in the magnificent drawing-room of his palace on East 47th Street.

Three days after his confession to Tictocq, he happened to look in the pockets of a discarded pair of pants and found twenty million francs in gold.

Suddenly the door opens and Tictocq, the detective, with a dozen gensd'arme, enters the room.

"You are my prisoners," says the detective.

"On what charge?"

"The murder of Marie Cusheau on the night of August 17th."

"Your proofs?"

"I saw you do it, and your own confession on the spire of Notadam."

The Count laughed and took a paper from his pocket.

"Read this," he said, "here is proof that Marie Cusheau died of heart failure."

Tictocq looked at the paper.

It was a check for 100,000 francs.

Tictocq dismissed the gensd'arme with a wave of his hand.

"We have made a mistake, monsieurs," he said, but as he turns to leave the room, Count Carnaignole stops him.

"One moment, monsieur."

The Count Carnaignole tears from his own face a false beard and reveals the flashing eyes and well-known features of Tictocq, the detective.

Then, springing forward, he snatches a wig and false eyebrows from his visitor, and the Gray Wolf, grinding his teeth in rage, stands before him.

The murderer of Marie Cusheau was never discovered.

A SNAPSHOT AT THE PRESIDENT

[This is the kind of waggish editorial O. Henry was writing in 1894 for the readers of *The Rolling Stone*. The reader will do well to remember that the paper was for local consumption and that the allusions are to a very special place and time.]

(It will be remembered that about a month ago there were special rates offered to the public for a round trip to the City of Washington. The price of the ticket being exceedingly low, we secured a loan of twenty dollars from a public-spirited citizen of Austin, by mortgaging our press and cow, with the additional security of our brother's name, and a slight draught on Major Hutchinson for $4,000.

We purchased a round trip ticket, two loaves of Vienna bread, and quite a large piece of cheese, which we handed to a member of our reportorial staff, with instructions to go to Washington, interview President Cleveland, and get a scoop, if possible, on all other Texas papers.

Our reporter came in yesterday morning, via the Manor dirt road, with a large piece of folded cotton bagging tied under each foot.

It seems that he lost his ticket in Washington, and having divided the Vienna bread and cheese with some disappointed office seekers who were coming home by the same route, he arrived home hungry, desiring food, and with quite an appetite.

Although somewhat late, we give his description of his interview with President Cleveland.)

I AM chief reporter on the staff of *The Rolling Stone*.

About a month ago the managing editor came into the room where we were both sitting engaged in conversation and said:

"Oh, by the way, go to Washington and interview President Cleveland."

167

"All right," said I. "Take care of yourself."

Five minutes later I was seated in a palatial drawing-room car bounding up and down quite a good deal on the elastic plush-covered seat.

I shall not linger upon the incidents of the journey. I was given carte blanche to provide myself with every comfort, and to spare no expense that I could meet. For the regalement of my inside the preparations had been lavish. Both Vienna and Germany had been called upon to furnish dainty viands suitable to my palate.

I changed cars and shirts once only on the journey. A stranger wanted me to also change a two-dollar bill, but I haughtily declined.

The scenery along the entire road to Washington is diversified. You find a portion of it on one hand by looking out of the window, and upon turning the gaze upon the other side the eye is surprised and delighted by discovering some more of it.

There were a great many Knights of Pythias on the train. One of them insisted upon my giving him the grip I had with me, but he was unsuccessful.

On arriving in Washington, which city I instantly recognized from reading the history of George, I left the car so hastily that I forgot to fee Mr. Pullman's representative.

I went immediately to the Capitol.

In a spirit of jeu d'esprit I had had made a globular representation of a "rolling stone." It was of wood, painted a dark color, and about the size of a small cannon ball. I had attached to it a twisted pendant about three inches long to indicate moss. I had resolved to use this in place of a card, thinking people would readily recognize it as an emblem of my paper.

I had studied the arrangement of the Capitol, and walked directly to Mr. Cleveland's private office.

I met a servant in the hall, and held up my card to him smilingly.

I saw his hair rise on his head, and he ran like a deer to the door, and, lying down, rolled down the long flight of steps into the yard.

"Ah," said I to myself, "he is one of our delinquent subscribers."

A little farther along I met the President's private secretary, who had been writing a tariff letter and cleaning a duck gun for Mr. Cleveland.

When I showed him the emblem of my paper he sprang out of a high window into a hothouse filled with rare flowers.

This somewhat surprised me.

I examined myself. My hat was on straight, and there was nothing at all alarming about my appearance.

I went into the President's private office.

He was alone. He was conversing with Tom Ochiltree. Mr. Ochiltree saw my little sphere, and with a loud scream rushed out of the room.

President Cleveland slowly turned his eyes upon me.

He also saw what I had in my hand, and said in a husky voice:

"Wait a moment, please."

He searched his coat pocket, and presently found a piece of paper on which some words were written.

He laid this on his desk and rose to his feet, raised one hand above him, and said in deep tones:

"I die for Free Trade, my country, and — and — all that sort of thing."

I saw him jerk a string, and a camera snapped on another table, taking our picture as we stood.

"Don't die in the House, Mr. President," I said. "Go over into the Senate Chamber."

"Peace, murderer!" he said. "Let your bomb do its deadly work."

"I'm no bum," I said, with spirit. "I represent *The Rolling Stone*, of Austin, Texas, and this I hold in my hand does the same thing, but, it seems, unsuccessfully."

The President sank back in his chair greatly relieved.

"I thought you were a dynamiter," he said. "Let me see; Texas! Texas!" He walked to a large wall map of the United States, and placing his finger thereon at about the location of Idaho, ran it down in a zigzag, doubtful way until he reached Texas.

"Oh, yes, here it is. I have so many things on my mind, I sometimes forget what I should know well.

"Let's see; Texas? Oh, yes, that's the State where Ida Wells and a lot of colored people lynched a socialist named Hogg for raising a riot at a camp-meeting. So you are from Texas. I know a man from Texas named Dave

Culberson. How is Dave and his family? Has Dave got any children?"

"He has a boy in Austin," I said, "working around the Capitol."

"Who is President of Texas now?"

"I don't exactly ——"

"Oh, excuse me. I forgot again. I thought I heard some talk of its having been made a Republic again."

"Now, Mr. Cleveland," I said, "you answer some of my questions."

A curious film came over the President's eyes. He sat stiffly in his chair like an automaton.

"Proceed," he said.

"What do you think of the political future of this country?"

"I will state that political exigencies demand emergentistical promptitude, and while the United States is indissoluble in conception and invisible in intent, treason and internecine disagreement have ruptured the consanguinity of patriotism, and ——"

"One moment, Mr. President," I interrupted; "would you mind changing that cylinder? I could have gotten all that from the American Press Association if I had wanted plate matter. Do you wear flannels? What is your favorite poet, brand of catsup, bird, flower, and what are you going to do when you are out of a job?"

"Young man," said Mr. Cleveland, sternly, "you are going a little too far. My private affairs do not concern the public."

I begged his pardon, and he recovered his good humor in a moment.

"You Texans have a great representative in Senator Mills," he said. "I think the greatest two speeches I ever heard were his address before the Senate advocating the removal of the tariff on salt and increasing it on chloride of sodium."

"Tom Ochiltree is also from our State," I said.

"Oh, no, he isn't. You must be mistaken," replied Mr. Cleveland, "for he says he is. I really must go down to Texas some time, and see the State. I want to go up into the Panhandle and see if it is really shaped like it is on the map."

"Well, I must be going," said I.

"When you get back to Texas," said the President, rising, "you must write to me. Your visit has awakened in me quite an interest in your State which I fear I have not given the attention it deserves. There are many historical and otherwise interesting places that you have revived in my recollection — the Alamo, where Davy Jones fell; Goliad, Sam Houston's surrender to Montezuma, the petrified boom found near Austin, five-cent cotton and the Siamese Democratic platform born in Dallas. I should so much like to see the gals in Galveston, and go to the wake in Waco. I am glad I met you. Turn to the left as you enter the hall and keep straight on out." I made a low bow to signify that the interview was at an end, and withdrew immediately. I had no difficulty in leaving the building as soon as I was outside.

I hurried downtown in order to obtain refreshments at some place where viands had been placed upon the free list.

I shall not describe my journey back to Austin. I lost my return ticket somewhere in the White House, and was forced to return home in a manner not especially beneficial to my shoes. Everybody was well in Washington when I left, and all send their love.

AN UNFINISHED CHRISTMAS STORY

[Probably begun several years before his death. Published, as it here appears, in *Short Stories*, January, 1911.]

NOW, a Christmas story should be one. For a good many years the ingenious writers have been putting forth tales for the holiday numbers that employed every subtle, evasive, indirect and strategic scheme they could invent to disguise the Christmas flavor. So far has this new practice been carried that nowadays when you read a story in a holiday magazine the only way you can tell it is a Christmas story is to look at the footnote which reads: ["The incidents in the above story happened on December 25th. — ED."]

There is progress in this; but it is all very sad. There are just as many real Christmas stories as ever, if we would only dig 'em up. Me, I am for the Scrooge and Marley Christmas story, and the Annie and Willie's prayer poem, and the long lost son coming home on the stroke of twelve to the poorly thatched cottage with his arms full of talking dolls and popcorn balls and — Zip! you hear the second mortgage on the cottage go flying off it into the deep snow.

So, this is to warn you that there is no subterfuge about this story — and you might come upon stockings hung to the mantel and plum puddings and hark! the chimes!

174

and wealthy misers loosening up and handing over penny whistles to lame newsboys if you read further.

Once I knocked at a door (I have so many things to tell you I keep on losing sight of the story). It was the front door of a furnished room house in West 'Teenth Street. I was looking for a young illustrator named Paley originally and irrevocably from Terre Haute. Paley doesn't enter even into the first serial rights of this Christmas story; I mention him simply in explaining why I came to knock at the door — some people have so much curiosity.

The door was opened by the landlady. I had seen hundreds like her. And I had smelled before that cold, dank, furnished draught of air that hurried by her to escape immurement in the furnished house.

She was stout, and her face and hands were as white as though she had been drowned in a barrel of vinegar. One hand held together at her throat a buttonless flannel dressing sacque whose lines had been cut by no tape or butterick known to mortal woman. Beneath this a too-long, flowered, black sateen skirt was draped about her, reaching the floor in stiff wrinkles and folds.

The rest of her was yellow. Her hair, in some bygone age, had been dipped in the fountain of folly presided over by the merry nymph Hydrogen; but now, except at the roots, it had returned to its natural grim and grizzled white.

Her eyes and teeth and finger nails were yellow. Her chops hung low and shook when she moved. The look

on her face was exactly that smileless look of fatal
melancholy that you may have seen on the countenance of a hound left sitting on the doorstep of a deserted
cabin.

I inquired for Paley. After a long look of cold suspicion the landlady spoke, and her voice matched the
dingy roughness of her flannel sacque.

Paley? Was I sure that was the name? And wasn't
it, likely, Mr. Sanderson I meant, in the third floor rear?
No; it was Paley I wanted. Again that frozen, shrewd,
steady study of my soul from her pale-yellow, unwinking
eyes, trying to penetrate my mask of deception and rout
out my true motives from my lying lips. There was a
Mr. Tompkins in the front hall bedroom two flights up.
Perhaps it was he I was seeking. He worked of nights;
he never came in till seven in the morning. Or if it was
really Mr. Tucker (thinly disguised as Paley) that I was
hunting I would have to call between five and ——

But no; I held firmly to Paley. There was no such name
among her lodgers. Click! the door closed swiftly in my
face; and I heard through the panels the clanking of
chains and bolts.

I went down the steps and stopped to consider. The
number of this house was 43. I was sure Paley had said 43
— or perhaps it was 45 or 47 — I decided to try 47, the
second house farther along.

I rang the bell. The door opened; and there stood the
same woman. I wasn't confronted by just a resemblance
— it was the *same* woman holding together the same old

A Page from the "Plunkville Patriot."

THe PLunKViLLe PaTRiOt,

o o Published nearly every Friday o o

COL. ARISTOLLE JORDAN,
Editor & candidate for COUNTY
JUDGE. —

Office next door to the colored Baptist graaeyarp, over Smith's Tin shop.

Subscription per year - - - $1.50.
"   ", six mos - : : $200.
ariteUp for Candidates Soper LiNE.
Obituary poetry   10 "   ,

☞ The great Statesmen and litterateur Oliver holmes VVendell is dead.

—The cash ballance in the treasury is $1187o,4 147. We need a few more loads of hickory wood, and Some potatoes or corn field peas at an early date.

The inauferable egotism and blunders to the bast interests of the country is rapidly leading Mr. Cleveland into the a multitude of most dannsable errors of Judgement. Last week be appointed Tobe Rogers P.M. of Plunkville; Everybopy knows Tobe has three wives in Georgia and cant read the address on a letter to save his life. VVe had over 3 hundred names signed to our petition for said Office. Aro the people of this country to going submit to such high handed Dictators's?

Miss Madalien Brackinridge, a relative of VV. C. P. Breckenridge the famous "sliver tongue orator o Kentucky has sued a man named Pollard for an old livery Bill for carriage hire.

The war between China and Japan continues to wage. The sooner these barbarious and uncivilized Nations wipe each other from off of the face of the earth the better. Our sympathies are decidedly with the Japanese however. Their manufacturies of Japanese hams Japaned tin, and Japonicas show them to be the superior nation. besides, that we have been forced to wear our coat buttoned up at the throat for more than an week on account of having lost a small piece of piece of paper, with a hieroglyphic on it supposed to represent the fact that we had deposited our shirt with a celness laundryman for it's customary cleansing. This Chinaman pos'tively and idiotically refus'd to deliver us said garment with the "oglyphics. We have written to the Secretarys of war and State, but they ignored our appeal. VVe in-

te nd to lay the matter before the Japanese charge de'affairs at VVashington; and if no results ensues we shall take the Matter in our own hands and said laundry. ☞ The Chinese must GO!

LoCaL IteMS

Did
You
Hear
the
Rain?

Go to the 4th methodist Church' supper to ni ght at freenaos ha ll. The ladies of the church prom lse to give you Bickles's arnica Salve for cuts, bruises a fine time. Oásterst urkey, cake, and skin eruptions, and corns or money and ice cream will be served. refused.

Miss Mattie Lungweiler a charming brunette of Hog prairie is on a visit to The Elite SaLOON. open day & Night her friecd, Miss Gussie Shaw.

A vanetity old Papers, turnip seed; vender slein notes, axie grease and aO. 16 collar's for sale at this okco.

CONTRIBUTED.

SUNSEt.

Airwart tne gouea n sun set bare;
Steal colors wan & faint
While purple shadow smook the light
And lo okjust like paint,

Now elves is booky doils hallo
And Pixies bind their hair
And little stars peep out in plaY,
And slyl≤ sav Ah' tgere:

The owl hoots in the popular tree
The riverm ists are cold,
The day has almost been tged its last
That is so I have been told.
EFFie LUSHiNGToN.
October the 10th. 1894.

$100,000 REWARD

For any case of Insomia, sleeplessness or Inability to slumber that We cannot sure. Price 5 cents. Address Ausano Daily Statesman. Send for clubbing Rates with Cocaino depw tment, Popular drug Store.

STOP AT the CRAWLEY hOUSE!

PLUNKViLLe Texas.
ROOMS WITH doors in them! Hot and Colp Gas !
o Not reSponcible for guests Left over Thirty (3o) dayS. o
No water on premises.   Malleable steaks.

RATES		
for comercial men	:	$2.00 per day,
" Clergymen	:	$2.00 "
		$2.00

THE Plunkville Patriot——   Est'd 1847.

SoLiDER than EVER !

We will soon begin the 46 th year of our existence and point with Pride to to the record we have made as well as to the gnancial basis on which we stand

Second to no Paper in the South ! ! !

We have the Srcet job offic nin the South south of St. Louis & are ready to do at short notice job Printing of all kinds A SLOW AS THE LOVVEST.
Subscribe now before the Rusq——

——Specoal features for 1895.

FOR SALE CHEAP!

one ¼ cash the rest in 1, 2, and 3 days.
THE
PLUNKViLLe PATRi-OT

oo The oldest paper int the state o o

Will be Sold Regardless of Price Hard Times The cause,
No offer Refused. ☞

MARRiED MEN—ATTENiON

MArveLLous discoVerY

Dr. Kings New Comsumption compo'd.
OR
The mother in law

EradIcatOr

Guaranteed to produce galloping Consum ption in any Female over 49 years age in 30 Minutes. Can be Administered in tea or coffee by any one so taste or smell Send for Sampee bottle to try on the man who borryws your paper.

GONE BEFoRE.

James sidebotham, our most prominent dealer in hides and futures succumbed on the 20' to the inevitabel; and leaves a widow to mourn his loss. Sueq however is Jabez's gain.

I will make you fuken, miss you
When the stars begin to shine,
In fact it will be hard to go along with—
o? you
But I only have to be resign—

Nou will wait for me in heaven
Just with in the pearly gates
He died just a vuarier past seven
gut Providence rules our fates

Bu t true hearts death cannot sever,
There securewas a kinder man,
I never expect to do better ever;
But I.ll try and do the best I can

The miserable subsidyid, cowarkly lying sycophants parasite who disgraces the editorlal chair of the Plunkville Heralp, has spread the report that we tried to commit suicide last friday night. It is true that we drankl about four ounce of embalming fluid at the Palace Drug Store, but we did so in good faith supposing same o be rve whiskey. We are not ready to commit suicide yet but would think very serlousyy of it if we wereas worthless, degraded and deprased as Col. (.) Montmorency(?) of the Herald. We suffered no inconvenience from the mistake we hope beyond a slight pain in the gastric region, and a somewhat awkward thirst which we found troublen in satisfying. we hereby warn the editor(?) of the Herald that if we see' proper to daink nitric acid or melted lead in the future we want no comment from any will promptly reason same.

Dr. Hoffer, a rising young physician of Plunkville; has gone on a short trip to New Orleans. Dame rumor has it that he will not come back alone. as the requisition papers were made out yesterday.

out at third, but the umpire refused. to change the decision. Dr. Sballen burger thinks the wound not serious.

Visitor—"Dear me, General, who is that dreadful man?"
General—"Oh, that's only the orderly sergeant."

UNCLE SAM—"Well, I declare, those gentlemen must be brothers

A humorous and a political cartoon from *The Rolling Stone.*

sacque at her throat and looking at me with the same
yellow eyes as if she had never seen me before on earth.
I saw on the knuckle of her second finger the same red-and-
black spot made, probably, by a recent burn against a hot
stove.

I stood speechless and gaping while one with moderate
haste might have told fifty. I couldn't have spoken
Paley's name even if I had remembered it. I did the
only thing that a brave man who believes there are mysterious forces in nature that we do not yet fully comprehend could have done in the circumstances. I backed
down the steps to the sidewalk and then hurried away
frontward, fully understanding how incidents like that
must bother the psychical research people and the census
takers.

Of course I heard an explanation of it afterward, as we
always do about inexplicable things.

The landlady was Mrs. Kannon; and she leased three
adjoining houses, which she made into one by cutting
arched doorways through the walls. She sat in the middle
house and answered the three bells.

I wonder why I have maundered so slowly through the
prologue. I have it! it was simply to say to you, in
the form of introduction rife through the Middle West:
"Shake hands with Mrs. Kannon."

For, it was in her triple house that the Christmas story
happened; and it was there where I picked up the incon-
trovertible facts from the gossip of many roomers and met
Stickney — and saw the necktie.

Christmas came that year on Thursday. And snow came with it.

Stickney (Harry Clarence Fowler Stickney to whomsoever his full baptismal cognominal burdens may be of interest) reached his address at six-thirty Wednesday afternoon. "Address" is New Yorkese for "home." Stickney roomed at 45 West 'Teenth Street, third floor rear hall room. He was twenty years and four months old, and he worked in a cameras-of-all-kinds, photographic supplies and films-developed store. I don't know what kind of work he did in the store; but you must have seen him. He is the young man who always comes behind the counter to wait on you and lets you talk for five minutes, telling him what you want. When you are done, he calls the proprietor at the top of his voice to wait on you, and walks away whistling between his teeth.

I don't want to bother about describing to you his appearance; but, if you are a man reader, I will say that Stickney looked precisely like the young chap that you always find sitting in your chair smoking a cigarette after you have missed a shot while playing pool — not billiards but pool — when you want to sit down yourself.

There are some to whom Christmas gives no Christmassy essence. Of course, prosperous people and comfortable people who have homes or flats or rooms with meals, and even people who live in apartment houses with hotel service get something of the Christmas flavor. They give one another presents with the cost mark scratched off with a penknife; and they hang holly wreaths in the front

windows and when they are asked whether they prefer
light or dark meat from the turkey they say: "Both,
please," and giggle and have lots of fun.   And the very
poorest people have the best time of it.   The Army gives
'em a dinner, and the 10 A. M. issue of the Night Final
edition of the newspaper with the largest circulation in
the city leaves a basket at their door full of an apple, a
Lake Ronkonkoma squab, a scrambled eggplant and a
bunch of Kalamazoo bleached parsley.   The poorer you
are the more Christmas does for you.

But, I'll tell you to what kind of a mortal Christmas
seems to be only the day before the twenty-sixth day of
December.   It's the chap in the big city earning sixteen
dollars a week, with no friends and few acquaintances,
who finds himself with only fifty cents in his pocket on
Christmas eve.   He can't accept charity; he can't borrow;
he knows no one who would invite him to dinner.   I have
a fancy that when the shepherds left their flocks to follow
the star of Bethlehem there was a bandy-legged young
fellow among them who was just learning the sheep business.   So they said to him, "Bobby, we're going to investigate this star route and see what's in it.   If it should
turn out to be the first Christmas day we don't want to
miss it.   And, as you are not a wise man, and as you
couldn't possibly purchase a present to take along,
suppose you stay behind and mind the sheep."   So as
we may say, Harry Stickney was a direct descendant
of the shepherd who was left behind to take care of the
flocks.

Getting back to facts, Stickney rang the doorbell of 45. He had a habit of forgetting his latchkey.

Instantly the door opened and there stood Mrs. Kannon, clutching her sacque together at the throat and gorgonizing him with her opaque, yellow eyes.

(To give you good measure, here is a story within a story. Once a roomer in 47 who had the Scotch habit not kilts, but a habit of drinking Scotch — began to figure to himself what might happen if two persons should ring the doorbells of 43 and 47 at the same time. Visions of two halves of Mrs. Kannon appearing respectively and simultaneously at the two entrances, each clutching at a side of an open, flapping sacque that could never meet, overpowered him. Bellevue got him.)

"Evening," said Stickney cheerlessly, as he distributed little piles of muddy slush along the hall matting. "Think we'll have snow?"

"You left your key," said ——

(Here the manuscript ends.)

THE UNPROFITABLE SERVANT

[Left unfinished, and published as it here appears in *Everybody's Magazine*, December, 1911.]

I AM the richer by the acquaintance of four newspaper men. Singly, they are my encyclopedias, friends, mentors, and sometimes bankers. But now and then it happens that all of them will pitch upon the same printworthy incident of the passing earthly panorama and will send in reportorial constructions thereof to their respective journals. It is then that, for me, it is to laugh. For it seems that to each of them, trained and skilled as he may be, the same occurrence presents a different facet of the cut diamond, life.

One will have it (let us say) that Mme. André Macarté's apartment was looted by six burglars, who descended via the fire-escape and bore away a ruby tiara valued at two thousand dollars and a five-hundred-dollar prize Spitz dog, which (in violation of the expectoration ordinance) was making free with the halls of the Wuttapesituckque-sunoowetunquah Apartments.

My second "chiel" will take notes to the effect that while a friendly game of pinochle was in progress in the tenement rooms of Mrs. Andy McCarty, a lady guest named Ruby O'Hara threw a burglar down six flights of stairs, where he was pinioned and held by a two-thousand-dollar English bulldog amid a crowd of five hundred excited spectators.

My third chronicler and friend will gather the news threads of the happening in his own happy way; setting forth on the page for you to read that the house of Antonio Macartini was blown up at 6 A. M., by the Black Hand Society, on his refusing to leave two thousand dollars at a certain street corner, killing a pet five-hundred-dollar Pomeranian belonging to Alderman Rubitara's little daughter (see photo and diagram opposite).

Number four of my history-makers will simply construe from the premises the story that while an audience of two thousand enthusiasts was listening to a Rubinstein concert on Sixth Street, a woman who said she was Mrs. Andrew M. Carter threw a brick through a plate-glass window valued at five hundred dollars. The Carter woman claimed that some one in the building had stolen her dog.

Now, the discrepancies in these registrations of the day's doings need do no one hurt. Surely, one newspaper is enough for any man to prop against his morning water-bottle to fend off the smiling hatred of his wife's glance. If he be foolish enough to read four he is no wiser than a Higher Critic.

I remember (probably as well as you do) having read the parable of the talents. A prominent citizen, about to journey into a far country, first hands over to his servants his goods. To one he gives five talents; to another two; to another one — to every man according to

his several ability, as the text has it. There are two
versions of this parable, as you well know. There may be
more — I do not know.

When the p. c. returns he requires an accounting. Two
servants have put their talents out at usury and gained
one hundred per cent. Good. The unprofitable one
simply digs up the talent deposited with him and hands it
out on demand. A pattern of behavior for trust companies
and banks, surely! In one version we read that he had
wrapped it in a napkin and laid it away. But the com-
mentator informs us that the talent mentioned was composed of 750 ounces of silver — about $900 worth. So
the chronicler who mentioned the napkin, had either to
reduce the amount of the deposit or do a lot of explaining
about the size of the napery used in those days. Therefore in his version we note that he uses the word "pound"
instead of "talent."

A pound of silver may very well be laid away — and
carried away — in a napkin, as any hotel or restaurant
man will tell you.

But let us get away from our mutton.

When the returned nobleman finds that the one-talented
servant has nothing to hand over except the original fund
entrusted to him, he is as angry as a multi-millionaire
would be if some one should hide under his bed and make
a noise like an assessment. He orders the unprofitable
servant cast into outer darkness, after first taking away
his talent and giving it to the one-hundred-per cent.
financier, and breathing strange saws, saying: "From him

that hath not shall be taken away even that which he hath." Which is the same as to say: "Nothing from nothing leaves nothing."

And now closer draw the threads of parable, precept allegory, and narrative, leading nowhere if you will, or else weaving themselves into the little fiction story about Cliff McGowan and his one talent. There is but a definition to follow; and then the homely actors trip on.

Talent: A gift, endowment or faculty; some peculiar ability, power, or accomplishment, natural or acquired. (A metaphor borrowed from the parable in Matt. XXV. 14–30.)

In New York City to-day there are (estimated) 125,000 living creatures training for the stage. This does not include seals, pigs, dogs, elephants, prize-fighters, Carmens, mind-readers, or Japanese wrestlers. The bulk of them are in the ranks of the Four Million. Out of this number will survive a thousand.

Nine hundred of these will have attained their fulness of fame when they shall dubiously indicate with the point of a hatpin a blurred figure in a flashlight photograph of a stage tout ensemble with the proud commentary: "That's me."

Eighty, in the pinkest of (male) Louis XIV court costumes, shall welcome the Queen of the (mythical) Pawpaw Isles in a few well-memorized words, turning a tip-tilted nose upon the nine hundred.

Ten, in tiny lace caps, shall dust Ibsen furniture for six minutes after the rising of the curtain.

Nine shall attain the circuits, besieging with muscle, skill, eye, hand, voice, wit, brain, heel and toe the ultimate high walls of stardom.

One shall inherit Broadway.   Sic venit gloria mundi.

Cliff McGowan and Mac McGowan were cousins. They lived on the West Side and were talented.   Singing, dancing, imitations, trick bicycle riding, boxing, German and Irish dialect comedy, and a little sleight-of-hand and balancing of wheat straws and wheelbarrows on the ends of their chins came as easy to them as it is for you to fix your rat so it won't show or to dodge a creditor through the swinging-doors of a well-lighted café — according as you may belong to the one or the other division of the greatest prestidigitators — the people.   They were slim, pale, consummately self-possessed youths, whose finger-nails were always irreproachably (and clothes seams reproachfully) shiny.   Their conversation was in sentences so short that they made Kipling's seem as long as court citations.

Having the temperament, they did no work.   Any afternoon you could find them on Eighth Avenue either in front of Spinelli's barber shop, Mike Dugan's place, or the Limerick Hotel, rubbing their forefinger nails with dingy silk handkerchiefs.   At any time, if you had happened to be standing, undecisive, near a pool-table, and Cliff and Mack had, casually, as it were, drawn near, mentioning something, disinterestedly, about a game, well, indeed, would it have been for you had you gone your way, unresponsive.   Which assertion, carefully considered, is a study in tense, punctuation, and advice to strangers.

Of all kinships it is likely that the closest is that of cousin. Between cousins there exist the ties of race, name, and favor — ties thicker than water, and yet not coagulated with the jealous precipitations of brotherhood or the enjoining obligations of the matrimonial yoke. You can bestow upon a cousin almost the interest and affection that you would give to a stranger; you need not feel toward him the contempt and embarrassment that you have for one of your father's sons — it is the closer clan-feeling that sometimes makes the branch of a tree stronger than its trunk.

Thus were the two McGowans bonded. They enjoyed a quiet celebrity in their district, which was a strip west of Eighth Avenue with the Pump for its pivot. Their talents were praised in a hundred "joints"; their friendship was famed even in a neighborhood where men had been known to fight off the wives of their friends — when domestic onslaught was being made upon their friends by the wives of their friends. (Thus do the limitations of English force us to repetends.)

So, side by side, grim, sallow, lowering, inseparable, undefeated, the cousins fought their way into the temple of Art — art with a big A, which causes to intervene a lesson in geometry.

One night at about eleven o'clock Del Delano dropped into Mike's place on Eighth Avenue. From that moment, instead of remaining a Place, the café became a Resort.

It was as though King Edward had condescended to mingle
with ten-spots of a different suit; or Joe Gans had casually
strolled in to look over the Tuskegee School; or Mr.
Shaw, of England, had accepted an invitation to read
selections from "Rena, the Snow-bird" at an unveiling
of the proposed monument to James Owen O'Connor at
Chinquapin Falls, Mississippi. In spite of these compari-
sons, you will have to be told why the patronizing of a
third-rate saloon on the West Side by the said Del Delano
conferred such a specific honor upon the place.

Del Delano could not make his feet behave; and so the
world paid him $300 a week to see them misconduct
themselves on the vaudeville stage. To make the matter
plain to you (and to swell the number of words), he was
the best fancy dancer on any of the circuits between
Ottawa and Corpus Christi. With his eyes fixed on va-
cancy and his feet apparently fixed on nothing, he "nightly
charmed thousands," as his press-agent incorrectly stated.
Even taking night performance and matinée together,
he scarcely could have charmed more than eighteen
hundred, including those who left after Zora, the Nautch
girl, had squeezed herself through a hoop twelve inches in
diameter, and those who were waiting for the moving
pictures.

But Del Delano was the West Side's favorite; and nowhere is there a more loyal Side. Five years before our
story was submitted to the editors, Del had crawled from
some Tenth Avenue basement like a lean rat and had
bitten his way into the Big Cheese. Patched, half-starved,

cuffless, and as scornful of the Hook as an interpreter of
Ibsen, he had danced his way into health (as you and I
view it) and fame in sixteen minutes on Amateur Night at
Creary's (Variety) Theatre in Eighth Avenue. A bookmaker (one of the kind that talent wins with instead of
losing) sat in the audience, asleep, dreaming of an impossible pick-up among the amateurs. After a snore, a glass
of beer from the handsome waiter, and a temporary
blindness caused by the diamonds of a transmontane
blonde in Box E, the bookmaker woke up long enough
to engage Del Delano for a three-weeks' trial engagement
fused with a trained-dog short-circuit covering the three
Washingtons — Heights, Statue, and Square.

By the time this story was read and accepted, Del
Delano was drawing his three-hundred dollars a week,
which, divided by seven (Sunday acts not in costume being
permissible), dispels the delusion entertained by most
of us that we have seen better days. You can easily
imagine the worshipful agitation of Eighth Avenue whenever Del Delano honored it with a visit after his terpsi-
chorean act in a historically great and vilely ventilated
Broadway theatre. If the West Side could claim forty-
two minutes out of his forty-two weeks' bookings every
year, it was on occasion for bonfires and repainting of
the Pump. And now you know why Mike's saloon is a
Resort, and no longer a simple Place.

Del Delano entered Mike's alone. So nearly concealed
in a fur-lined overcoat and a derby two sizes too large for
him was Prince Lightfoot that you saw of his face only

his pale, hatchet-edged features and a pair of unwinking, cold, light blue eyes. Nearly every man lounging at Mike's bar recognized the renowned product of the West Side. To those who did not, wisdom was conveyed by prodding elbows and growls of one-sided introduction.

Upon Charley, one of the bartenders, both fame and fortune descended simultaneously. He had once been honored by shaking hands with the great Delano at a Seventh Avenue boxing bout. So with lungs of brass he now cried: "Hallo, Del, old man; what 'll it be?"

Mike, the proprietor, who was cranking the cash register, heard. On the next day he raised Charley's wages five a week.

Del Delano drank a pony beer, paying for it carelessly out of his nightly earnings of $42.85⅞. He nodded amiably but coldly at the long line of Mike's patrons and strolled past them into the rear room of the café. For he heard in there sounds pertaining to his own art — the light, stirring staccato of a buck-and-wing dance.

In the back room Mac McGowan was giving a private exhibition of the genius of his feet. A few young men sat at tables looking on critically while they amused themselves seriously with beer. They nodded approval at some new fancy steps of Mac's own invention.

At the sight of the great Del Delano, the amateur's feet stuttered, blundered, clicked a few times, and ceased to move. The tongues of one's shoes become tied in the presence of the Master. Mac's sallowface took on a slight flush.

From the uncertain cavity between Del Delano's hat brim and the lapels of his high fur coat collar came a thin puff of cigarette smoke and then a voice:

"Do that last step over again, kid. And don't hold your arms quite so stiff. Now, then!"

Once more Mac went through his paces. According to the traditions of the man dancer, his entire being was transformed into mere feet and legs. His gaze and expression became cataleptic; his body, unbending above the waist, but as light as a cork, bobbed like the same cork dancing on the ripples of a running brook. The beat of his heels and toes pleased you like a snare-drum obligato. The performance ended with an amazing clatter of leather against wood that culminated in a sudden flat-footed stamp, leaving the dancer erect and as motionless as a pillar of the colonial portico of a mansion in a Kentucky prohibition town. Mac felt that he had done his best and that Del Delano would turn his back upon him in derisive scorn.

An approximate silence followed, broken only by the mewing of a café cat and the hubbub and uproar of a few million citizens and transportation facilities outside.

Mac turned a hopeless but nervy eye upon Del Delano's face. In it he read disgust, admiration, envy, indifference, approval, disappointment, praise, and contempt.

Thus, in the countenances of those we hate or love we find what we most desire or fear to see. Which is an assertion equalling in its wisdom and chiaroscuro the most famous sayings of the most foolish philosophers that the world has ever known.

Del Delano retired within his overcoat and hat. In two minutes he emerged and turned his left side to Mac. Then he spoke.

"You've got a foot movement, kid, like a baby hippopotamus trying to side-step a jab from a humming-bird. And you hold yourself like a truck driver having his picture taken in a Third Avenue photograph gallery. And you haven't got any method or style. And your knees are about as limber as a couple of Yale pass-keys. And you strike the eye as weighing, let us say, 450 pounds while you work. But, say, would you mind giving me your name?"

"McGowan," said the humbled amateur —"Mac McGowan."

Delano the Great slowly lighted a cigarette and continued, through its smoke:

"In other words, you're rotten. You can't dance. But I'll tell you one thing you've got."

"Throw it all off of your system while you're at it," said Mac. "What've I got?"

"Genius," said Del Delano. "Except myself, it's up to you to be the best fancy dancer in the United States, Europe, Asia, and the colonial possessions of all three."

"Smoke up!" said Mac McGowan.

"Genius," repeated the Master — "you've got a talent for genius. Your brains are in your feet, where a dancer's ought to be. You've been self-taught until you're almost ruined, but not quite. What you need is a trainer. I'll take you in hand and put you at the top of the profession.

There's room there for the two of us. You may beat me," said the Master, casting upon him a cold, savage look combining so much rivalry, affection, justice, and human hate that it stamped him at once as one of the little great ones of the earth —"you may beat me; but I doubt it. I've got the start and the pull. But at the top is where you belong. Your name, you say, is Robinson?"

"McGowan," repeated the amateur, "Mac McGowan."

"It don't matter," said Delano. "Suppose you walk up to my hotel with me. I'd like to talk to you. Your footwork is the worst I ever saw, Madigan — but — well, I'd like to talk to you. You may not think so, but I'm not so stuck up. I came off of the West Side myself. That overcoat cost me eight hundred dollars; but the collar ain't so high but what I can see over it. I taught myself to dance, and I put in most of nine years at it before I shook a foot in public. But I had genius. I didn't go too far wrong in teaching myself as you've done. You've got the rottenest method and style of anybody I ever saw."

"Oh, I don't think much of the few little steps I take," said Mac, with hypocritical lightness.

"Don't talk like a package of self-raising buckwheat flour," said Del Delano. "You've had a talent handed to you by the Proposition Higher Up; and it's up to you to do the proper thing with it. I'd like to have you go up to my hotel for a talk, if you will.

In his rooms in the King Clovis Hotel, Del Delano put on a scarlet house coat bordered with gold braid and set out Apollinaris and a box of sweet crackers.

Mac's eye wandered.

"Forget it," said Del. "Drink and tobacco may be all right for a man who makes his living with his hands; but they won't do if you're depending on your head or your feet. If one end of you gets tangled, so does the other. That's why beer and cigarettes don't hurt piano players and picture painters. But you've got to cut 'em out if you want to do mental or pedal work. Now, have a cracker, and then we'll talk some."

"All right," said Mac. "I take it as an honor, of course, for you to notice my hopping around. Of course I'd like to do something in a professional line. Of course I can sing a little and do card tricks and Irish and German comedy stuff, and of course I'm not so bad on the trapeze and comic bicycle stunts and Hebrew monologues and ——"

"One moment," interrupted Del Delano, "before we begin. I said you couldn't dance. Well, that wasn't quite right. You've only got two or three bad tricks in your method. You're handy with your feet, and you belong at the top, where I am. I'll put you there. I've got six weeks continuous in New York; and in four I can shape up your style till the booking agents will fight one another to get you. And I'll do it, too. I'm of, from, and for the West Side. 'Del Delano' looks good on billboards, but the family name's Crowley. Now, Mackintosh — McGowan, I mean — you've got your chance — fifty times a better one than I had."

"I'd be a shine to turn it down," said Mac. "And I hope you understand I appreciate it. Me and my cousin

Cliff McGowan was thinking of getting a try-out at Creary's on amateur night a month from to-morrow."

"Good stuff!" said Delano. "I got mine there. Junius T. Rollins, the booker for Kuhn & Dooley, jumped on the stage and engaged me after my dance. And the boards were an inch deep in nickels and dimes and quarters. There wasn't but nine penny pieces found in the lot."

"I ought to tell you," said Mac, after two minutes of pensiveness, "that my cousin Cliff can beat me dancing. We've always been what you might call pals. If you'd take him up instead of me, now, it might be better. He's invented a lot of steps that I can't cut."

"Forget it," said Delano. "Mondays, Wednesdays, Fridays, and Saturdays of every week from now till amateur night, a month off, I'll coach you. I'll make you as good as I am; and nobody could do more for you. My act's over every night at 10:15. Half an hour later I'll take you up and drill you till twelve. I'll put you at the top of the bunch, right where I am. You've got talent. Your style's bum; but you've got the genius. You let me manage it. I'm from the West Side myself, and I'd rather see one of the same gang win out before I would an East-Sider, or any of the Flatbush or Hackensack Meadow kind of butt-iners. I'll see that Junius Rollins is present on your Friday night; and if he don't climb over the footlights and offer you fifty a week as a starter, I'll let you draw it down from my own salary every Monday night. Now, am I talking on the level or am I not?"

Amateur night at Creary's Eighth Avenue Theatre is cut by the same pattern as amateur nights elsewhere. After the regular performance the humblest talent may, by previous arrangement with the management, make its début upon the public stage. Ambitious non-professionals, mostly self-instructed, display their skill and powers of entertainment along the broadest lines. They may sing, dance, mimic, juggle, contort, recite, or disport themselves along any of the ragged boundary lines of Art. From the ranks of these anxious tyros are chosen the professionals that adorn or otherwise make conspicuous the full-blown stage. Press-agents delight in recounting to open-mouthed and closed-eared reporters stories of the humble beginnings of the brilliant stars whose orbits they control.

Such and such a prima donna (they will tell you) made her initial bow to the public while turning handsprings on an amateur night. One great matinée favorite made his début on a generous Friday evening singing coon songs of his own composition. A tragedian famous on two continents and an island first attracted attention by an amateur impersonation of a newly landed Scandinavian peasant girl. One Broadway comedian that turns 'em away got a booking on a Friday night by reciting (seriously) the graveyard scene in "Hamlet."

Thus they get their chance. Amateur night is a kindly boon. It is charity divested of almsgiving. It is a brotherly hand reached down by members of the best united band of coworkers in the world to raise up less fortunate ones without labelling them beggars. It gives you the chance, if you can grasp it, to step for a few minutes before some badly painted scenery and, during the playing by the orchestra of some ten or twelve bars of music, and while the soles of your shoes may be clearly holding to the uppers, to secure a salary equal to a Congressman's or any orthodox minister's. Could an ambitious student of literature or financial methods get a chance like that by spending twenty minutes in a Carnegie library? I do not trow so.

But shall we look in at Creary's? Let us say that the specific Friday night had arrived on which the fortunate Mac McGowan was to justify the flattering predictions of his distinguished patron and, incidentally, drop his silver talent into the slit of the slot-machine of fame and fortune that gives up reputation and dough. I offer, sure of your acquiescence, that we now forswear hypocritical philosophy and bigoted comment, permitting the story to finish itself in the dress of material allegations — a medium more worthy, when held to the line, than the most laborious creations of the word-milliners. . . .

(Page of manuscript missing here.)

easily among the wings with his patron, the great Del Delano. For, wherever footlights shone in the City-That Would-Be-Amused, the freedom of their unshaded side was Del's. And if he should take up an amateur — see? and bring him around — see? and, winking one of his cold blue eyes, say to the manager: "Take it from me — he's got the goods — see?" you wouldn't expect that ama-

teur to sit on an unpainted bench sudorifically awaiting
his turn, would you? So Mac strolled around largely with
the nonpareil; and the seven waited, clammily, on the
bench.

A giant in shirt-sleeves, with a grim, kind face in which
many stitches had been taken by surgeons from time to
time, *i. e.*, with a long stick, looped at the end. He was
the man with the Hook. The manager, with his close-
smoothed blond hair, his one-sided smile, and his abnor-
mally easy manner, pored with patient condescension over
the difficult program of the amateurs. The last of the
professional turns — the Grand March of the Happy
Huzzard — had been completed; the last wrinkle and darn
of their blue silkolene cotton tights had vanished from the
stage. The man in the orchestra who played the kettle-
drum, cymbals, triangle, sandpaper, whangdoodle, hoofbeats, and catcalls, and fired the pistol shots, had wiped
his brow. The illegal holiday of the Romans had arrived.

While the orchestra plays the famous waltz from "The
Dismal Wife," let us bestow two hundred words upon the
psychology of the audience.

The orchestra floor was filled by People. The boxes
contained Persons. In the galleries was the Foreordained
Verdict. The claque was there as it had originated in the
Stone Age and was afterward adapted by the French.
Every Micky and Maggie who sat upon Creary's amateur
bench, wise beyond their talents, knew that their success
or doom lay already meted out to them by that crowded,
whistling, roaring mass of Romans in the three galleries.

They knew that the winning or the losing of the game for each one lay in the strength of the "gang" aloft that could turn the applause to its favorite.   On a Broadway first night a wooer of fame may win it from the ticket buyers over the heads of the cognoscenti.   But not so at Creary's. The amateur's fate is arithmetical.   The number of his supporting admirers present at his try-out decides it in advance.   But how these outlying Friday nights put to a certain shame the Mondays, Tuesdays, Wednesdays, Thursdays, Saturdays, and matinées of the Broadway stage you should know.   .   .   .

(Here the manuscript ends.)

ARISTOCRACY VERSUS HASH

[From *The Rolling Stone*.]

THE snake reporter of *The Rolling Stone* was wandering up the avenue last night on his way home from the Y. M. C. A. rooms when he was approached by a gaunt, hungry-looking man with wild eyes and dishevelled hair. He accosted the reporter in a hollow, weak voice.

"'Can you tell me, Sir, where I can find in this town a family of scrubs?'

"'I don't understand exactly.'

"'Let me tell you how it is,' said the stranger, inserting his forefinger in the reporter's buttonhole and badly damaging his chrysanthemum. 'I am a representative from Soapstone County, and I and my family are house-less, homeless, and shelterless. We have not tasted food for over a week. I brought my family with me, as I have indigestion and could not get around much with the boys. Some days ago I started out to find a boarding house, as I cannot afford to put up at a hotel. I found a nice aristocratic-looking place, that suited me, and went in and asked for the proprietress. A very stately lady with a Roman nose came in the room. She had one hand laid across her stom — across her waist, and the other held a lace handkerchief. I told her I wanted board for myself

199

and family, and she condescended to take us. I asked for her terms, and she said $300 per week.

"'I had two dollars in my pocket and I gave her that for a fine teapot that I broke when I fell over the table when she spoke.'

"'You appear surprised,' says she. 'You will please remembah that I am the widow of Governor Riddle of Georgiah; my family is very highly connected; I give you board as a favah; I nevah considah money any equivalent for the advantage of my society, I ——'

"'Well, I got out of there, and I went to some other places. The next lady was a cousin of General Mahone of Virginia, and wanted four dollars an hour for a back room with a pink motto and a Burnet granite bed in it. The next one was an aunt of Davy Crockett, and asked eight dollars a day for a room furnished in imitation of the Alamo, with prunes for breakfast and one hour's conversation with her for dinner. Another one said she was a descendant of Benedict Arnold on her father's side and Captain Kidd on the other.

"'She took more after Captain Kidd.

"'She only had one meal and prayers a day, and counted her society worth $100 a week.

"'I found nine widows of Supreme Judges, twelve relicts of Governors and Generals, and twenty-two ruins left by various happy Colonels, Professors, and Majors, who valued their aristocratic worth from $90 to $900 per week, with weak-kneed hash and dried apples on the side. I admire people of fine descent, but my stomach yearns for pork and beans instead of culture. Am I not right?'

"'Your words,' said the reporter, 'convince me that you have uttered what you have said.'

"'Thanks. You see how it is. I am not wealthy; I have only my per diem and my per quisites, and I cannot afford to pay for high lineage and moldy ancestors. A little corned beef goes further with me than a coronet, and when I am cold a coat of arms does not warm me.'

"'I greatly fear,' said the reporter, with a playful hic-cough, 'that you have run against a high-toned town. Most all the first-class boarding houses here are run by ladies of the old Southern families, the very first in the land.'

"'I am now desperate,' said the Representative, as he chewed a tack awhile, thinking it was a clove. 'I want to find a boarding house where the proprietress was an orphan found in a livery stable, whose father was a dago from East Austin, and whose grandfather was never placed on the map. I want a scrubby, ornery, low-down, snuff-dipping, back-woodsy, piebald gang, who never heard of finger bowls or Ward McAllister, but who can get up a mess of hot cornbread and Irish stew at regular market quotations.

"'Is there such a place in Austin?'

"The snake reporter sadly shook his head. 'I do not know,' he said, 'but I will shake you for the beer.'

"Ten minutes later the slate in the Blue Ruin saloon bore two additional characters: 10.''

THE PRISONER OF ZEMBLA

[From *The Rolling Stone*.]

So THE king fell into a furious rage, so that none durst go near him for fear, and he gave out that since the Princess Ostla had disobeyed him there would be a great tourney, and to the knight who should prove himself of the greatest valor he would give the hand of the princess.

And he sent forth a herald to proclaim that he would do this.

And the herald went about the country making his desire known, blowing a great tin horn and riding a noble steed that pranced and gambolled; and the villagers gazed upon him and said: "Lo, that is one of them tin horn gamblers concerning which the chroniclers have told us."

And when the day came, the king sat in the grandstand, holding the gage of battle in his hand, and by his side sat the Princess Ostla, looking very pale and beautiful, but with mournful eyes from which she scarce could keep the tears. And the knights which came to the tourney gazed upon the princess in wonder at her beauty, and each swore to win her so that he could marry her and board with the king. Suddenly the heart of the princess gave a great bound, for she saw among the knights one of the poor students with whom she had been in love.

202

The knights mounted and rode in a line past the grandstand, and the king stopped the poor student, who had the worst horse and the poorest caparisons of any of the knights and said:

"Sir Knight, prithee tell me of what that marvellous shacky and rusty-looking armor of thine is made?"

"Oh, king," said the young knight, "seeing that we are about to engage in a big fight, I would call it scrap iron, wouldn't you?"

"Ods Bodkins!" said the king. "The youth hath a pretty wit."

About this time the Princess Ostla, who began to feel better at the sight of her lover, slipped a piece of gum into her mouth and closed her teeth upon it, and even smiled a little and showed the beautiful pearls with which her mouth was set. Whereupon, as soon as the knights perceived this, 217 of them went over to the king's treasurer and settled for their horse feed and went home.

"It seems very hard," said the princess, "that I cannot marry when I chews."

But two of the knights were left, one of them being the princess' lover.

"Here's enough for a fight, anyhow," said the king. "Come hither, O knights, will ye joust for the hand of this fair lady?"

"We joust will," said the knights.

The two knights fought for two hours, and at length the princess' lover prevailed and stretched the other upon the ground. The victorious knight made his horse caracole before the king, and bowed low in his saddle.

On the Princess Ostla's cheeks was a rosy flush; in her eyes the light of excitement vied with the soft glow of love; her lips were parted, her lovely hair unbound, and she grasped the arms of her chair and leaned forward with heaving bosom and happy smile to hear the words of her lover.

"You have foughten well, sir knight," said the king. "And if there is any boon you crave you have but to name it."

"Then," said the knight, "I will ask you this: I have bought the patent rights in your kingdom for Schneider's celebrated monkey wrench, and I want a letter from you endorsing it."

"You shall have it," said the king, "but I must tell you that there is not a monkey in my kingdom."

With a yell of rage the victorious knight threw himself on his horse and rode away at a furious gallop.

The king was about to speak, when a horrible suspicion flashed upon him and he fell dead upon the grandstand.

"My God!" he cried. "He has forgotten to take the princess with him!"

A STRANGE STORY

[From *The Rolling Stone*.]

IN THE northern part of Austin there once dwelt an honest family by the name of Smothers. The family consisted of John Smothers, his wife, himself, their little daughter, five years of age, and her parents, making six people toward the population of the city when counted for a special write-up, but only three by actual count.

One night after supper the little girl was seized with a severe colic, and John Smothers hurried down town to get some medicine.

He never came back.

The little girl recovered and in time grew up to womanhood.

The mother grieved very much over her husband's disappearance, and it was nearly three months before she married again, and moved to San Antonio.

The little girl also married in time, and after a few years had rolled around, she also had a little girl five years of age.

She still lived in the same house where they dwelt when her father had left and never returned.

One night by a remarkable coincidence her little girl was taken with cramp colic on the anniversary of the disappearance of John Smothers, who would now have been her grandfather if he had been alive and had a steady job.

"I will go downtown and get some medicine for her," said John Smith (for it was none other than he whom she had married).

"No, no, dear John," cried his wife. "You, too, might disappear forever, and then forget to come back."

So John Smith did not go, and together they sat by the bedside of little Pansy (for that was Pansy's name).

After a little Pansy seemed to grow worse, and John Smith again attempted to go for medicine, but his wife would not let him.

Suddenly the door opened, and an old man, stooped and bent, with long white hair, entered the room.

"Hello, here is grandpa," said Pansy. She had recognized him before any of the others.

The old man drew a bottle of medicine from his pocket and gave Pansy a spoonful.

She got well immediately.

"I was a little late," said John Smothers, "as I waited for a street car."

FICKLE FORTUNE OR HOW GLADYS HUSTLED

[From *The Rolling Stone*.]

PRESS me no more Mr. Snooper," said Gladys Vavasour-Smith. "I can never be yours."

"You have led me to believe different, Gladys," said Bertram D. Snooper.

The setting sun was flooding with golden light the oriel windows of a magnificent mansion situated in one of the most aristocratic streets west of the brick yard.

Bertram D. Snooper, a poor but ambitious and talented young lawyer, had just lost his first suit. He had dared to aspire to the hand of Gladys Vavasour-Smith, the beautiful and talented daughter of one of the oldest and proudest families in the county. The bluest blood flowed in her veins. Her grandfather had sawed wood for the Hornsbys and an aunt on her mother's side had married a man who had been kicked by General Lee's mule.

The lines about Bertram D. Snooper's hands and mouth were drawn tighter as he paced to and fro, waiting for a reply to the question he intended to ask Gladys as soon as he thought of one.

At last an idea occurred to him.

"Why will you not marry me?" he asked in an inaudible tone.

"Because," said Gladys firmly, speaking easily with great difficulty, "the progression and enlightenment that the woman of to-day possesses demand that the man shall bring to the marriage altar a heart and body as free from the debasing and hereditary iniquities that now no longer exist except in the chimerical imagination of enslaved custom."

"It is as I expected," said Bertram, wiping his heated brow on the window curtain. "You have been reading books."

"Besides that," continued Gladys, ignoring the deadly charge, "you have no money."

The blood of the Snoopers rose hastily and mantled the cheek of Bertram D. He put on his coat and moved proudly to the door.

"Stay here till I return," he said, "I will be back in fifteen years."

When he had finished speaking he ceased and left the room.

When he had gone, Gladys felt an uncontrollable yearning take possession of her. She said slowly, rather to herself than for publication, "I wonder if there was any of that cold cabbage left from dinner."

She then left the room.

When she did so, a dark-complexioned man with black hair and gloomy, desperate looking clothes, came out of the fireplace where he had been concealed and stated:

"Aha! I have you in my power at last, Bertram D. Snooper. Gladys Vavasour-Smith shall be mine. I am in the possession of secrets that not a soul in the world suspects. I have papers to prove that Bertram Snooper is the heir to the *Tom Bean estate, and I have discovered that Gladys' grandfather who sawed wood for the Hornsby's was also a cook in Major Rhoads Fisher's command during the war. Therefore, the family repudiate her, and she will marry me in order to drag their proud name down in the dust. Ha, ha, ha!"

As the reader has doubtless long ago discovered, this man was no other than Henry R. Grasty. Mr. Grasty then proceeded to gloat some more, and then with a sardonic laugh left for New York.

* * * * * * *

Fifteen years have elapsed.

Of course, our readers will understand that this is only supposed to be the case.

It really took less than a minute to make the little stars that represent an interval of time.

We could not afford to stop a piece in the middle and wait fifteen years before continuing it.

We hope this explanation will suffice. We are careful not to create any wrong impressions.

Gladys Vavasour-Smith and Henry R. Grasty stood at the marriage altar.

Mr. Grasty had evidently worked his rabbit's foot successfully, although he was quite a while in doing so.

---

*An estate famous in Texas legal history. It took many, many years for adjustment and a large part of the property was, of course, consumed as expenses of litigation.

Just as the preacher was about to pronounce the fatal words on which he would have realized ten dollars and had the laugh on Mr. Grasty, the steeple of the church fell off and Bertram D. Snooper entered.

The preacher fell to the ground with a dull thud. He could ill afford to lose ten dollars. He was hastily removed and a cheaper one secured.

Bertram D. Snooper held a *Statesman* in his hand.

"Aha!" he said, "I thought I would surprise you. I just got in this morning. Here is a paper noticing my arrival."

He handed it to Henry R. Grasty.

Mr. Grasty looked at the paper and turned deadly pale. It was dated three weeks after Mr. Snooper's arrival.

"Foiled again!" he hissed.

"Speak, Bertram D. Snooper," said Gladys, "why have you come between me and Henry?"

"I have just discovered that I am the sole heir to Tom Bean's estate and am worth two million dollars."

With a glad cry Gladys threw herself in Bertram's arms.

Henry R. Grasty drew from his breast pocket a large tin box and opened it, took therefrom 467 pages of closely written foolscap.

"What you say is true, Mr. Snooper, but I ask you to read that," he said, handing it to Bertram Snooper.

Mr. Snooper had no sooner read the document than he uttered a piercing shriek and bit off a large chew of tobacco.

"All is lost," he said.

"What is that document?" asked Gladys. "Governor Hogg's message?"

"It is not as bad as that," said Bertram, "but it deprives me of my entire fortune. But I care not for that, Gladys, since I have won you."

"What is it? Speak, I implore you," said Gladys.

"Those papers," said Henry R. Grasty, "are the proofs of my appointment as administrator of the Tom Bean estate."

With a loving cry Gladys threw herself in Henry R. Grasty's arms.

    *   *   *   *   *   *   *

Twenty minutes later Bertram D. Snooper was seen deliberately to enter a beer saloon on Seventeenth Street.

AN APOLOGY

[This appeared in *The Rolling Stone* shortly before it "suspended publication" never to resume.]

THE person who sweeps the office, translates letters from foreign countries, deciphers communications from graduates of business colleges, and does most of the writing for this paper, has been confined for the past two weeks to the under side of a large red quilt, with a joint caucus of la grippe and measles.

We have missed two issues of *The Rolling Stone*, and are now slightly convalescent, for which we desire to apologize and express our regrets.

Everybody's term of subscription will be extended enough to cover all missed issues, and we hope soon to report that the goose remains suspended at a favorable altitude. People who have tried to run a funny paper and entertain a congregation of large piebald measles at the same time will understand something of the tact, finesse, and hot sassafras tea required to do so. We expect to get out the paper regularly from this time on, but are forced to be very careful, as improper treatment and deleterious after-effects of measles, combined with the high price of paper and presswork, have been known to cause a relapse. Any one not getting their paper regularly will please come down and see about it, bringing with them a ham or any little delicacy relished by invalids.

LORD OAKHURST'S CURSE

[This story was sent to Dr. Beall of Greensboro, N. C., in a letter in 1883, and so is one of O. Henry's earliest attempts at writing.]

I

LORD OAKHURST lay dying in the oak chamber in the eastern wing of Oakhurst Castle. Through the open window in the calm of the summer evening, came the sweet fragrance of the early violets and budding trees, and to the dying man it seemed as if earth's loveliness and beauty were never so apparent as on this bright June day, his last day of life.

His young wife, whom he loved with a devotion and strength that the presence of the king of terrors himself could not alter, moved about the apartment, weeping and sorrowful, sometimes arranging the sick man's pillow and inquiring of him in low, mournful tones if anything could be done to give him comfort, and again, with stifled sobs, eating some chocolate caramels which she carried in the pocket of her apron. The servants went to and fro with that quiet and subdued tread which prevails in a house where death is an expected guest, and even the crash of broken china and shivered glass, which announced their approach, seemed to fall upon the ear with less violence and sound than usual.

Lord Oakhurst was thinking of days gone by, when he wooed and won his beautiful young wife, who was then but a charming and innocent girl. How clearly and minutely those scenes rose up at the call of his memory: He seemed to be standing once more beneath the old chestnut grove where they had plighted their troth in the twilight under the stars; while the rare fragrance of the June roses and the smell of supper came gently by on the breeze. There he had told her his love; how that his whole happiness and future joy lay in the hope that he might win her for a bride; that if she would trust her future to his care the devotedness of his lifetime should be hers, and his only thought would be to make her life one long day of sunshine and peanut candy.

How plainly he remembered how she had, with girlish shyness and coyness, at first hesitated, and murmured something to herself about "an old bald-headed galoot," but when he told her that to him life without her would be a blasted mockery, and that his income was £50,000 a year, she threw herself on to him and froze there with the tenacity of a tick on a brindled cow, and said, with tears of joy, "Hen-ery, I am thine."

And now he was dying. In a few short hours his spirit would rise up at the call of the Destroyer and, quitting his poor, weak, earthly frame, would go forth into that dim and dreaded Unknown Land, and solve with certainty that Mystery which revealeth itself not to mortal man.

II

A carriage drove rapidly up the avenue and stopped at the door. Sir Everhard FitzArmond, the famous London physician, who had been telegraphed for, alighted and quickly ascended the marble steps. Lady Oakhurst met him at the door, her lovely face expressing great anxiety and grief. "Oh, Sir Everhard, I am so glad you have come. He seems to be sinking rapidly. Did you bring the cream almonds I mentioned in the telegram?"

Sir Everhard did not reply, but silently handed her a package, and, slipping a couple of cloves into his mouth, ascended the stairs that led to Lord Oakhurst's apartment. Lady Oakhurst followed.

Sir Everhard approached the bedside of his patient and laid his hand gently on this sick man's diagnosis. A shade of feeling passed over his professional countenance as he gravely and solemnly pronounced these words: "Madam, your husband has croaked."

Lady Oakhurst at first did not comprehend his technical language, and her lovely mouth let up for a moment on the cream almonds. But soon his meaning flashed upon her, and she seized an axe that her husband was accustomed to keep by his bedside to mangle his servants with, and struck open Lord Oakhurst's cabinet containing his private papers, and with eager hands opened the document which she took therefrom. Then, with a wild, unearthly shriek that would have made a steam piano go out behind a barn and kick itself in despair, she fell senseless to the floor.

Sir Everhard FitzArmond picked up the paper and read its contents. It was Lord Oakhurst's will, bequeathing all his property to a scientific institution which should have for its object the invention of a means for extracting peach brandy from sawdust.

Sir Everhard glanced quickly around the room. No one was in sight. Dropping the will, he rapidly transferred some valuable ornaments and rare specimens of gold and silver filigree work from the centre table to his pockets, and rang the bell for the servants.

III — THE CURSE

Sir Everhard FitzArmond descended the stairway of Oakhurst Castle and passed out into the avenue that led from the doorway to the great iron gates of the park. Lord Oakhurst had been a great sportsman during his life and always kept a well-stocked kennel of curs, which now rushed out from their hiding places and with loud yelps sprang upon the physician, burying their fangs in his lower limbs and seriously damaging his apparel.

Sir Everhard, startled out of his professional dignity and usual indifference to human suffering, by the personal application of feeling, gave vent to a most horrible and blighting CURSE and ran with great swiftness to his carriage and drove off toward the city.

BEXAR SCRIP NO. 2692

[From *The Rolling Stone*, Saturday, March 5, 1894]

WHENEVER you visit Austin you should by all means go to see the General Land Office.

As you pass up the avenue you turn sharp round the corner of the court house, and on a steep hill before you you see a mediæval castle.

You think of the Rhine; the "castled crag of Drachenfels"; the Lorelei; and the vine-clad slopes of Germany. And German it is in every line of its architecture and design.

The plan was drawn by an old draftsman from the "Vaterland," whose heart still loved the scenes of his native land, and it is said he reproduced the design of a certain castle near his birthplace, with remarkable fidelity.

Under the present administration a new coat of paint has vulgarized its ancient and venerable walls. Modern tiles have replaced the limestone slabs of its floors, worn in hollows by the tread of thousands of feet, and smart and gaudy fixtures have usurped the place of the time-worn furniture that has been consecrated by the touch of hands that Texas will never cease to honor.

But even now, when you enter the building, you lower

217

your voice, and time turns backward for you, for the atmosphere which you breathe is cold with the exudations of buried generations.

The building is stone with a coating of concrete; the walls are immensely thick; it is cool in the summer and warm in the winter; it is isolated and sombre; standing apart from the other state buildings, sullen and decaying, brooding on the past.

Twenty years ago it was much the same as now; twenty years from now the garish newness will be worn off and it will return to its appearance of gloomy decadence.

People living in other states can form no conception of the vastness and importance of the work performed and the significance of the millions of records and papers composing the archives of this office.

The title deeds, patents, transfers and legal documents connected with every foot of land owned in the state of Texas are filed here.

Volumes could be filled with accounts of the knavery, the double-dealing, the cross purposes, the perjury, the lies, the bribery, the alteration and erasing, the suppressing and destroying of papers, the various schemes and plots that for the sake of the almighty dollar have left their stains upon the records of the General Land Office.

No reference is made to the employees. No more faithful, competent and efficient force of men exists in the clerical portions of any government, but there is — or was, for their day is now over — a class of land speculators commonly called land sharks, unscrupulous and greedy,

who have left their trail in every department of this office,
in the shape of titles destroyed, patents cancelled, homes
demolished and torn away, forged transfers and lying
affidavits.

Before the modern tiles were laid upon the floors, there
were deep hollows in the limestone slabs, worn by the
countless feet that daily trod uneasily through its echoing
corridors, pressing from file room to business room, from
commissioner's sanctum to record books and back again.

The honest but ignorant settler, bent on saving the
little plot of land he called home, elbowed the wary land
shark who was searching the records for evidence to oust
him; the lordly cattle baron, relying on his influence and
money, stood at the Commissioner's desk side by side with
the preëmptor, whose little potato patch lay like a minute
speck of island in the vast, billowy sea of his princely
pastures, and, played the old game of "freeze-out," which
is as old as Cain and Abel.

The trail of the serpent is through it all.

Honest, earnest men have wrought for generations
striving to disentangle the shameful coil that certain
years of fraud and infamy have wound. Look at the
files and see the countless endorsements of those in
authority:

"Transfer doubtful — locked up."

"Certificate a forgery — locked up."

"Signature a forgery."

"Patent refused — duplicate patented elsewhere."

"Field notes forged."

"Certificates stolen from office" — and soon ad infinitum.

The record books, spread upon long tables, in the big room upstairs, are open to the examination of all.

Open them, and you will find the dark and greasy finger prints of half a century's handling. The quick hand of the land grabber has fluttered the leaves a million times; the damp clutch of the perturbed tiller of the soil has left traces of his calling on the ragged leaves.

Interest centres in the file room.

This is a large room, built as a vault, fireproof, and entered by but a single door.

There is "No Admission" on the portal; and the precious files are handed out by a clerk in charge only on presentation of an order signed by the Commissioner or chief clerk.

In years past too much laxity prevailed in its management, and the files were handled by all comers, simply on their request, and returned at their will, or not at all.

In these days most of the mischief was done. In the file room, there are about —— files, each in a paper wrapper, and comprising the title papers of a particular tract of land.

You ask the clerk in charge for the papers relating to any survey in Texas. They are arranged simply in districts and numbers.

He disappears from the door, you hear the sliding of a tin box, the lid snaps, and the file is in your hand.

Go up there some day and call for Bexar Scrip No. 2692.

The file clerk stares at you for a second, says shortly:
"Out of file."

It has been missing twenty years.

The history of that file has never been written before.

Twenty years ago there was a shrewd land agent living in Austin who devoted his undoubted talents and vast knowledge of land titles, and the laws governing them, to the locating of surveys made by illegal certificates, or improperly made, and otherwise of no value through non-compliance with the statutes, or whatever flaws his ingenious and unscrupulous mind could unearth.

He found a fatal defect in the title of the land as on file in Bexar Scrip No. 2692 and placed a new certificate upon the survey in his own name.

The law was on his side.

Every sentiment of justice, of right, and humanity was against him.

The certificate by virtue of which the original survey had been made was missing.

It was not to be found in the file, and no memorandum or date on the wrapper to show that it had ever been filed.

Under the law the land was vacant, unappropriated public domain, and open to location.

The land was occupied by a widow and her only son, and she supposed her title good.

The railroad had surveyed a new line through the property, and it had doubled in value.

Sharp, the land agent, did not communicate with her in any way until he had filed his papers, rushed his claim through the departments and into the patent room for patenting.

Then he wrote her a letter, offering her the choice of buying from him or vacating at once.

He received no reply.

One day he was looking through some files and came across the missing certificate. Some one, probably an employee of the office, had by mistake, after making some examination, placed it in the wrong file, and curiously enough another inadvertence, in there being no record of its filing on the wrapper, had completed the appearance of its having never been filed.

Sharp called for the file in which it belonged and scrutinized it carefully, fearing he might have overlooked some endorsement regarding its return to the office.

On the back of the certificate was plainly endorsed the date of filing, according to law, and signed by the chief clerk.

If this certificate should be seen by the examining clerk, his own claim, when it came up for patenting, would not be worth the paper on which it was written.

Sharp glanced furtively around. A young man, or rather a boy about eighteen years of age, stood a few feet away regarding him closely with keen black eyes.

Sharp, a little confused, thrust the certificate into the file where it properly belonged and began gathering up the other papers.

The boy came up and leaned on the desk beside him.

"A right interesting office, sir!" he said. "I have never

been in here before. All those papers, now, they are about lands, are they not? The titles and deeds, and such things?"

"Yes," said Sharp. "They are supposed to contain all the title papers."

"This one, now," said the boy, taking up Bexar Scrip No. 2692, "what land does this represent the title of ? Ah, I see 'Six hundred and forty acres in B —— country? Absalom Harris, original grantee.' Please tell me, I am so ignorant of these things, how can you tell a good survey from a bad one. I am told that there are a great many illegal and fraudulent surveys in this office. I suppose this one is all right?"

"No," said Sharp. "The certificate is missing. It is invalid."

"That paper I just saw you place in that file, I suppose is something else — field notes, or a transfer probably?"

"Yes," said Sharp, hurriedly, "corrected field notes. Excuse me, I am a little pressed for time."

The boy was watching him with bright, alert eyes.

It would never do to leave the certificate in the file; but he could not take it out with that inquisitive boy watching him.

He turned to the file room, with a dozen or more files in his hands, and accidentally dropped part of them on the floor. As he stooped to pick them up he swiftly thrust Bexar Scrip No. 2692 in the inside breast pocket of his coat.

This happened at just half-past four o'clock, and when

the file clerk took the files he threw them in a pile in his room, came out and locked the door.

The clerks were moving out of the doors in long, straggling lines.

It was closing time.

Sharp did not desire to take the file from the Land Office. The boy might have seen him place the file in his pocket, and the penalty of the law for such an act was very severe.

Some distance back from the file room was the draftsman's room now entirely vacated by its occupants.

Sharp dropped behind the outgoing stream of men, and slipped slyly into this room.

The clerks trooped noisily down the iron stairway, singing, whistling, and talking.

Below, the night watchman awaited their exit, ready to close and bar the two great doors to the south and east.

It is his duty to take careful note each day that no one remains in the building after the hour of closing.

Sharp waited until all sounds had ceased.

It was his intention to linger until everything was quiet, and then to remove the certificate from the file, and throw the latter carelessly on some draftsman's desk, as if it had been left there during the business of the day.

He knew also that he must remove the certificate from the office or destroy it, as the chance finding of it by a clerk would lead to its immediately being restored to its proper place, and the consequent discovery that his location over the old survey was absolutely worthless.

As he moved cautiously along the stone floor the loud

barking of the little black dog, kept by the watchmen, told
that his sharp ears had heard the sounds of his steps.

The great, hollow rooms echoed loudly, move as lightly
as he could.

Sharp sat down at a desk and laid the file before him.

In all his queer practices and cunning tricks he had not
yet included any act that was downright criminal.

He had always kept on the safe side of the law, but in
the deed he was about to commit there was no compro-
mise to be made with what little conscience he had left.

There is no well-defined boundary line between honesty
and dishonesty.

The frontiers of one blend with the outside limits of the
other, and he who attempts to tread this dangerous
ground may be sometimes in one domain and sometimes
in the other; so the only safe road is the broad highway
that leads straight through and has been well defined by
line and compass.

Sharp was a man of what is called high standing in the
community. That is, his word in a trade was as good as
any man's; his check was as good as so much cash, and so
regarded; he went to church regularly; went in good
society and owed no man anything.

He was regarded as a sure winner in any land trade he
chose to make, but that was his occupation.

The act he was about to commit now would place him
forever in the ranks of those who choose evil for their
portion — if it was found out.

More than that, it would rob a widow and her son

of property soon to be of great value, which, if not legally theirs, was theirs certainly by every claim of justice.

But he had gone too far to hesitate.

His own survey was in the patent room for patenting. His own title was about to be perfected by the State's own hand.

The certificate must be destroyed.

He leaned his head on his hands for a moment, and as he did so a sound behind him caused his heart to leap with guilty fear, but before he could rise, a hand came over his shoulder and grasped the file.

He rose quickly, as white as paper, rattling his chair loudly on the stone floor.

The boy who had spoken to him earlier stood contemplating him with contemptuous and flashing eyes, and quietly placed the file in the left breast pocket of his coat.

"So, Mr. Sharp, by nature as well as by name," he said, "it seems that I was right in waiting behind the door in order to see you safely out. You will appreciate the pleasure I feel in having done so when I tell you my name is Harris. My mother owns the land on which you have filed, and if there is any justice in Texas she shall hold it. I am not certain, but I think I saw you place a paper in this file this afternoon, and it is barely possible that it may be of value to me. I was also impressed with the idea that you desired to remove it again, but had not the opportunity. Anyway, I shall keep it until to-morrow and let the Commissioner decide."

Far back among Mr. Sharp's ancestors there must have

been some of the old berserker blood, for his caution, his presence of mind left him, and left him possessed of a blind, devilish, unreasoning rage that showed itself in a moment in the white glitter of his eye.

"Give me that file, boy," he said, thickly, holding out his hand.

"I am no such fool, Mr. Sharp," said the youth. "This file shall be laid before the Commissioner to-morrow for examination. If he finds —— Help! Help!"

Sharp was upon him like a tiger and bore him to the floor. The boy was strong and vigorous, but the suddenness of the attack gave him no chance to resist. He struggled up again to his feet, but it was an animal, with blazing eyes and cruel-looking teeth that fought him, instead of a man.

Mr. Sharp, a man of high standing and good report, was battling for his reputation.

Presently there was a dull sound, and another, and still one more, and a blade flashing white and then red, and Edward Harris dropped down like some stuffed effigy of a man, that boys make for sport, with his limbs all crumpled and lax, on the stone floor of the Land Office.

The old watchman was deaf, and heard nothing.

The little dog barked at the foot of the stairs until his master made him come into his room.

Sharp stood there for several minutes holding in his hand his bloody clasp knife, listening to the cooing of the pigeons on the roof, and the loud ticking of the clock above the receiver's desk.

A map rustled on the wall and his blood turned to ice; a rat ran across some strewn papers, and his scalp prickled, and he could scarcely moisten his dry lips with his tongue.

Between the file room and the draftsman's room there is a door that opens on a small dark spiral stairway that winds from the lower floor to the ceiling at the top of the house.

This stairway was not used then, nor is it now.

It is unnecessary, inconvenient, dusty, and dark as night, and was a blunder of the architect who designed the building.

This stairway ends above at the tent-shaped space between the roof and the joists.

That space is dark and forbidding, and being useless is rarely visited.

Sharp opened this door and gazed for a moment up this narrow, cobwebbed stairway.

.   .   .   .   .   .

After dark that night a man opened cautiously one of the lower windows of the Land Office, crept out with great circumspection and disappeared in the shadows.

.   .   .   .   .   .

One afternoon, a week after this time, Sharp lingered behind again after the clerks had left and the office closed.

The next morning the first comers noticed a broad mark in the dust on the upstairs floor, and the same mark was observed below stairs near a window.

It appeared as if some heavy and rather bulky object had been dragged along through the limestone dust.

A memorandum book with "E. Harris" written on the flyleaf was picked up on the stairs, but nothing particular was thought of any of these signs.

Circulars and advertisements appeared for a long time in the papers asking for information concerning Edward Harris, who left his mother's home on a certain date and had never been heard of since.

After a while these things were succeeded by affairs of more recent interest, and faded from the public mind.

. . . .

Sharp died two years ago, respected and regretted. The last two years of his life were clouded with a settled melancholy for which his friends could assign no reason.

The bulk of his comfortable fortune was made from the land he obtained by fraud and crime.

The disappearance of the file was a mystery that created some commotion in the Land Office, but he got his patent.

. . . .

It is a well-known tradition in Austin and vicinity that there is a buried treasure of great value somewhere on the banks of Shoal Creek, about a mile west of the city.

Three young men living in Austin recently became possessed of what they thought was a clue of the whereabouts of the treasure, and Thursday night they repaired to the place after dark and plied the pickaxe and shovel with great diligence for about three hours.

At the end of that time their efforts were rewarded by

the finding of a box buried about four feet below the surface, which they hastened to open.

The light of a lantern disclosed to their view the flesh-less bones of a human skeleton with clothing still wrapping its uncanny limbs.

They immediately left the scene and notified the proper authorities of their ghastly find.

On closer examination, in the left breast pocket of the skeleton's coat, there was found a flat, oblong packet of papers, cut through and through in three places by a knife blade, and so completely soaked and clotted with blood that it had become an almost indistinguishable mass.

With the aid of a microscope and the exercise of a little imagination this much can be made out of the letters at the top of the papers:

B — x a — —— rip N — 3 — 92.

QUERIES AND ANSWERS

[From *The Rolling Stone*, June 23, 1894.]

Can you inform me where I can buy an interest in a newspaper of some kind? I have some money and would be glad to invest it in something of the sort, if some one would allow me to put in my capital against his experience.   COLLEGE GRADUATE.

Telegraph us your address at once, day message. Keep telegraphing every ten minutes at our expense until we see you. Will start on first train after receiving your wire.

Who was the author of the line, "Breathes there a man with soul so dead?"   G. F.

This was written by a visitor to the State Saengerfest of 1892 while conversing with a member who had just eaten a large slice of limburger cheese.

Where can I get the "Testimony of the Rocks"?
                    GEOLOGIST.

See the reports of the campaign committees after the election in November.

Please state what the seven wonders of the world are. I know five of them, I think, but can't find out the other two.   SCHOLAR.

The Temple of Diana, at Lexington, Ky.; the Great Wall of China; Judge Von Rosenberg (the Colossus of Roads); the Hanging Gardens at Albany; a San Antonio Sunday school; Mrs. Frank Leslie, and the Populist party.

———————

What day did Christmas come on in the year 1847?

CONSTANT READER.

The 25th of December.

———————

What does an F. F. V. mean?   IGNORANT.

What does he mean by what? If he takes you by the arm and tells you how much you are like a brother of his in Richmond, he means Feel For Your Vest, for he wants to borrow a five. If he holds his head high and don't speak to you on the street he means that he already owes you ten and is Following a Fresh Victim.

———————

Please decide a bet for us. My friend says that the sentence, "The negro bought the watermelon *of* the farmer" is correct, and I say it should be "The negro bought the watermelon from the farmer." Which is correct?   R.

Neither. It should read, "The negro stole the watermelon from the farmer."

———————

When do the Texas game laws go into effect?

HUNTER.

When you sit down at the table.

VOL. II. NO. 12.

PRICE FIVE CENTS.

THE ROLLING STONE

AUSTIN, TEXAS, SATURDAY, APRIL 27, 1895.

THE TEXAS WAY.

MISS POTTER: "Oh papa, what is that?"

MR. POTTER of Texas: "That's a live Count I bought for you in New York."

MISS POTTER: "Oh, how nice, and Uncle George gave me a new six shooter, and the dogs haven't had any exercise in a week. Won't it be fun?"

THE ROLLING STONE

VOL. I. No. 27.   AUSTIN, TEXAS, SATURDAY, OCTOBER 13, 1894.   Price 5c.

CAN HE MAKE THE JUMP?

Do you know where I can trade a section of fine Panhandle land for a pair of pants with a good title?

LAND AGENT.

We do not. You can't raise anything on land in that section. A man can always raise a dollar on a good pair of pants.

Name in order the three best newspapers in Texas.

ADVERTISER.

Well, the Galveston *News* runs about second, and the San Antonio *Express* third. Let us hear from you again.

Has a married woman any rights in Texas?

PROSPECTOR.

Hush, Mr. Prospector. Not quite so loud, if you please. Come up to the office some afternoon, and if everything seems quiet, come inside, and look at our eye, and our suspenders hanging on to one button, and feel the lump on the top of our head. Yes, she has some rights of her own, and everybody else's she can scoop in.

Who was the author of the sayings, "A public office is a public trust," and "I would rather be right than President"?

Eli Perkins.

Is the Lakeside Improvement Company making anything out of their town tract on the lake?

Inquisitive.

Yes, lots.

POEMS

[This and the other poems that follow have been found in files of *The Rolling Stone*, in the Houston *Post's* Postscripts and in manuscript. There are many others, but these few have been selected rather arbitrarily, to round out this collection.]

THE PEWEE

In the hush of the drowsy afternoon,
When the very wind on the breast of June
Lies settled, and hot white tracery
Of the shattered sunlight filters free
Through the unstinted leaves to the pied cool sward;
On a dead tree branch sings the saddest bard
   Of the birds that be;
    'Tis the lone Pewee.
It's note is a sob, and it's note is pitched
In a single key, like a soul bewitched
   To a mournful minstrelsy.

"Pewee, Pewee," doth it ever cry;
A sad, sweet minor threnody
That threads the aisles of the dim hot grove
Like a tale of a wrong or a vanished love;
And the fancy comes that the wee dun bird
Perchance was a maid, and her heart was stirred

By some lover's rhyme
In a golden time,
And broke when the world turned false and cold;
And her dreams grew dark and her faith grew cold
In some fairy far-off clime.

And her soul crept into the Pewee's breast;
And forever she cries with a strange unrest
For something lost, in the afternoon;
For something missed from the lavish June;
For the heart that died in the long ago;
For the livelong pain that pierceth so:
Thus the Pewee cries,
While the evening lies
Steeped in the languorous still sunshine,
Rapt, to the leaf and the bough and the vine
Of some hopeless paradise.

NOTHING TO SAY

"You can tell your paper," the great man said,
  "I refused an interview.
I have nothing to say on the question, sir;
  Nothing to say to you."

And then he talked till the sun went down
  And the chickens went to roost;
And he seized the collar of the poor young man,
  And never his hold he loosed.

And the sun went down and the moon came up,
  And he talked till the dawn of day;
Though he said, "On this subject mentioned by you,
  I have nothing whatever to say."

And down the reporter dropped to sleep
  And flat on the floor he lay;
And the last he heard was the great man's words,
  "I have nothing at all to say."

THE MURDERER

"I push my boat among the reeds;
   I sit and stare about;
Queer slimy things crawl through the weeds,
   Put to a sullen rout.
I paddle under cypress trees;
   All fearfully I peer
Through oozy channels when the breeze
   Comes rustling at my ear.

"The long moss hangs perpetually;
   Gray scalps of buried years;
Blue crabs steal out and stare at me,
   And seem to gauge my fears;
I start to hear the eel swim by;
   I shudder when the crane
Strikes at his prey; I turn to fly
   At drops of sudden rain.

"In every little cry of bird
   I hear a tracking shout;
From every sodden leaf that's stirred
   I see a face frown out;
My soul shakes when the water rat
   Cowed by the blue snake flies;
Black knots from tree holes glimmer at
   Me with accusive eyes.

"Through all the murky silence rings
   A cry not born of earth;
An endless, deep, unechoing thing
   That owns not human birth.
I see no colors in the sky
   Save red, as blood is red;
I pray to God to still that cry
   From pallid lips and dead.

"One spot in all that stagnant waste
   I shun as moles shun light,
And turn my prow to make all haste
   To fly before the night.
A poisonous mound hid from the sun,
   Where crabs hold revelry;
Where eels and fishes feed upon
   The Thing that once was He.

"At night I steal along the shore;
   Within my hut I creep;
But awful stars blink through the door,
   To hold me from my sleep.
The river gurgles like his throat,
   In little choking coves,
And loudly dins that phantom note
   From out the awful groves.

"I shout with laughter through the night,
   I rage in greatest glee;
My fears all vanish with the light
   Oh! splendid nights they be!

I see her weep; she calls his name;
  He answers not, nor will;
My soul with joy is all aflame;
  I laugh, and laugh, and thrill.

"I count her teardrops as they fall;
  I flout my daytime fears;
I mumble thanks to God for all
  These gibes and happy jeers.
But, when the warning dawn awakes,
  Begins my wandering;
With stealthy strokes through tangled brakes,
  A wasted, frightened thing."

SOME POSTSCRIPTS

TWO PORTRAITS

Wild hair flying, in a matted maze,
Hand firm as iron, eyes all ablaze;
Bystanders timidly, breathlessly gaze,
As o'er the keno board boldly he plays.
        — That's Texas Bill.

Wild hair flying, in a matted maze,
Hand firm as iron, eyes all ablaze;
Bystanders timidly, breathlessly gaze,
As o'er the keyboard boldly he plays.
        —That's Paderewski.

A CONTRIBUTION

There came unto ye editor
    A poet, pale and wan,
And at the table sate him down,
    A roll within his hand.

Ye editor accepted it,
    And thanked his lucky fates;
Ye poet had to yield it up
    To a king full on eights.

THE OLD FARM

Just now when the whitening blossoms flare
  On the apple trees and the growing grass
Creeps forth, and a balm is in the air;
    With my lighted pipe and well-filled glass
      Of the old farm I am dreaming,
      And softly smiling, seeming
      To see the bright sun beaming
    Upon the old home farm.

And when I think how we milked the cows,
  And hauled the hay from the meadows low;
And walked the furrows behind the plows,
    And chopped the cotton to make it grow
      I'd much rather be here dreaming
      And smiling, only seeming
      To see the hot sun gleaming
    Upon the old home farm.

VANITY

A Poet sang so wondrous sweet
  That toiling thousands paused and listened long;
So lofty, strong and noble were his themes,
  It seemed that strength supernal swayed his song.

He, god-like, chided poor, weak, weeping man,
  And bade him dry his foolish, shameful tears;
Taught that each soul on its proud self should lean,
  And from that rampart scorn all earth-born fears.

The Poet grovelled on a fresh heaped mound,
  Raised o'er the clay of one he'd fondly loved;
And cursed the world, and drenched the sod with tears;
  And all the flimsy mockery of his precepts proved.

THE LULLABY BOY

The lullaby boy to the same old tune
  Who abandons his drum and toys
For the purpose of dying in early June
  Is the kind the public enjoys.

But, just for a change, please sing us a song,
  Of the sore-toed boy that's fly,
And freckled and mean, and ugly, and bad,
  And positively will not die.

CHANSON DE BOHÊME

Lives of great men all remind us
  Rose is red and violet's blue;
Johnny's got his gun behind us
  'Cause the lamb loved Mary too.
    — Robert Burns' "Hocht Time in the aud Town."

I'd rather write this, as bad as it is
  Than be Will Shakespeare's shade;
I'd rather be known as an F. F. V.
  Than in Mount Vernon laid.
I'd rather count ties from Denver to Troy
  Than to head Booth's old programme;
I'd rather be special for the New York *World*
  Than to lie with Abraham.

May 19th 1901

My Dear Margaret

Here it is summertime, and the bees are blooming and the flowers are singing and the birds making honey. and we haven't been fishing yet Well, there's only one more month till July, and then we'll go, and no mistake I thought you would write and tell me about the high water around Pittsburg some time ago, and whether it came up to where you live, or not. And I haven't heard a thing about Easter, and about the rabbit's eggs — but I suppose you have learned by this time that eggs grow on egg plants and are not laid by rabbits.

I would like very much to hear from you oftener, it has been more than a month now since you wrote Write soon and tell me how you are, and when school will be out, for we want plenty of holidays in July so we can have a good time I am going to send you something nice the last of this week, what do you guess it will be? Lovingly,

Papa

A letter to his daughter Margaret.

PAGE FROM

THE JUNKVILLE PATRIOT.

THe PlunkVille Patriot,

o o Published nearly every Friday. o o

COL. ARISTOTLE JORDAN,
Editor & Excandidate for COUNTY
JUDGE. —

Office next door to the colored gap-
graneyarp, over Smith's Tin shop.

Subscription per Year • • $1.00
" 6 moS • ; . .200

writeUp for candipates 5c per lines.
Obituary poetry IOc "

R. R. timetable.
N. bound arr. Plunkville 7-15 AM
" leaves " 7-15½ "

Hide and Bone Market in the
County.

Every Advantage Offered to Persons
Coming to Stay Over Night

A Sketch of Plunkville as it is Today.

When in 1857 Silas Q. Plunk
laid out the then little town
of Plunkville little did he think it would be the city it is today. It
he had he would have kicked himself
down avenue C, torn up his plans and
saved trouble. General Plunk came
to Texas in 1427 about one mile in
advance of the sheriff of Sangaree Co.
Ohio. He and the sheriff made friends
and laid out the town of Plunkvile.
Some difficulty arising about corner
lots, the sheriff laid our Colonel Plunk.

COLONEL MOSES MORDECAI,
President of the 2nd Nat'l Bank.

OTR. PROMINENT BUILDINGS.

There are many magnificent buildings in Plunkville. The Court house,
Judge perkins's barn McCrackin's
Slaughter House, the Blue Mass can-
ning factory, widow Pogram's residence and Hefflinger's faro rooms are

in 1890 of heart failure while trying to
play the joker as a side card with four
aces against five jacks. Mrs. Pogram
takes a few boarders as a relief from
ennui. Her home is a model of neat-
ness and luxury. We have boarded
there three years and know whereof
we speak. We owe the widow 97$
which we have never been pressed for.
Stop at the Pogram House.

The largest and most enterprising
firm of grocers in our city is the firm
of

JONES and POTTS.

They had quite a stock of goods on
hand when we came here four years
ago, and we believe have them yet.
the only advertising they have ever
been guilty of was free, an don tha
occasion when Mr. Pot's was sued for
divorce by his wife on grounds of cru-

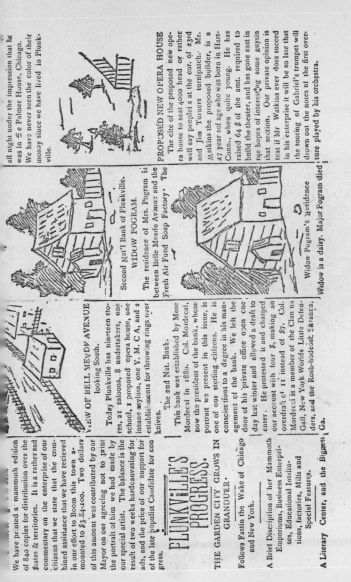

We have printed a mammoth edition of 840 copies for distribution over the state & territories. It is a rather sad commentary on the enterprise of our citizens that we state that the combined assistance that we have recieved in our effort to Boom this town amounted to $3.84-100. Two dollars of this amount was contributed by our Mayor on our agreeing not to print the portrait of him we had made by our special artist. The balance is the result of two weeks hardcanvasing for ads, and the price of our support for of the late populist Caudidate for congress.

PLUNKVILLE'S PROGRESS.

THE GARDEN CITY GROWS IN GRANDUER.

Follows Fastin the Wake of Chicago and New York.

A Brief Discription of her Mammoth Emporiums, Business Enterprises, Educational Institutions, factories, Mills and Special Features.

A Literary Center, and the Biggest Ga.

VIEW OF BELL MEVDE AVENUE looking South.

Today Plunkville has nineteen stores, 21 saloons, 8 undertakers, one school, 1 proposed opera house, one insane asylum, one Y. M. C A, and 2 establishments for throwing rings over knives.

The 2nd Nat. Bank.

This bank was established by Mose Mordecai in 1880. Col. Mordecai, now the president of the bank, whose portrait we present in this issue, is one of our sterling citizens. He is conscientious to a degree in his management of the bank. We left the door of his private office open one day last winter and allowed a draft to enter. He protested it and charged our account with four $, making an overdraft of 11 instead of $7. Col. Mordecai is a member of the Clan na Gail, New York Worlds Little Defenders, and the Rosh-hodeosh Savanna, Ga.

Second Nat'l Bank of Plunkville. WIDOW POGRAM.

The residence of Mrs. Pogram is between Belle Meade Avanu and the Fresh Air Fund Soap Factory. The

Widow Pogram's Residence

Widow is a daisy. Major Pogram died all night under the impression that he was in ɛ e Palmer House, Chicago. We have never seen the color of their money since we have lived in Plunkville.

PROPOSED NEW OPERA HOUSE

The cite of the proposed new opera house to seat 4000 head or rather well say people s at the cor. of 23rd and Jim Turners turnipatch. Mr. Matkins the proposed builder, is a 47 year sof age who was born in Hartford, Conn., when quite young. He has raised 64 $ of the amt. required to build the theater, and has gone east in the hopes of interesting some guys in that section. Our private opinion is teat if Mr Watkins ever does succeed in his enterprise it will be so late that the tooting of Gabriel's trumpet will drown out the notes nf the first overture played by his orchestra.

"Ikey, this is mine vater from Waco, come to visit me. Bring us two goot dinners und der dice-box"

(One of The Rolling Stone pictures, 1894)

For there's stuff in the can, there's Dolly and Fan,
   And a hundred things to choose;
There's a kiss in the ring, and every old thing
   That a real live man can use.

I'd rather fight flies in a boarding house
   Than fill Napoleon's grave,
And snuggle up warm in my three slat bed
   Than be André the brave.
I'd rather distribute a coat of red
   On the town with a wad of dough
Just now, than to have my cognomen
   Spelled "Michael Angelo."

For a small live man, if he's prompt on hand
   When the good things pass around,
While the world's on tap has a better snap
   Than a big man under ground.

HARD TO FORGET

I'm thinking to-night of the old farm, Ned,
   And my heart is heavy and sad
As I think of the days that by have fled
   Since I was a little lad.
There rises before me each spot I know
   Of the old home in the dell,
The fields, and woods, and meadows below
   That memory holds so well.

The city is pleasant and lively, Ned,
   But what to us is its charm?
To-night all my thoughts are fixed, instead,
   On our childhood's old home farm.
I know you are thinking the same, dear Ned,
   With your head bowed on your arm,
For to-morrow at four we'll be jerked out of bed
   To plow on that darned old farm.

DROP A TEAR IN THIS SLOT

He who, when torrid Summer's sickly glare
Beat down upon the city's parched walls,
Sat him within a room scarce 8 by 9,
And, with tongue hanging out and panting breath,
Perspiring, pierced by pangs of prickly heat,
Wrote variations of the seaside joke
We all do know and always loved so well,
And of cool breezes and sweet girls that lay
In shady nooks, and pleasant windy coves
Anon
Will in that self-same room, with tattered quilt
Wrapped round him, and blue stiffening hands,
All shivering, fireless, pinched by winter's blasts,
Will hale us forth upon the rounds once more,
So that we may expect it not in vain,
The joke of how with curses deep and coarse
Papa puts up the pipe of parlor stove.
So ye
Who greet with tears this olden favorite,
Drop one for him who, though he strives to please,
Must write about the things he never sees

TAMALES

This is the Mexican
Don José Calderon
One of God's countrymen,
Land of the buzzard.
Cheap silver dollar, and
Cacti and murderers.
Why has he left his land
Land of the lazy man,
Land of the pulque
Land of the bull fight,
Fleas and revolution.

This is the reason,
Hark to the wherefore;
Listen and tremble.
One of his ancestors,
Ancient and garlicky,
Probably grandfather,
Died with his boots on.
Killed by the Texans,
Texans with big guns,
At San Jacinto.
Died without benefit
Of priest or clergy;

Died full of minie balls,
Mescal and pepper.

Don José Calderon
Heard of the tragedy.
Heard of it, thought of it,
Vowed a deep vengeance;
Vowed retribution
On the Americans,
Murderous gringos,
Especially Texans.
"Valga me Dios! que
Ladrones, diablos,
Matadores, mentidores,
Caraccos y perros,
Voy a matarles,
Con solos mis manos,
Toditas sin falta."
Thus swore the Hidalgo
Don José Calderon.

He hied him to Austin.
Bought him a basket,
A barrel of pepper,
And another of garlic;
Also a rope he bought.
That was his stock in trade;
Nothing else had he.
Nor was he rated in

Dun or in Bradstreet,
Though he meant business,
Don José Calderon,
Champion of Mexico,
Don José Calderon,
Seeker of vengeance.

With his stout lariat,
Then he caught swiftly
Tomcats and puppy dogs,
Caught them and cooked them,
Don José Calderon,
Vower of vengeance.
Now on the sidewalk
Sits the avenger
Selling Tamales to
Innocent purchasers.
Dire is thy vengeance,
Oh, José Calderon,
Pitiless Nemesis
Fearful Redresser
Of the wrongs done to thy
Sainted grandfather.

Now the doomed Texans,
Rashly hilarious,
Buy of the deadly wares,
Buy and devour.
Rounders at midnight,

Citizens solid,
Bankers and newsboys,
Bootblacks and preachers,
Rashly importunate,
Courting destruction.
Buy and devour.
Beautiful maidens
Buy and devour,
Gentle society youths
Buy and devour.

Buy and devour
This thing called Tamale;
Made of rat terrier,
Spitz dog and poodle.
Maltese cat, boarding house
Steak and red pepper.
Garlic and tallow,
Corn meal and shucks.
Buy without shame
Sit on store steps and eat,
Stand on the street and eat,
Ride on the cars and eat,
Strewing the shucks around
Over creation.

Dire is thy vengeance.
Don José Calderon.
For the slight thing we did

Killing thy grandfather.
What boots it if we killed
Only one greaser,
Don Jose Calderon?
This is your deep revenge,
You have greased all of us,
Greased a whole nation
With your Tamales,
Don Jose Calderon.
Santos Esperition,
Vincente Camillo,
Quitana de Rios,
De Rosa y Ribera.

LETTERS

[Letter to Mr. Gilman Hall, O. Henry's friend and Associate Editor of *Everybody's Magazine*.]

"the Callie" —
Excavation Road —   Sundy.
my dear mr. hall:

in your october E'bodys' i read a story in which i noticed some sentences as follows:

"Day in, day out, day in, day out, day in, day out, day in, day out, day in, day out, it had rained, rained, and rained and rained & rained & rained & rained & rained till the mountains loomed like a chunk of rooined velvet."

And the other one was: "i don't keer whether you are any good or not," she cried. "You're alive! You're alive! You're alive! You're alive! You're alive! You're alive! You're alive! You're alive! You're alive! You're alive! You're alive! You're alive! You're alive! You're alive! You're alive! You're alive!"

I thought she would never stop saying it, on and on and on and on and on and on and on and on and on and on and on. "You're alive! You're alive! You're alive! You're alive! You're alive! You're alive! You're alive! You're ALIVE!

"You're alive! You're alive! You're alive! You're

alive! You're alive! You're alive! You're alive! You're ALIVE!

"YOU'RE ALIVE!"

Say, bill; do you get this at a rate, or does every word go?

i want to know, because if the latter is right i'm going to interduce in my compositions some histerical personages that will loom up large as repeeters when the words are counted up at the polls.

Yours truly
O. henry
28 West 26th St.,
West of broadway

Mr. hall,
 part editor
  of everybody's.

KYNTOEKNEEYOUGH RANCH, November 31, 1883.

[Letter to Mrs. Hall, a friend back in North Carolina. This is one of the earliest letters found.]

Dear Mrs. Hall:

As I have not heard from you since the shout you gave when you set out from the station on your way home I guess you have not received some seven or eight letters from me, and hence your silence. The mails are so unreliable that they may all have been lost. If you don't get this you had better send to Washington and get them to look over the dead letter office for the others. I have nothing to tell you of any interest, except that we all nearly froze to death last night, thermometer away below 32 degrees in the shade all night.

You ought by all means to come back to Texas this winter; you would love it more and more; that same little breeze that you looked for so anxiously last summer is with us now, as cold as Callum Bros. suppose their soda water to be.

My sheep are doing finely; they never were in better condition. They give me very little trouble, for I have never been able to see one of them yet. I will proceed to give you all the news about this ranch. Dick has got his new house well under way, the pet lamb is doing finely, and I take the cake for cooking mutton steak and fine gravy. The chickens are doing mighty well, the garden produces magnificent prickly pears and grass; onions are worth two for five cents, and Mr. Haynes has shot a Mexican.

Please send by express to this ranch 75 cooks and 200 washwomen, blind or wooden legged ones preferred. The climate has a tendency to make them walk off every two or three days, which must be overcome. Ed Brockman has quit the store and I think is going to work for Lec among the cows. Wears a red sash and swears so fluently that he has been mistaken often for a member of the Texas Legislature.

If you see Dr. Beall bow to him for me, politely but distantly; he refuses to waste a line upon me. I suppose he is too much engaged in courting to write any letters.

Give Dr. Hall my profoundest regards. I think about him invariably whenever he is occupying my thoughts.

Influenced by the contents of the *Bugle*, there is an impression general at this ranch that you are president, secretary, and committee, &c., of the various associations of fruit fairs, sewing societies, church fairs, Presbytery, general assembly, conference, medical conventions, and baby shows that go to make up the glory and renown of North Carolina in general, and while I heartily congratulate the aforesaid institutions on their having such a zealous and efficient officer, I tremble lest their requirements leave you not time to favor me with a letter in reply to this, and assure you that if you would so honor me I would highly appreciate the effort. I would rather have a good long letter from you than many *Bugles*. In your letter be certain to refer as much as possible to the advantages of civilized life over the barbarous; you might mention the theatres you see there, the nice things you eat, warm fires, niggers to cook and bring in wood; a special reference to nice beef-steak would be advisable. You know our being reminded of these luxuries makes us contented and happy. When we hear of you people at home eating turkeys and mince pies and getting drunk Christmas and having a fine time generally we become more and more reconciled to this country and would not leave it for anything.

I must close now as I must go and dress for the opera. Write soon.   Yours very truly,

W. S. PORTER.

TO DR. W. P. BEALL

[Dr. Beall, of Greensboro, N. C., was one of young Porter's dearest friends. Between them there was an almost regular correspondence during Porter's first years in Texas.

LA SALLE COUNTY, Texas, December 8, 1883.

Dear Doctor: I send you a play — a regular high art full orchestra, gilt-edged drama. I send it to you because of old acquaintance and as a revival of old associations. Was I not ever ready in times gone by to generously fur- nish a spatula and other assistance when you did buy the succulent watermelon? And was it not by my connivance and help that you did oft from the gentle Oscar Mayo skates entice? But I digress. I think that I have so concealed the identity of the characters introduced that no one will be able to place them, as they all appear under fictitious names, although I admit that many of the inci- dents and scenes were suggested by actual experiences of the author in your city.

You will, of course, introduce the play upon the stage if proper arrangements can be made. I have not yet had an opportunity of ascertaining whether Edwin Booth, John McCullough or Henry Irving can be secured. However, I will leave all such matters to your judg- ment and taste. Some few suggestions I will make with regard to the mounting of the piece which may be of value to you. Discrimination will be necessary in selecting a fit person to represent the character of Bill Slax, the tramp. The part is that of a youth of great beauty and noble manners, temporarily under a cloud, and is generally rather difficult to fill properly.   The other minor characters, such as damfools, citizens, police, customers, countrymen, &c., can be very easily supplied, especially the first.

Let it be announced in the *Patriot* for several days that in front of Benbow Hall, at a certain hour, a man will walk a tight rope seventy feet from the ground who has never made the attempt before; that the exhibition will be FREE, and that the odds are 20 to 1 that the man will be killed.   A large crowd will gather.   Then let the Guilford Grays charge one side, the Reidsville Light Infantry the other, with fixed bayonets, and a man with a hat commence taking up a collection in the rear.   By this means they can be readily driven into the hall and the door locked.

I have studied a long time about devising a plan for obtaining pay from the audience and have finally struck upon the only feasible one I think.

After the performance let some one come out on the stage and announce that James Forbis will speak two hours.   The result, easily explainable by philosophical and psychological reasons, will be as follows: The minds of the audience, elated and inspired by the hope of immediate departure when confronted by such a terror-inspiring and dismal prospect, will collapse with the fearful reaction which will take place, and for a space of time they will remain in a kind of comatose, farewell-vain-world condition.   Now, as this is the time when the interest of the evening is at its highest pitch, let the melodious strains of the orchestra steal forth as a committee appointed by the managers of lawyers, druggists, doctors, and revenue officers, go around and relieve the audience of the price of admission for each one. Where one person has no money let it be made up from another, but on no account let the whole sum taken be more than the just amount at usual rates.

As I said before, the characters in the play are purely imaginary, and therefore not to be confounded with real persons. But lest any one, feeling some of the idiosyncrasies and characteristics apply too forcibly to his own high moral and irreproachable self, should allow his warlike and combative spirits to arise, you might as you go, kind of casually like, produce the impression that I rarely miss my aim with a Colt's forty-five, but if that does not have the effect of quieting the splenetic individual, and he still thirsts for Bill Slax's gore, just inform him that if he comes out here he can't get any whiskey within two days' journey of my present abode, and water will have to be his only beverage while on the warpath. This, I am sure, will avert the bloody and direful conflict.

Accept my lasting regards and professions of respect.

Ever yours,

BILL SLAX.

TO DR. W. P. BEALL

My Dear Doctor: I wish you a happy, &c., and all that sort of thing, don't you know, &c., &c., I send you a few little productions in the way of poetry, &c., which, of course, were struck off in an idle moment. Some of the pictures are not good likenesses, and so I have not labelled them, which you may do as fast [as] you discover whom they represent, as some of them resemble others more than themselves, but the poems are good without exception, and will compare favorably with Baron Alfred's latest on spring.

I have just come from a hunt, in which I mortally wounded a wild hog, and as my boots are full of thorns I can't write any longer than this paper will contain, for it's all I've got, because I'm too tired to write any more for the reason that I have no news to tell.

I see by the *Patriot* that you are Superintendent of Public Health, and assure you that all such upward rise as you make like that will ever be witnessed with interest and pleasure by me, &c., &c. Give my regards to Dr. and Mrs. Hall. It would be uncomplimentary to your powers of perception as well as superfluous to say that I will now close and remain, yours truly,

W. S. PORTER.

LETTER TO DR. W. P. BEALL

LA SALLE COUNTY, Texas, February 27, 1884.

My Dear Doctor: Your appreciated epistle of the 18th received. I was very glad to hear from you. I hope to hear again if such irrelevant correspondence will not interfere with your duties as Public Health Eradicator, which I believe is the office you hold under county authority. I supposed the very dramatic Shakespearian comedy to be the last, as I heard nothing from you previous before your letter, and was about to write another of a more exciting character, introducing several bloody single combats, a dynamite explosion, a ladies' oyster supper for charitable purposes, &c., also comprising some mysterious sub rosa transactions known only to myself and a select few, new songs and dances, and the Greensboro Poker Club. Having picked up a few points myself relative to this latter amusement, I feel competent to give a lucid, glittering portrait of the scenes presented under its auspices. But if the former drama has reached you safely, I will refrain from burdening you any more with the labors of general stage manager, &c.

If long hair, part of a sombrero, Mexican spurs, &c., would make a fellow famous, I already occupy a topmost niche in the Temple Frame. If my wild, untamed aspect had not been counteracted by my well-known benevolent and amiable expression of countenance, I would have been arrested long ago by the Rangers on general suspicions of murder and horse stealing. In fact, I owe all my present means of lugubrious living to my desperate and blood-thirsty appearance, combined with the confident and easy way in which I tackle a Winchester rifle. There is a gentleman who lives about fifteen miles from the ranch, who for amusement and recreation, and not altogether without an eye to the profit, keeps a general merchandise store. This gent, for the first few months has been trying very earnestly to sell me a little paper, which I would like much

to have, but am not anxious to purchase. Said paper is
my account, receipted. Occasionally he is absent, and
the welcome news coming to my ear, I mount my fiery
hoss and gallop wildly up to the store, enter with something of the sang froid, grace, abandon and récherché
nonchalance with which Charles Yates ushers ladies and
gentlemen to their seats in the opera-house, and, nervously
fingering my butcher knife, fiercely demand goods and
chattels of the clerk. This plan always succeeds. This
is by way of explanation of this vast and unnecessary
stationery of which this letter is composed. I am always
in too big a hurry to demur at kind and quality, but when
I get to town I will write you on small gilt-edged paper
that would suit even the fastidious and discriminating
taste of a Logan.

When I get to the city, which will be shortly, I will send
you some account of this country and its inmates.

You are right, I have almost forgotten what a regular
old, gum-chewing, ice-cream destroying, opera ticket
vortex, ivory-clawing girl looks like. Last summer a very
fair specimen of this kind ranged over about Fort Snell,
and I used to ride over twice a week on mail days and
chew the end of my riding whip while she "Stood on the
Bridge" and "Gathered up Shells on the Sea Shore" and
wore the "Golden Slippers." But she has vamoosed, and
my ideas on the subject are again growing dim.

If you see anybody about to start to Texas to live,
especially to this part, if you will take your scalpyouler
and sever the jugular vein, cut the brachiopod artery and

hamstring him, after he knows what you have done for him he will rise and call you blessed. This country is a silent but eloquent refutation of Bob Ingersoll's theory; a man here gets prematurely insane, melancholy and unreliable and finally dies of lead poisoning, in his boots, while in a good old land like Greensboro a man can die, as they do every day, with all the benefits of the clergy.

W. S. PORTER.

AUSTIN, Texas, April 21, 1885.

Dear Dave: I take my pen in hand to let you know that I am well, and hope these few lines will find you as well as can be expected.

I carried out your parting injunction of a floral nature with all the solemnity and sacredness that I would have bestowed upon a dying man's last request. Promptly at half-past three I repaired to the robbers' den, commonly known as Radams Horticultural and Vegetable Emporium, and secured the high-priced offerings, according to promise. I asked if the bouquets were ready, and the polite but piratical gentleman in charge pointed proudly to two objects on the counter reposing in a couple of vases, and said they were.

I then told him I feared there was some mistake, as no buttonhole bouquets had been ordered, but he insisted on his former declaration, and so I brought them away and sent them to their respective destinations.

I thought it a pity to spoil a good deck of cards by taking out only one, so I bundled up the whole deck, and inserted them in the bouquet, but finally concluded it would not be right to *violet* (JOKE) my promise and I *rose* (JOKE) superior to such a mean trick and sent only one as directed.

I have a holiday to-day, as it is San Jacinto day. Thermopylae had its messenger of defeat, but the Alamo had none. Mr. President and fellow citizens, those glorious heroes who fell for their country on the bloody field of San Jacinto, etc.

There is a bazaar to-night in the representatives' hall. You people out in Colorado don't know anything. A bazaar is cedar and tacks and girls and raw-cake and stepladders and Austin Grays and a bass solo by Bill Stacy, and net profits $2.65.

Albert has got his new uniform and Alf Menille is in town, and the store needs the "fine Italian hand" of the bookkeeper very much, besides some of his plain Anglo-Saxon conversation.

Was interviewed yesterday by Gen'l Smith, Clay's father. He wants Jim S. and me to represent a manufactory in Jeff. City: Convict labor. Says parties in Galveston and Houston are making good thing of it. Have taken him up. Hope to be at work soon. Glad, by jingo! Shake. What'll you have? Claret and sugar? Better come home. Colorado no good.

Strange thing happened in Episcopal Church Sunday. Big crowd. Choir had sung jolly tune and preacher come from behind scenes. Everything quiet. Suddenly fellow comes down aisle. Late. Everybody looks. Disappointment. It is a stranger. Jones and I didn't go. Service proceeds.

Jones talks about his mashes and Mirabeau B. Lamar, daily. Yet there is hope. Cholera infantum; Walsh's crutch; Harvey, or softening of the brain may carry him off yet.

Society notes are few. Bill Stacy is undecided where to spend the summer. Henry Harrison will resort at Wayland and Crisers. Charlie Cook will not go near a watering place if he can help it.

If you don't strike a good thing out West, I hope we will see you soon.

Yours as ever,

W. S. P.

AUSTIN, Texas, April 28, 1885.

Dear Dave: I received your letter in answer to mine, which you never got till sometime after you had written.

I snatch a few moments from my arduous labors to reply. The Colorado has been on the biggest boom I have seen since '39. In the pyrotechnical and not strictly grammatical language of the *Statesman* — "The cruel, devastating flood swept, on a dreadful holocaust of swollen, turbid waters, surging and dashing in mad fury which have never been equalled in human history. A pitiable sight was seen the morning after the flood. Six hundred men, out of employment, were seen standing on the banks of the river, gazing at the rushing stream, laden with débris of every description. A wealthy New York Banker, who was present, noticing the forlorn appearance of these men, at once began to collect a subscription for them, appealing in eloquent terms for help for these poor sufferers by the flood. He collected one dollar, and five horn buttons. The dollar he had given himself. He learned on inquiry that these men had not been at any employment in six years, and all they had lost by the flood was a few fishing poles. The Banker put his dollar in his pocket and stepped up to the Pearl Saloon.

As you will see by this morning's paper, there is to be a minstrel show next Wednesday for benefit of Austin Grays.

I attended the rehearsal last night, but am better this morning, and the doctor thinks I will pull through with careful attention.

The jokes are mostly mildewed, rockribbed, and ancient as the sun. I can give you no better idea of the tout ensemble and sine die of the affair than to state that Scuddy is going to sing a song. . . .

Mrs. Harrell brought a lot of crystallized fruits from New Orleans for you. She wants to know if she shall send them around on Bois d'arc or keep them 'til you return. Answer.

Write to your father. He thinks you are leaving him out, writing to everybody else first. Write.

We have the boss trick here now. Have sold about ten boxes of cigars betting on it in the store.

Take four nickels, and solder them together so the solder will not appear. Then cut out of three of them a square hole like this: (Illustration.) Take about twelve other nickels, and on top of them you lay a small die with the six up, that will fit easily in the hole without being noticed. You lay the four nickels over this, and all presents the appearance of a stack of nickels. You do all this privately so everybody will suppose it is nothing but a stack of five-cent pieces. You then lay another small die on top of the stack with the ace up. You have a small tin cup shaped like this (Illustration) made for the purpose. You let everybody see the ace, and then say you propose to turn the ace into a six. You lay the tin cup carefully over the stack this way, and feel around in your pocket for a pencil and not finding one. . . .

(The rest of this letter is lost)

AUSTIN, Texas, May 10, 1885.

Dear Dave: I received your two letters and have commenced two or three in reply, but always failed to say what I wanted to, and destroyed them all. I heard from Joe that you would probably remain in Colorado. I hope you will succeed in making a good thing out of it, if you conclude to do so, but would like to see you back again in Austin. If there is anything I can do for you here, let me know.

Town is fearfully dull, except for the frequent raids of the Servant Girl Annihilators, who make things lively during the dead hours of the night; if it were not for them, items of interest would be very scarce, as you may see by the *Statesman.*

Our serenading party has developed new and alarming modes of torture for our helpless and sleeping victims. Last Thursday night we loaded up a small organ on a hack and with our other usual instruments made an assault upon the quiet air of midnight that made the atmosphere turn pale.

After going the rounds we were halted on the Avenue by Fritz Hartkopf and ordered into his *salon*. We went in, carrying the organ, etc. A large crowd of bums immediately gathered, prominent among which, were to be seen Percy James, Theodore Hillyer, Randolph Burmond, Charlie Hicks, and after partaking freely of lemonade we wended our way down, and were duly halted and treated in the same manner by other hospitable gentlemen.

We were called in at several places while wit and champagne, Rhein Wine, etc., flowed in a most joyous and hilarious manner. It was one of the most recherché and per diem affairs ever known in the city. Nothing occurred to mar the pleasure of the hour, except a trifling incident that might be construed as malapropos and post-meridian by the hypercritical. Mr. Charles Sims on attempting to introduce Mr. Charles Hicks and your humble servant to young ladies, where we had been invited inside, forgot our names and required to be informed on the subject before proceeding.

Yours

W. S. P.

AUSTIN, Texas, December 22, 1885.

Dear Dave: Everything wept at your departure. Especially the clouds. Last night the clouds had a silver lining, three dollars and a half's worth. I fulfilled your engagement in grand, tout ensemble style, but there is a sad bon jour look about the thirty-eight cents left in my vest pocket that would make a hired man weep. All day long the heavens wept, and the heavy, sombre clouds went drifting about over head, and the north wind howled in maniacal derision, and the hack drivers danced on the pavements in wild, fierce glee, for they knew too well what the stormy day betokened. The hack was to call for me at eight. At five minutes to eight I went upstairs and dressed in my usual bijou and operatic style, and rolled away to the opera. Emma sang finely. I applauded at the wrong times, and praised her rendering of the chromatic scale when she was performing on "c" flat andante pianissimo, but otherwise the occasion passed off without anything to mar the joyousness of the hour. Everybody was there. Isidor Moses and John Ireland, and Fritz Hartkopf and Prof. Herzog and Bill Stacy and all the bong ton elight. You will receive a draft to-day through the First National Bank of Colorado for $3.65, which you will please honor.

There is no news, or there are no news, either you like to tell. Lavaca Street is very happy and quiet and enjoys life, for Jones was sat on by his Uncle Wash and feels humble and don't sing any more, and the spirit of

peace and repose broods over its halls.   Martha rings the
matin bell, it seems to me before cock crow or ere the first
faint streaks of dawn are limned in the eastern sky by the
rosy fingers of Aurora.   At noon the foul ogre cribbage
stalks rampant, and seven-up for dim, distant oysters that
only the eye of faith can see.

The hour grows late.   The clock strikes!   Another day
has vanished.   Gone into the dim recesses of the past,
leaving its record of misspent hours, false hopes, and
disappointed expectations.   May a morrow dawn that will
bring recompense and requital for the sorrows of the days
gone by, and a new order of things when there will be
more starch in cuff and collar, and less in handkerchiefs.

Come with me out into the starlight night.   So calm,
so serene, ye lights of heaven, so high above earth; so pure
and majestic and mysterious; looking down on the mad
struggle of life here below, is there no pity in your never
closing eyes for us mortals on which you shine?

Come with me on to the bridge.   Ah, see there, far
below, the dark, turbid stream.   Rushing and whirling
and eddying under the dark pillars with ghostly murmur
and siren whisper.   What shall we find in your depths?
The stars do not reflect themselves in your waters, they
are too dark and troubled and swift!   What shall we
find in your depths?   Rest? — Peace? — catfish?   Who
knows?   'Tis but a moment.   A leap!   A plunge! — and
— then oblivion or another world?   Who can tell?   A
A man once dived into your depths and brought up a

horse collar and a hoop-skirt. Ah! what do we know of the beyond? We know that death comes, and we return no more to our world of trouble and care — but where do we go? Are there lands where no traveller has been? A chaos — perhaps where no human foot has trod — perhaps Bastrop — perhaps New Jersey! Who knows? Where do people go who are in McDade? Do they go where they have to fare worse? They cannot go where they have worse fare!

Let us leave the river. The night grows cold. We could not pierce the future or pay the toll. Come, the ice factory is deserted! No one sees us. My partner, W. P. Anderson, will never destroy himself. Why? His credit is good. No one will sue a side-partner of mine!

You have heard of a brook murmuring, but you never knew a sewer sighed! But we digress! We will no longer pursue a side issue like this. Au revoir. I will see you later.   Yours truly,

WILLIAM SHAKESPEARE INGOMAR JUNIUS
    BRUTUS CALLIOPE SIX-HANDED EUCHRE
    GROVER CLEVELAND HILL CITY QUARTETTE
    JOHNSON.

AN EARLY PARABLE

In one of his early letters, written from Austin, O. Henry wrote a long parable that was evidently to tell his correspondent some of the local gossip. Here it is:

Once upon a time there was a maiden in a land not far

away — a maiden of much beauty and rare accomplish-
ments. She was beloved by all on account of her goodness
of heart, and her many charms of disposition. Her father
was a great lord, rich and powerful, and a mighty man, and
he loved his daughter with exceeding great love, and he
cared for her with jealous and loving watchfulness, lest
any harm should befall her, or even the least discomfort
should mar her happiness and cause any trouble in her
smooth and peaceful life. The cunningest masters were
engaged to teach her from her youngest days; she played
upon the harpsichord the loveliest and sweetest music;
she wrought fancy work in divers strange and wonderful
forms that might puzzle all beholders as to what manner
of things they might be; she sang; and all listeners heark-
ened thereunto, as to the voice of an angel; she danced
stately minuets with the gay knights as graceful as a queen
and as light as the thistledown borne above the clover
blossoms by the wind; she could paint upon china, rare
and unknown flowers the like unto which man never saw
in colors, crimson and blue and yellow, glorious to behold;
she conversed in unknown tongues whereof no man knew
the meaning and sense; and created wild admiration in all,
by the ease and grace with which she did play upon a new
and strange instrument of wondrous sound and structure
which she called a banjo.

She had gone into a strange land, far away beyond the
rivers that flowed through her father's dominion — farther
than one could see from the highest castle tower — up into
the land of ice and snow, where wise men, famous for learn-

ing and ancient lore had gathered together from many lands and countries the daughters of great men. Kings and powerful rulers, railroad men, bankers, mighty men who wished to bring up their children to be wise and versed in all things old and new. Here, the Princess abode for many seasons, and she sat at the feet of old wise men, who could tell of the world's birth, and the stars, and read the meaning of the forms of the rocks that make the high mountains and knew the history of all created things that are; and here she learned to speak strange tongues, and studied the deep mysteries of the past — the secrets of the ancients; Chaldaic lore; Etruscan inscription; hidden and mystic sciences, and knew the names of all the flowers and things that grow in fields or wood; even unto the tiniest weed by the brook.

In due time the Princess came back to her father's castle. The big bell boomed from the high tower; the heavy iron gates were thrown open; banners floated all along the battlemented walls, and in the grand hall, servants and retainers hurried to and fro, bearing gold dishes, and great bowls of flaming smoking punch, while oxen were roasted whole and hogsheads of ale tapped on the common by the castle walls, and thither hied them the villagers one and all to make merry at the coming of the dear Princess again. "She will come back so wise and learned," they said, "so far above us that she will not notice us as she did once," but not so: the Princess with a red rose in her hair, and dressed so plain and neat that she looked more like a farmer's daughter than a great

king's, came down among them from her father's side
with nods of love and welcome on her lips, and a smile
upon her face, and took them by the hands as in the old
days, and none among them so lowly or so poor but what
received a kind word from the gracious Princess, and
carried away in their hearts glad feelings that she was still
the same noble and gracious lady she always was.   Then
night came, and torches by thousands lit up the great
forest, and musicians played and bonfires glowed, with
sparks flying like myriads of stars among the gloomy trees.

In the great castle hall were gathered the brave knights
and the fairest ladies in the kingdom.   The jolly old King,
surrounded by the wise men and officers of state moved
about among his guests, stately and courteous, ravishing
music burst forth from all sides, and down the hall moved
the fair Princess in the mazy dance, on the arm of a Knight
who gazed upon her face in rapt devotion and love.   Who
was he that dared to look thus upon the daughter of the
King, sovereign prince of the kingdom, and the heiress of
her father's wealth and lands.

He had no title, no proud name to place beside a royal
one, beyond that of an honorable knight, but who says
that that is not a title that, borne worthily, makes a man
the peer of any that wears a crown?

He had loved her long.   When a boy they had roamed
together in the great forest about the castle, and played
among the fountains of the court like brother and sister.
The King saw them together often and smiled and went
his way and said nothing.   The years went on and they

were together as much as they could be. The summer
days when the court went forth into the forest mounted
on prancing steeds to chase the stags with hounds; all clad
in green and gold with waving plumes and shining silver
and ribbons of gay colors, this Knight was by the Princess'
side to guide her through the pathless swamps where the
hunt ranged, and saw that no harm came to her. And
now that she had come back after years of absence, he
went to her with fear lest she should have changed from her
old self, and would not be to him as she was when they
were boy and girl together. But no, there was the same
old kindly welcome, the same smiling greeting, the warm
pressure of the hand, the glad look in the eyes as of yore.
The Knight's heart beat wildly and a dim new-awakened
hope arose in him. Was she too far away, after all?

He felt worthy of her, and of any one in fact, but he was
without riches, only a knight-errant with his sword for his
fortune, and his great love his only title; and he had always
refrained from ever telling her anything of his love, for
his pride prevented him, and you know a poor girl even
though she be a princess cannot say to a man, "I am rich,
but, let that be no bar between us, I am yours and will
let my wealth pass if you will give up your pride." No
princess can say this, and the Knight's pride would not
let him say anything of the kind and so you see there was
small chance of their ever coming to an understanding.

Well, the feasting and dancing went on, and the Knight
and the Princess danced and sang together, and walked
out where the moon was making a white wonder of the

great fountain, and wandered under the rows of great oaks,
but spoke no word of love, though no mortal man knows
what thoughts passed in their heads; and she gave long
accounts of the wonders she had seen in the far, icy north,
in the great school of wise men, and the Knight talked
of the wild and savage men he had seen in the Far West,
where he had been in battles with the heathen in a wild
and dreary land; and she heard with pity his tales of suffering and trials in the desert among wild animals and fierce
human kings; and inside the castle the music died away
and the lights grew dim and the villagers had long since
gone to their homes and the Knight and the Princess still
talked of old times, and the moon climbed high in the
eastern sky.

One day there came news from a country far to the west
where lay the possessions of the Knight. The enemy had
robbed him of his treasure, driven away his cattle, and he
found it was best to hie him away and rescue his inheritance and goods. He buckled on his sword and mounted
his good war-horse. He rode to the postern gate of the
castle to make his adieus to the Princess.

When he told her he was going away to the wild western
country to do battle with the heathen, she grew pale, and
her eyes took on a look of such pain and fear that the
Knight's heart leaped and then sank in his bosom, as his
pride still kept him from speaking the words that might
have made all well.

She bade him farewell in a low voice, and tears even
stood in her eyes, but what could she say or do?

The Knight put spurs to his horse, and dashed away over the hills without ever looking back, and the Princess stood looking over the gate at him till the last sight of his plume below the brow of the hill. The Knight was gone. Many suitors flocked about the Princess. Mighty lords and barons of great wealth were at her feet and attended her every journey. They came and offered themselves and their fortunes again and again, but none of them found favor in her eyes. "Will the Princess listen to no one," they began to say among themselves. "Has she given her heart to some one who is not among us?" No one could say.

A great and mighty physician, young and of wondrous power in his art, telephoned to her every night if he might come down. How his suit prospered no one could tell, but he persevered with great and astonishing diligence. A powerful baron who assisted in regulating the finances of the kingdom and who was a direct descendant of a great prince who was cast into a lion's den, knelt at her feet.

A gay and lively lord who lived in a castle hung with ribbons and streamers and gay devices of all kinds, with other nobles of like character, prostrated themselves before her, but she would listen to none of them.

The Princess rode about in quiet ways in the cool evenings upon a gray palfrey, alone and very quiet, and she seemed to grow silent and thoughtful as time went on and no news came from the western wars, and the Knight came not back again.

[Written to his daughter Margaret.]

TOLEDO, Ohio, Oct. 1, 1900.

Dear Margaret: I got your very nice, long letter a good many days ago. It didn't come straight to me, but went to a wrong address first. I was very glad indeed to hear from you, and very, very sorry to learn of your getting your finger so badly hurt. I don't think you were to blame at all, as you couldn't know just how that villainous old "hoss" was going to bite. I do hope that it will heal up nicely and leave your finger strong. I am learning to play the mandolin, and we must get you a guitar, and we will learn a lot of duets together when I come home which will certainly not be later than next summer, and maybe earlier.

I suppose you have started to school again some time ago. I hope you like to go, and don't have to study too hard. When one grows up, a thing they never regret is that they went to school long enough to learn all they could. It makes everything easier for them, and if they like books and study they can always content and amuse themselves that way even if other people are cross and tiresome, and the world doesn't go to suit them.

You mustn't think that I've forgotten somebody's birthday. I couldn't find just the thing I wanted to send, but I know where it can be had, and it will reach you in a few days. So, when it comes you'll know it is for a birthday remembrance.

I think you write the prettiest hand of any little girl (or big one, either) I ever knew. The letters you make are as even and regular as printed ones. The next time you write, tell me how far you have to go to school and whether you go alone or not.

I am busy all the time writing for the papers and magazines all over the country, so I don't have a chance to come home, but I'm going to try to come this winter. If I don't I will by summer *sure*, and then you'll have somebody to boss and make trot around with you.

Write me a letter whenever you have some time to spare, for I am always glad and anxious to hear from you. Be careful when you are on the streets not to feed shucks to strange dogs, or pat snakes on the head or shake hands with cats you haven't been introduced to, or stroke the noses of electric car horses.

Hoping you are well and your finger is getting all right, I am, with much love, as ever, PAPA.

My Dear Margaret: Here it is summertime, and the bees are blooming and the flowers are singing and the birds making honey, and we haven't been fishing yet. Well, there's only one more month till July, and then we'll go, and no mistake. I thought you would write and tell me about the high water around Pittsburg some time ago, and whether it came up to where you live, or not. And I haven't heard a thing about Easter, and about the rabbit's eggs — but I suppose you have learned by this time that eggs grow on egg plants and are not laid by rabbits.

I would like very much to hear from you oftener, it has been more than a month now since you wrote. Write soon and tell me how you are, and when school will be out, for we want plenty of holidays in July so we can have a good time. I am going to send you something nice the last of this week. What do you guess it will be?

Lovingly,   PAPA.

The Caledonia
WEDNESDAY.

My Dear Mr. Jack:

I owe Gilman Hall $175 (or mighty close to it) pusson‑ally — so he tells me. I thought it was only about $30, but he has been keeping the account.

He's just got to have it to-day. *McClure's* will pay me some money on the 15th of June, but I can't get it until then. I was expecting it before this — anyhow before Gilman left, but they stick to the letter.

I wonder if you could give me a check for that much to pay him to-day. If you will I'll hold up my right hand — thus: that I'll have you a *first-class story on your desk before the last of this week.*

I reckon I'm pretty well overdrawn, but I've sure got to see that Hall gets his before he leaves. I don't want anything for myself.

Please, sir, let me know right away, by return boy if you'll do it.

If you can't, I'll have to make a quick dash at the three-ball magazines; and I do hate to tie up with them for a story.

The Same

Mr. J. O. H. COSGRAVE,   SYDNEY PORTER.
    at this time editor of *Everybody's Magazine.*

A letter to Gilman Hall, written just before the writer's marriage to Miss Sara Lindsay Coleman of Asheville, N. C.

WEDNESDAY.

Dear Gilman:

Your two letters received this A. M. Mighty good letters, too, and cheering.

Mrs. Jas. Coleman is writing Mrs. Hall to-day. She is practically the hostess at Wynn Cottage where the hullabaloo will occur.

Say, won't you please do one or two little things for me before you leave, as you have so kindly offered?

(1) Please go to Tiffany's and get a wedding ring, size 5¼. Sara says the bands worn now are quite narrow —and that's the kind she wants.

(2) And bring me a couple of dress collars, size 16½. I have ties.

(3) And go to a florist's — there is one named Mackintosh (or something like that) on Broadway, East side of street five or six doors north of 26th St., where I used to buy a good many times. He told me he could ship flowers in good shape to Asheville — you might remind him that I used to send flowers to 36 West 17th Street some time ago. I am told by the mistress of ceremonies that I am to furnish two bouquets — one of lilies of the valley and one of pale pink roses. Get plenty of each — say enough lilies to make a large bunch to be carried in the hand, and say three or four dozen of the roses.

I note what you say about hard times and will take heed. I'm not going into any extravagances at all, and I'm going to pitch into hard work just as soon as I get the rice grains out of my ear.

I wired you to-day "MS. mailed to-day, please rush one century by wire."

That will exhaust the Reader check — if it isn't too exhausted itself to come. You, of course, will keep the check when it arrives — I don't think they will fall down on it surely. I wrote Howland a pretty sharp letter and ordered him to send it at once care of *Everybody's*.

When this story reaches you it will cut down the overdraft "right smart," but if the house is willing I'd mighty well like to run it up to the limit again, because cash is sure scarce, and I'll have to have something like $300 more to see me through. The story I am sending is a new one; I still have another partly written for you, which I shall finish and turn in before I get back to New York and then we'll begin to clean up all debts.

Just after the wedding we are going to Hot Spring, N. C., only thirty-five miles from Asheville, where there is a big winter resort hotel, and stay there about a week or ten days. Then back to New York.

Please look over the story and arrange for bringing me the $300 when you come—it will still keep me below the allowed limit and thereafter I will cut down instead of raising it.

Just had a 'phone message from S. L. C. saying how pleased she was with your letter to her.

I'm right with you on the question of the "home-like"

system of having fun. I think we'll all agree beautifully on that. I've had all the cheap bohemia that I want. I can tell you, none of the "climbers" and the cocktail crowd are going to bring their *vaporings* into my house. It's for the clean, merry life, with your best friends in the game and a general concentration of energies and aims. I am having a cedarwood club cut from the mountains with knots on it, and I am going to stand in my hallway (when I have one) and edit with it the cards of all callers. You and Mrs. will have latchkeys, of course.

Yes, I think you'd better stay at the hotel—— Of course they'd want you out at Mrs. C's. But suppose we take Mrs. Hall out there, and you and I remain at the B. P. We'll be out at the Cottage every day anyhow, and it'll be scrumptious all round.

I'm simply tickled to death that "you all" are coming.

The protoplasm is in Heaven; all's right with the world. Pippa passes. Yours as ever,

BILL.

FRIDAY.

My Dear Col. Griffith:

Keep your shirt on. I found I had to re-write the story when it came in. I am sending you part of it just so you will have something tangible to remind you that you can't measure the water from the Pierian Spring in spoonfuls.

I've got the story in much better form; and I'll have the rest of it ready this evening.

I'm sorry to have delayed it; but it's best for both of us
to have it a little late and a good deal better.

I'll send over the rest before closing time this afternoon
or the first thing in the morning.

In its revised form I'm much better pleased with it.

> Yours truly,
>
> SYDNEY PORTER.

Mr. Al. Jennings. of Oklahoma City, was an early
friend of O. Henry's. Now, in 1912, a prominent attorney,
Mr. Jennings, in his youth, held up trains.

28 W. 26.   N. Y., SUNDAY.

ALGIE JENNINGS, ESQ., THE WEST.

DEAR BILL:

Glad you've been sick too. I'm well again. Are you?

Well, as I had nothing to do I thought I would write
you a letter; and as I have nothing to say I will close.

How are ye, Bill? How's old Initiative and Referen-
dum? When you coming back to Manhattan? You
wouldn't know the old town now. Main Street is building
up, and there is talk of an English firm putting up a new
hotel. I saw Duffy a few days ago. He looks kind of
thoughtful as if he were trying to calculate how much he'd
have been ahead on Gerald's board and clothes by now
if you had taken him with you. Mrs. Hale is up in Maine
for a 3 weeks' vacation.

Say, Bill, I'm sending your MS. back by mail to-day.
I kept it a little longer after you sent for it because one of
the McClure & Phillips firm wanted to see it first. Every-

body says it is full of good stuff, but thinks it should be put in a more connected shape by some skilful writer who has been trained to that sort work.

It seems to me that you ought to do better with it out there than you could here. If you can get somebody out there to publish it it ought to sell all right. N. Y. is a pretty cold proposition and it can't see as far as the Oklahoma country when it is looking for sales. How about trying Indianapolis or Chicago? Duffy told me about the other MS sent out by your friend Abbott. Kind of a bum friendly trick, wasn't it?

Why don't you get "Arizona's Hand" done and send it on? Seems to me you could handle a short story all right.

My regards to Mrs. Jennings and Bro. Frank. Write some more. Still

BILL.

N. Y., May 23, '05.

Dear Jennings:

Got your letter all right. Hope you'll follow it soon.

I'd advise you not to build any high hopes on your book — just consider that you're on a little pleasure trip, and taking it along as a side line. Mighty few MSS. ever get to be books, and mighty few books pay.

I have to go to Pittsburg the first of next week to be gone about 3 or 4 days. If you decide to come here any time after the latter part of next week I will be ready to meet you. Let me know in advance a day or two.

Gallot is in Grand Rapids — maybe he will run over for a day or two.

In haste and truly yours,
W. S. P.

[It was hard to get O. Henry to take an interest in his books. He was always eager to be at the undone work, to be writing a new story instead of collecting old ones. This letter came from North Carolina. It shows how much thought he gave always to titles.]

LAND O' THE SKY, Monday, 1909.

My Dear Colonel Steger: As I wired you to-day, I like "Man About Town" for a title.

But I am sending in a few others for you to look at; and if any other suits you better, I'm agreeable. Here they are, in preferred order:

The Venturers.

Transfers.

Merry-Go-Rounds.

Babylonica.

Brickdust from Babel.

Babes in the Jungle.

If none of these hit you right, let me know and I'll get busy again. But I think "Man About Town" is about the right thing. It gives the city idea without using the old hackneyed words.

I am going to write you a letter in a day or so "touchin' on and appertainin' to" other matter and topics. I am still improving and feeling pretty good. Colonel Bingham has put in a new ash-sifter and expects you to come down and see that it works all right.

All send regards to you. You seem to have made quite a hit down here for a Yankee.

Salutations and good wishes. Yours, S. P.

[This letter was found unfinished, among his papers after his death. His publishers had discussed many times his writing of a novel, but the following letter constitutes the only record of his own opinions in the matter. The date is surely 1909 or 1910.]

My Dear Mr. Steger: My idea is to write the story of a man — an individual, not a type — but a man who, at the same time, I want to represent a "human nature type," if such a person could exist. The story will teach no lesson, inculcate no moral, advance no theory.

I want it to be something that it won't or can't be — but as near as I can make it — the *true* record of a man's thoughts, his description of his mischances and adventures, his *true* opinions of life as he has seen it and his *absolutely honest* deductions, comments, and views upon the different phases of life that he passes through.

I do not remember ever to have read an autobiography, a biography, or a piece of fiction that told the *truth*. Of course, I have read stuff such as Rousseau and Zola and George Moore and various memoirs that were supposed to be window panes in their respective breasts; but, mostly, all of them were either liars, actors, or posers. (Of course, I'm not trying to belittle the greatness of their literary expression.)

All of us have to be prevaricators, hypocrites and liars every day of our lives; otherwise the social structure would fall into pieces the first day. We must act in one

another's presence just as we must wear clothes. It is
for the best.

The trouble about writing the truth has been that the
writers have kept in their minds one or another or all of
three thoughts that made a handicap — they were trying
either to do a piece of immortal literature, or to shock
the public or to please editors. Some of them suc
ceeded in all three, but they did not write the *truth*.
Most autobiographies are insincere from beginning to end.
About the only chance for the truth to be told is in fiction.

It is well understood that "all the truth" cannot be
told in print — but how about "nothing but the truth"?
That's what I want to do.

I want the man who is telling the story to tell it — not
as he would to a reading public or to a confessor — but
something in this way: Suppose he were marooned on an
island in mid-ocean with no hope of ever being rescued;
and, in order to pass away some of the time he should tell
a story *to himself* embodying his adventure and experiences and opinions. Having a certain respect for
himself (let us hope) he would leave out the "realism"
that he would have no chance of selling in the market;
he would omit the lies and self-conscious poses, and
would turn out to his one auditor something real and true.

So, as truth is not to be found in history, autobiography, press reports (nor at the bottom of an H. G.
Wells), let us hope that fiction may be the means of bringing out a few grains of it.

The "hero" of the story will be a man born and "raised"

in a somnolent little southern town. His education is about a common school one, but he learns afterward from reading and life. I'm going to try to give him a "style" in narrative and speech — the best I've got in the shop. I'm going to take him through all the main phases of life — wild adventure, city, society, something of the "under world," and among many characteristic planes of the phases. I want him to acquire all the sophistication that experience can give him, and always preserve his individual honest *human* view, and have him tell the *truth* about everything.

It is time to say now, that by the "truth" I don't mean the objectionable stuff that so often masquerades under the name. I mean true opinions a true estimate of all things as they seem to the "hero." If you find a word or a suggestive line or sentence in any of my copy, you cut it out and deduct it from the royalties.

I want this man to be a man of natural intelligence, of individual character, absolutely open and broad minded; and show how the Creator of the earth has got him in a rat trap — put him here "willy nilly" (you know the Omar verse); and then I want to show what he does about it. There is always the eternal question from the Primal Source — "What are you going to do about it?"

Please don't think for the half of a moment that the story is going to be anything of an autobiography. I have a distinct character in my mind for the part, and he does not at all

(Here the letter ends. He never finished it.)

THE STORY OF "HOLDING UP A TRAIN"

In "Sixes and Sevens" there appears an article entitled "Holding Up a Train." Now the facts were given to O. Henry by an old and dear friend who, in his wild avenging youth, had actually held up trains. To-day he is Mr. Al. Jennings, of Oklahoma City, Okla., a prominent attorney. He has permitted the publication of two letters O. Henry wrote him, the first outlining the story as he thought his friend Jennings ought to write it, and the second announcing that, with O. Henry's revision, the manuscript had been accepted.

From W. S. Porter to Al. Jennings, September 21st (year not given but probably 1902).

Dear Pard:

In regard to that article — I will give you my idea of what is wanted. Say we take for a title "The Art and Humor of the Hold-up" — or something like that. I would suggest that in writing you assume a character. We have got to respect the conventions and delusions of the public to a certain extent. An article written as you would naturally write it would be regarded as a fake and an imposition. Remember that the traditions must be preserved wherever they will not interfere with the truth. Write in as simple, plain and unembellished a style as you know how. Make your sentences short. Put in as much realism and as many facts as possible. Where you want to express an opinion or comment on the matter do it as practically and plainly as you can. Give it *life* and the vitality of *facts*.

Now, I will give you a sort of general synopsis of my idea — of course, everything is subject to your own revision and change. The article, we will say, is written by a *typical* train hoister — one without your education and powers of expression (bouquet) but intelligent enough to convey his ideas from *his standpoint* — not from John Wanamaker's. Yet, in order to please John, we will have to assume a virtue that we do not possess. Comment on the moral side of the proposition as little as possible. Do not claim that holding up trains is the only business a gentleman would engage in, and, on the contrary, do not depreciate a profession that is really only financiering with spurs on. Describe the *facts* and *details* — all that part of the proceedings that the passenger sitting with his hands up in a Pullman looking into the end of a tunnel in the hands of one of the performers does not see. Here is a rough draft of my idea: Begin abruptly, without any philosophizing, with your idea of the best times, places and conditions for the hold-up — compare your opinions of this with those of others — mention some poorly conceived attempts and failures of others, giving your opinion why — as far as possible refer to actual occurrences, and incidents — describe the manner of a hold-up, how many men is best, where they are stationed, how do they generally go into it, nervous? or joking? or solemnly. The details of stopping the train, the duties of each man of the gang — the behavior of the train crew and passengers (here give as many brief odd and humorous incidents as you can think of). Your opinions on going through the passengers, when is it done and when not done. How is the boodle gotten at? How does the express clerk generally take it? Anything done with the mail car? *Under what circumstances will a train robber shoot a passenger or a train man* — suppose a man refuses to throw up his hands? Queer articles found on passengers (a chance here for some imaginative work) — queer and laughable incidents of any kind. Refer whenever apropos to actual hold-ups and facts concerning them of interest. What could two or three brave and determined passengers do if they were to try? Why don't they try? How long does it take to do the business. Does the train man ever stand in¯with the hold-up? Best means of getting away — how and when is the money divided. How is it mostly spent. Best way to manœuvre afterward. How to get caught and how not to. Comment on the methods of officials who try to capture. (Here's your chance to get even.)

These ideas are some that occur to me casually. You will, of course, have many far better. I suggest that you make the article anywhere from 4,000 to 6,000 words. Get as much meat in it as you can, and, by the way — stuff it full of western *genuine* slang — (not the eastern story paper kind). Get all the quaint cowboy expressions and terms of speech you can think of.

Information is what we want, clothed in the peculiar

western style of the character we want to present. The main idea is to be *natural, direct,* and *concise.*

I hope you will understand what I say. I don't. But try her a whack and send it along as soon as you can, and let's see what we can do. By the way, Mr. "Everybody" pays good prices. I thought I would, when I get your story, put it into the shape my judgment decides upon, and then send both your MS. and mine to the magazine. If he uses mine, we'll whack up shares on the proceeds, If he uses yours, you get the check direct. If he uses neither, we are out only a few stamps.

Sincerely your friend,
W. S. P.

And here is the letter telling his "pard" that the article had been bought by *Everybody's Magazine.* This is dated Pittsburg, October 24th, obviously the same year:

DEAR PARD:

You're It. I always told you you were a genius. All you need is to succeed in order to make a success.

I enclose pub[rs] letter which explains itself. When you see your baby in print don't blame me if you find strange ear marks and brands on it. I slashed it and cut it and added lots of stuff that never happened, but I followed your facts and ideas, and that is what made it valuable. I'll think up some other idea for an article and we'll collaborate again some time — eh?

I have all the work I can do, and am selling it right along. Have averaged about $150 per month since

August 1st.   And yet I don't overwork — don't think
I ever will.   I commence about 9 A. M. and generally
knock off about 4 or 5 P. M.

As soon as check mentioned in letter comes I'll send you
your "sheer" of the boodle.

By the way, please keep my *nom de plume* strictly to
yourself.   I don't want any one to know just yet.

Give my big regards to Billy.   Reason with him and
try to convince him that we believe him to be pure merino
and of more than average width.   With the kindest
remembrances to yourself I remain,

Your friend,
W. S. P.

At this time O. Henry was unknown and thought himself lucky to sell a story at any price.

THE END

THE COUNTRY LIFE PRESS
GARDEN CITY, N. Y.